MAKE ME A MONSTER

MAKE ME A MONSTER

A

MONSTER

KALYNN BAYRON

BLOOMSBURY

LONDON OXFORD NEW YORK NEW DELHI SYDNEY

BLOOMSBURY YA
Bloomsbury Publishing Plc
50 Bedford Square, London WC1B 3DP, UK
Bloomsbury Publishing Ireland Limited
29 Earlsfort Terrace, Dublin 2, D02 AY28, Ireland

BLOOMSBURY, BLOOMSBURY YA and the Diana logo are
trademarks of Bloomsbury Publishing Plc

First published in the United States of America in 2025 by Bloomsbury YA
First published in Great Britain in 2025 by Bloomsbury Publishing Plc

A catalogue record for this book is available from the British Library

ISBN: PB: 978-1-5266-8046-4; eBook: 978-1-5266-8043-3; ePDF: 978-1-5266-8045-7

2 4 6 8 10 9 7 5 3

Typeset by Westchester Publishing Services

Printed and bound in India by Thomson Press India Ltd

To find out more about our authors and books visit
www.bloomsbury.com and sign up for our newsletters
For product safety related questions contact productsafety@bloomsbury.com

For sale in the Indian subcontinent only

To Mary Shelley
You would have loved gel pens,
Ziploc bags, and The Cure

It is true, we shall be monsters, cut off from all the world; but on that account we shall be more attached to one another.

—Mary Shelley, *Frankenstein*

"Ghastly grim and ancient Raven wandering from the Nightly shore— Tell me what thy lordly name is on the Night's Plutonian shore!" Quoth the Raven, "Nevermore."

—Edgar Allan Poe, *The Raven*

PROLOGUE

In the dream, I'm always sitting in the back seat. Dad is driving and Mom is in the front passenger seat. A song plays on the radio. I can't make out the words. Mom looks back at me. There is an expression on her face that I can't place. Then, there's a flash, like a lightning bolt. It tears through the car as an undulating orange haze surrounds me—panic sets in. My father's cries split the air and when the smoke clears and I finally see him, he is crouched over my mom's lifeless body on the side of some rain-slick road.

This is usually where I wake up.

But not this time.

Now, for the first time in what feels like forever, there is something new in this hellscape between sleeping and waking. I'm outside on the ground, lying on my back, looking up at a starry night sky. I turn my head and pain rockets up my neck. I cry out in agony.

This is the dream I've been having for years. The same sequence. The same creeping dread. The all-encompassing terror. Always the same.

Now it has a horrifying new chapter. I have no idea what it means. All I know for sure is that watching my mother die in my dreams makes me feel like a hole is being punched directly through my chest. In the gaping wound, there is only despair.

CHAPTER 1

WELCOME TO REDWOOD FUNERAL HOME

There's a dead body waiting for me at home and I'm excited to see her.

It's not what most people look forward to when they get home after a long day at school, but for me, I know it'll be a nice quiet afternoon of prepping our newest guest.

Guest.

Dead body. Decedent. Corpse. Cadaver.

There are lots of names for the dearly departed, but *guest* just sounds more professional.

I run up the front steps of my house and stick my key in the door.

"I'm home!" I call as I go in. It's mostly silent aside from the ticking of the large grandfather clock in the front hall. "Mom! Dad!"

Silence.

I kick off my shoes and put my coat and backpack on the hook in the entryway. I hit the light switch and it clicks but the light doesn't flicker on. I glance around. None of the lights are on— the usual hum of the fridge, the computer in my dad's first-floor office, they're all silent.

I peek into the first room off the main hall. The mahogany catafalque is sitting there empty. No casket perched atop it . . . yet.

"Mom," I call again. "You here?" The boards creak under my feet as I step back toward the hall. "Dad?"

I catch something in the air.

"Meka," a voice calls.

It's less like a call and more like a whisper. It filters through the silence like a puff of smoke, there and gone in the space of a breath. I hit the light switch in the viewing room and . . . nothing.

"Meka," a voice says again.

I step back into the main hall and stand still, listening.

"Meka."

I have a choice to make. Run or investigate. I've seen enough horror movies to know what I'm not gonna do. I sprint to the front door when a rush of running footsteps comes bounding down the hall behind me. I glance back.

"Caleb?" I ask, confused.

Caleb, one of my best friends, is stumbling out of my kitchen and down the hall straight toward me, a terrified expression plastered on his face.

"Girl, move!" he says as he pushes me out of the way and runs into the street.

My mom, Dad, my boyfriend Noah, and my other friend Cipriana come tumbling out of the kitchen.

"Caleb!" Noah yells. "You're ruining the surprise!"

Noah jogs up to me and kisses me gently on the cheek. He's wearing a black suit and his face is painted ghostly white. The hollows under his eyes are darkened with black face paint.

"Ummmm," I say, bewildered at why he looks like a walking corpse. "Somebody wanna tell me what's going on?"

Cipriana gives me a big hug. "Caleb is a crybaby." She leans out the front door. "Caleb! Get your scary ass back inside!"

"Language," my mom says as she breezes up to me.

"Sorry, Mrs. Redwood," Cipriana says, heat rising in her face. "He's ridiculous."

"He's scared," my dad says. He hangs back near the kitchen, clearly uncomfortable with so many people being in the house. I'm still a little confused as to why everybody is here.

"We were planning a surprise for you," Noah says.

"What kind of surprise?" I ask. "Why do you look like a zombie?"

"I'm not a zombie," he says, laughing. "I'm dead."

"Oh, right," I say. "Because that makes sense."

I stare up into his big brown eyes, and a little flutter invades my stomach. My mom goes out and guides Caleb back inside. I put my arm around him.

"Sorry," Caleb says. "Your mom was whispering your name and we were tryna get you to come to the kitchen and she cut off the power so it would be dark but then I saw the hearse outside and I got scared and I know you got dead bodies in the freezer and—"

"Caleb," I say, interrupting his spiral. "It's okay. I promise. Try to breathe."

"And why did we have to cut all the lights out anyway?" Caleb asks.

"Ambience," Cipriana says. "And it worked. Look at yourself. A mess."

Caleb takes a few deep breaths as he tries to calm himself down. Caleb almost never comes to my house because he's scared to death of dead bodies—a very unfortunate thing to be when, as one of his best friends, I live in a funeral home.

"Everybody into the kitchen," my mom says. "I got cupcakes!"

I grab Caleb by one arm and Noah takes him by the other. We steer him into the kitchen and prop him on a stool in the corner. A handmade sign hangs across the kitchen window and it reads Congrats, Meka! A paper chain of little tombstones dangles from the edge of the counter.

The kitchen counter is cleared and Noah hops up and lies back, crossing his hands over his chest like a corpse lying in state. My mom places a cupcake with a single black candle stuck in the middle on his chest.

"We're so proud of you," my mom says, beaming. "Make a wish and blow out the candle."

I wish for the same thing I wish for at every birthday or when the clock says 11:11 or any other time a wish is required—that my mom stays safe and that the dream that haunts me will never come true. I blow out the candle.

I am officially Ithaca, New York's youngest certified mortician's assistant. At seventeen, I just received my certification and clearly, my friends and family want to celebrate. Everything is weird but I wouldn't have it any other way.

We divvy up the other cupcakes and Cipriana tries to sing a song to the tune of "Happy Birthday" but makes up some lyrics about doing makeup on the dead and Caleb almost passes out, so we stop. My mom scrapes the icing off her cupcake, then decides to abandon the whole thing so she doesn't get an upset stomach. Caleb doesn't eat at all and spends the whole time holding my hand like his life depends on it. He is scared to death of what goes on in my house but the fact that he tries to set his feelings aside to be here to celebrate my accomplishment means a lot to me. If I'm honest, my other friends feel the same way Caleb does, but they're better at hiding it.

I can't say I blame them. Death is my life and for most people, that is simply too much to handle.

Mrs. Lang lies stiff and cold on the mortuary prep table. My mom had applied the woman's foundation perfectly. I'm following up by painting on a rosy-pink lip lacquer with a brush intended for an artist's canvas. I guess technically, I *am* an artist, only I'm painting dead people's skin instead of a stretched canvas.

The lips are very delicate. They tend to flake and sometimes they're so dry they peel back, exposing the teeth. A thick layer of moisturizer must be applied first, and the lip stain glides on like butter. I attach a few individual lashes. Mrs. Lang's are sparse, and her daughter told me she loved to wear falsies because she loved that old Hollywood movie-star look. I gently glue the hairs on and paint them with a layer of mascara before clamping them between an eyelash curler. I dust a fine layer of blush over her cheekbones and temples. I think she's done. She looks good, rejuvenated even. She's ready for her big—and last—entrance.

"All done, Mrs. Lang," I say. "I hope your homegoing is peaceful."

At the foot of the prep table I slip on her shoes. Grasping her discolored ankles, it takes a firm shove to get her feet in—this is why shoes are almost always a no-go but her family had insisted. There is a small rustle from the head of the table. I glance up. Mrs. Lang's head has shifted slightly to the right. I huff, move back to her side, and readjust her head but her lids are now slightly parted, revealing the little white eye caps covering her actual eyes.

"No peeking," I say as I close her open lids with the tips of my fingers.

I don't know if it's healthy to think about death as much as I do. I can't get away from the dead no matter how hard I try. And the thing is . . . I don't really want to.

I've watched corpses get wheeled into the prep room in the basement of my house for as long as I can remember. When I was little, I used to try and guess who was in the body bag based on how lumpy it was. Was it a tall person? Somebody's grandma or uncle? A short person? A kid? The images I conjured up were always worse than the reality—dead people don't look dead. They don't look like zombies, all rotting skin and tattered clothing. Most of the time they just look empty. Those little things that make them human leave when the heart stops and the brain shuts down. Some people call it a spark, a flame, a soul. Whatever it is, whatever it's called, it leaves when a person dies and it's impossible to put back once it has departed.

It's not all gloom and sadness, though. There are perks to this job, this life, too. A decommissioned autopsy table makes a really great sled in the winter. Scalpels and bone saws make excellent pumpkin carving tools and I'm never short on makeup during Halloween. It's all in how you look at it. That is the tale I tell myself because deep inside, I know that riding autopsy tables down snow-covered hills and carving pumpkins with bone saws is weird. And maybe that means I'm weird too.

My circle of friends is less of a circle and more like a square. Everyone who was at the little surprise party make up the four corners—Noah, Caleb, Cip, and me. I like it that way and besides, nobody else is fighting to be friends with a girl who spends most of her days in the company of corpses. I've lost count of the number of times somebody from school spotted me pushing a body into the basement of my house while they were out for a walk or driving by. I try to see myself through their eyes and when I'm out moving bodies with my hair wrapped up, in sweats, pimple patches on my face, I probably look scary as hell. I'm fine with that. Hauling bodies isn't even the strangest part of my job.

On this gray afternoon in early January, I'm staring down at Mrs. Lang one final time before we move her upstairs and place her casket on the raised platform in the viewing room. Her hair and makeup are finished, and she looks stunning.

The cool flush of the AC causes a few loose strands of her hair to dance across her forehead. I gently tuck them back into place and put my hand on her shoulder. Her family is probably already missing her so much. My chest aches a little at the thought. I shut my eyes and take a deep breath.

When I open my eyes, Mrs. Lang's lids are parted again. I sigh. I grab a small tube of superglue and gently lift one of Mrs. Lang's lids. I apply one small bead of the stuff to her waterline, then reclose the lid. Repeating the process on her other eye solves the problem and she still looks great.

I hang my plastic apron on a hook and toss away the mostly empty tube of superglue. There's suddenly a loud, metallic-sounding groan. I spin around to find that the table Mrs. Lang is resting on has rolled slightly to the right. My heart crashes in my chest as I quickly grab hold of the table's edge. The metal tables are solid but can move if a body is shifted around on it. I check the wheel locks and find that two of them are not snapped in place. I shove the table back into position and set the locks, pushing on it to make sure it doesn't move. Mrs. Lang's body rocks stiffly but the table stays in place. I hiss out a long, slow breath, then head upstairs.

There, I finish prepping the front room of our house for Mrs. Lang's wake—lining up the chairs and arranging flowers on the table near the back. Bool's Flower Shop provides most of our funeral arrangements but sometimes we get stuff shipped from Bri's in Brooklyn or their sister shop in Rhinebeck. I inspect the large bouquet of white mums and rearrange the vases of lilies and carnations in a way that allows for a little stack of programs to sit among them. Mrs. Lang's antemortem face is on the front surrounded by a wreath of white and pink peonies. The whole setup is beautiful, and I think it's a shame Mrs. Lang is too dead to see it.

One thing I know for certain is that people need something when a person dies. They need to mourn, to feel like other people see their pain, and ultimately, they take part in these rituals— embalming, a wake, a burial, a repast, the whole homegoing process—to make themselves feel better. These death rituals are mostly for the living, not the dead, but that doesn't make them any less necessary or important.

"Meka!" my mom calls from somewhere in the house.

"Ma'am?" I call back.

"Put out the sign, would you?"

"I'll do it right now," I say.

I pull the sandwich board out of the closet and drag it down the front steps. I prop it in front of the house. It reads Redwood

Funeral Home, Service in Progress, Please Be Respectful in scrawling burgundy script. The sign was my mom's idea. A while ago, we had a man show up selling Kirby vacuum cleaners right in the middle of a service. The sales guy would not take no for an answer even though we had Mr. Eddelston's body laid out in the viewing room. The man even offered to demonstrate the Kirby's legendary suction strength on the carpet in the hallway. I didn't even know people sold vacuums door-to-door anymore. I don't know if the sign would have kept the guy away to begin with but if Mom says put it up, that's what I'm going to do.

I adjust the sign and tuck my arms in close as I glance up and down East Court Street. Things are quiet. It's one of those frigid but beautifully overcast days. A perfect day for a funeral. I hustle back in to finish up.

Part of my job also includes distracting kids in an adjacent playroom, who are too little to handle seeing their dead relatives lying stiff in a coffin. Babysitting used to be my main job, but now that I have my official license I get to make our guests feel welcome whether they're living or dead.

After I've checked the playroom, I go into the viewing room directly across the hall and peer down at Mrs. Lang after she's been moved into position.

"She looks great," my mom says.

I try to keep my heart from leaping into my throat. "You scared me," I say, grabbing my chest dramatically.

"Sorry," she says.

She stands in the doorway like a burst of sunshine in an environment that feels like a gray storm cloud a lot of the time. She checks her makeup in the large mirror that hangs just inside the viewing room and touches up her lipstick before joining me at the coffin side.

I reach into the coffin and adjust a large brooch on Mrs. Lang's knitted sweater. It's a gaudy thing with an emerald-colored stone at the center. It doesn't go with what she's wearing, but her oldest son insisted we put it on her. In fact, he'd been the one who insisted on us putting her shoes on too. He'd been wearing a suit that looked like he'd stolen it off a dead body when he dropped off his mother's things. I should have known he was going to have his poor mother looking a mess.

"Having to take fashion advice from a man even when you're dead has gotta be some kind of punishment, right?" I ask.

"Depends on the man," Mom says. She eyes the brooch. "In this case, yes. A punishment."

I continue primping Mrs. Lang, making sure everything is just right. "I think we did good," I say.

"We always do," says Mom. "I thought the skin slippage would be an issue, but I put a little Dryene on her. The wax covered it right up."

"You did that," I say, smiling.

My mom pretends like she doesn't want the compliment, but only for a second. She isn't the type of person who believes in being overly humble.

"I can't take all the credit," she says. "Her pallor was tough to correct but *you* did that. You get better and better every time, Meka."

Now it's my turn to poke out my chest a little. I had worked really hard on the color matching and texture to make sure it was flawless. Mrs. Lang's skin felt like it came alive under my brush. She was pale with blue-green undertones and her skin was dry and rough. Burst capillaries had made little reddish webs of the broken vessels around her nose and under her eyes. We could have slapped on some foundation in a near-match color and called it a day but that's not what we do here.

As Mom admires our work, something catches my eye—a small wire, maybe as long and thin as an eyelash, protrudes from the skin above Mrs. Lang's top lip on the side of her face closest to the inside of her coffin. It looks like a metallic whisker.

"Oh no," I say, leaning in to get a better look. "Why is it sticking out like that?"

I pinch the wire and tug it. Mrs. Lang's perfectly painted lips bulge. I sigh. Dead bodies tend to open their mouths if they aren't sewn shut. I can't think of anything more traumatic than looking into your loved one's coffin only to find their mouth agape in a silent scream. We keep that from happening by using a needle injector to place two lengths of wire in the upper and lower lip; then we twist them together, cut off the excess, and fill the divots with mortuary wax. Problem solved. No more silently screaming corpses.

"We need to clip the loose ends a little bit shorter," Mom says. She gently touches her own lip as if she's calculating the adjustments that need to be made in the same place on Mrs. Lang.

I reach into my pocket and take out a tiny pair of shears. My mom gifted them to me when I first started assisting her. They're shaped like a bird, a crane, I think. The wings make up the handles and the scissor mechanism is in the shape of a beak. I clip the ends of the wire and re-form the wax around Mrs. Lang's lip.

"Picture perfect," my mom says, smiling. "You didn't even need to touch up her makeup." She glances at my shears and then back to Mrs. Lang. "You've got the magic touch, baby."

She readjusts the big loopy bow at her collar and smooths out the front of her pleated pants.

"You look really nice," I say.

She laughs lightly and kisses me on the top of my head. "I try, baby. It's getting harder and harder to do the older I get."

I hug her tight. "Stop. You look like we could be in class together. You know how many seniors have asked me if they can get your number thinking you're my sister or something?" I cringe. "It's annoying."

"Yeah, that's not cool," she says. "But you really think I look like I could be one of your little friends?"

I nod and laugh. "Yup."

"Hmm," she says thoughtfully. "I don't know how I feel about that but I'll take it as a compliment for now."

My mom is always dressed to impress, no matter the occasion. She's particular about the way she looks because she's the face of Redwood Funeral Home. She handles almost all our face-to-face meetings with clients because my dad is whatever the opposite of a people person is. She always tells me that you only get one chance to make a good first impression. She's the kindest, gentlest person I know but she's hard on herself no matter how much me and my dad tell her she doesn't need to be. Working on dead bodies all day probably isn't helping the issue. Nothing will give you a complex faster than seeing, up close and in person, the way time ravages the body. I give her a hug, breathing her in. She smells like flowers, like roses. Anybody who doesn't work in a funeral home every day of their life might think it's just a nice floral perfume. They would never guess it was the scent of the mortuary paint we use to prep the bodies.

An hour later, Mrs. Lang's family begins to trickle in, and I herd the smaller kids into the playroom while the adults grieve openly at the coffin. They wail and sob, and I know my mom will pat them on their backs and offer them words of comfort. I can hear them even through the closed door so I put on music as the kids play with our assortment of battered toys and draw pictures of their recently deceased grandma. I settle myself in a child-size chair at the low table and a little girl in a frilly black dress with a head full of brown ringlets scoots up next to me. She hands me a piece of paper.

"Is this your artwork?" I ask, smiling at her.

She nods and smiles back.

Stick figures clearly meant to represent Mrs. Lang and the little girl are holding hands, but they are far beneath the grass rendered in evergreen crayon.

"What's going on here?" I ask.

She curls her little hands around my arm as she looks at the picture and then back to me like it should be obvious. "That's me and my grandma. We're holding hands."

"I can see that," I say gently. "But why are you both under the ground?"

"She's dead. She's going under the ground forever," the little girl says so matter-of-factly all I can do is stare blankly at her for a moment.

"Oh, right," I say. Images of me and my mom handling Mrs. Lang's mortal remains in the previous days flood my brain. Stuffing her stiffened limbs into her clothes and shoes . . .

I push those thoughts aside and lean toward the girl, cupping my hand over hers. "But you're still here, right? You're okay."

The little girl looks thoughtful and then tenderly leans her head against my arm. "I wanna hold her hand even when she's under the ground," she says. "She can be dead and I can be alive. It's okay."

Kids are so nonchalant about death sometimes, it's actually a little unnerving.

"You want me to draw you a picture too?" she asks.

"No, that's okay, I—"

She either doesn't hear me or she doesn't care what my answer is because she immediately grabs a crayon and a piece of blank paper. She sets to work, drawing the arms and legs of a figure that's supposed to be me. She glances at me, studying my face, and then back to the paper, scribbling in the curly black hair slicked back in a bun. She continues on to the gray pantsuit, the shiny black shoes and finally, a six-sided shape completely surrounding the figure.

"Is this me?" I ask.

"That's you," she says, grinning.

"And what's that shape around me?" I ask.

The little girl looks up at me, her big brown eyes shining. "That's your coffin," she says. "You're dead."

CHAPTER 2

AN UNKINDNESS OF RAVENS

I wait for her to say she's joking or that the hexagonal shape surrounding me is something else, but she just laughs and skips over to the other side of the room to play Legos with her cousin like she hadn't admitted to wanting to hold hands with her dead grandma's corpse and then drawn me inside a coffin. I push the drawing as far away from me on the table as I can.

My phone buzzes in my pocket and I'm happy to have a distraction from the little girl and her weird drawing. I glance at the screen and see a text from Noah.

NOAH: I'm starving. I got some tacos. You want me to bring some over?
ME: We're doing a service.
NOAH: NEVERMIND

He sends a GIF of somebody screaming in terror.

ME: You're just as bad as Caleb.
NOAH: Nobody is as bad as Caleb.

He has a point.

Mrs. Lang's viewing comes to a close and the children's caregivers collect them. They leave in a tangle of tearstained faces and embracing arms. Mrs. Lang's body is loaded into the hearse and taken away for the graveside service. As I straighten up the playroom I consider tossing all the crayons in the trash since people's kids want to draw creepy pictures of me.

"I appreciate you watching out for the kids, baby," my mom says.

I spin around and find her propping the door open.

"Not a problem," I say. "Look at this." I hand her the pictures the little girl had left behind. "Weird, right? It's her and her dead grandma holding hands." I show her the other drawing. "This one's supposed to be me."

Mom studies the drawing, then touches her quivering bottom lip.

I gently put my hand on her shoulder. "You okay?"

She pats my hand and folds the drawings in half, handing them back to me. "Kids, right? They don't know what's going on sometimes. Or maybe they do. Who knows." She clears her throat and smiles at me. "Makes me sad, that's all."

I think seeing people's grieving families bothers her more than anything else in our profession.

"Throw that picture away," my mom says.

She doesn't have to ask me twice. I crumple the paper up and toss it into the trash can.

That evening, Mom orders takeout and I'm setting the plastic containers at the dining room table when the front door creaks open. My dad, clad in black, his briefcase dangling from his hand, trudges in. He slips off his shoes and hangs his coat on a hook in the entryway.

His job in the funeral home is hands-on, technical. He preserves bodies and handles the legal paperwork. His work outside the house is a never-ending series of conferences and lectures. When I was little he taught gothic literature in addition to his duties as a mortician. Every once in a while he picks up teaching a class or giving a talk but it comes second to his work with the faculty in Cornell's anatomy and physiology departments. He's constantly honing his mortuary craft and learning the latest and greatest in preservation techniques for the dead. He's a perfectionist and he doesn't like feeling as if he's behind the curve in any way. If it's new in the world of mortuary techniques, he knows about it and is already figuring out a way to incorporate it into the care of our guests.

Basically, he's the opposite of my mom. Where she's the bubbly face of our business, willing to talk to anyone, he keeps his head down and avoids interacting with anyone who still has a pulse. He likes it that way. He and my mom are like two pieces of a very strange puzzle.

"Hey," I say.

He jumps even though he's looking right at me, almost like my regular speaking voice is too loud. "Oh, hey," he says softly as he runs his hand over the day's worth of stubble dotting his chin, then rests it on his chest like he's trying to calm his racing heart. "How'd it go today?"

"Everything went smooth. Mrs. Lang's family was really happy." I pause. "Happy isn't the right word."

"I know what you mean," he says. "Happy with the work, devastated that it needs to be done in the first place." He smiles in that way that's all mouth and no eyes. Like he's got something else on his mind and is just going through the motions.

When I was younger, I thought moping around was just the way you had to act if you were an undertaker. Dealing in death takes its toll, but melancholy clings to him like a heavy blanket most days. He is haunted.

What I've come to understand is that it isn't just death and dying that overwhelm my dad—it's life, too. Death is final and the processes after a death are predictable—bodies decay at a certain rate under certain circumstances, they come to us to be preserved and restored, there's a homegoing, and then the bodies go into the ground or a crypt or to cremation. He's good at those details because he knows exactly what to expect at every turn.

It's regular everyday life that stumps him sometimes. He doesn't really know what to say or do during the planning of a funeral. He's not great at talking to people and his whole demeanor is a little too on the nose for most folks. It's always been like that, though. He has always seemed out of place. He stuck out like a weed at my piano recitals and my school plays. Mom was always there to remind him that *he* wasn't actually a corpse, but he always seemed surprised to remember that little fact.

"How are my babies?" he asks, glancing toward the back door.

"You know they don't like me," I say.

"Not true," my dad says. "They love you. Why wouldn't they?"

His *babies* are an unkindness of ravens that he's been feeding and caring for, for years. He'd always been fascinated by them and their myths. They circle battlefields and often pick at dead and decaying things. They symbolize death and so it's not surprising that they gather here at our funeral home. Where it goes a little off the rails is when my dad spent a week carefully cutting a hole in the wall next to our back door and fitting it with a small window he could open and close from the inside. It has a platform about the size of a sheet of printer paper that sticks out of it, a feeding station for the ravens. He leaves them seeds and they bring him shiny little trinkets—coins, buttons, the odd ring or bracelet. The happiest I ever see him is when he's tending to his birds.

He goes to the little window and opens it. He scoops out a heaping half cup of birdseed from a bag on the floor and scatters it across the platform. Not a second later two large ravens, black as night, eyes like glinting black beads, descend and begin to peck at the feed. My dad smiles. I think he could reach out and pet them if he wanted to.

"You know there's this old movie called *The Birds*," I say. "It's about a bunch of birds that attack people."

Dad gives his ravens a quizzical look, then shuts the little window. "Where'd you see a movie like that?"

"Film studies," I say. It's one of the classes I'd been wanting to take and there had been a wait list, but my English teacher, Mr. Brennan, put in a good word for me and my name got bumped up the list. "It's a horror movie."

"Movies exaggerate things," my dad says. "They never quite get it right."

"Get what right?" I ask. "They're scary movies. They just make stuff up."

My dad looks thoughtful, then comes over and puts his hand on my shoulder. "Where's your mom?"

"Changing," I say. "We got takeout."

He surveys the assortment of plastic containers, fold-top boxes, and plastic cutlery. "Looks good. I'm starving."

We sit next to each other and serve ourselves, hoping Mom won't mind too much, but when her footsteps sound on the stairs we both put our hands in our laps.

Mom comes downstairs in a pair of high-waisted jeans, a cropped navy sweater with bat-wing sleeves, and a pair of gold flats. Even after work, she is dressed to impress.

"I wanna be like you when I grow up," I tease.

"Oh, I know," she says, jokingly. "Give it time, baby. You might catch up." She winks at me.

She stands by the table and pushes her hand down on her hip, striking a little pose and smiling.

"You look amazing," my dad says as his eyes grow wide. A soft smile breaks across his face. One thing that can always get him out of a funk is my mom.

She smiles back at him. "Thanks, babe. Looks like you two started without me."

"Want me to make you a plate?" Dad asks.

"No, I'm okay," she says.

"There's steamed rice," I say. "I know your stomach's been bothering you. You really gotta get the doctor to figure it out. It's been years."

"Who you tellin'?" Mom huffs.

My dad reaches out and takes my mom's hand, squeezing it gently, as she sits down. He doesn't look her in the eye, though.

Mom shakes her head and spoons some white rice out onto her plate. "Don't worry about me. I just need to be more careful about what I eat, that's all. Doc thinks maybe it's a gluten allergy. I don't know. He says I'd need a biopsy of my small intestine to know for sure."

My parents exchange a look that's a cross between worry and sadness. I glance at my mom. If something was wrong—really wrong—I'd know.

"You're seeing somebody good, right?" I ask. "Somebody who knows what they're doing?"

Mom waves off my concerns. "Dr. Albert Hayes. He's a specialist. I have an appointment next week, just to follow up."

That makes me feel a little better.

Mom shrugs and gives a little laugh. "It's fine, and I'm tired of trying to figure it out anyway." She sighs. "That's really the last thing I need."

She collects food allergies the way Thanos collects infinity stones. She's deathly allergic to shellfish, nuts, and eggs. She can't tolerate lactose in any form. If she adds in a gluten allergy, her list of food options will get even smaller. She loves to cook but rarely partakes in the meals she puts together because there's always something in it she can't have. Most of the time she eats before we all sit together. She rarely complains but I see her eyeing my pad thai. It's sprinkled with peanuts and chunks of fried egg poke out from between the noodles. I slide my plate as far away from her as I can.

She laughs lightly. "I'm not going to have a reaction just from looking at it, baby."

She raises her spoon to her mouth as the doorbell rings.

"I got it," I say.

My dad rests his hand on my shoulder before I can stand up. "You stay here and eat. I'll go." He pushes his chair away from the table and goes to the front door.

My mom leans across the table and cups her hand over mine. "Meka, baby. You look really tired. How'd you sleep?"

A heavy silence wraps itself around us. She knows about the dream. I've been having it for years but what she doesn't know is how lately, I've been having it almost every night. And then last night . . . it changed. For the first time ever, it was different.

"I had a rough night," I say.

Mom narrows her gaze at me. "The dream?"

I nod. She sits very still for a moment. It's like she's not even breathing and then she sighs and reaches out to touch the back of my hand.

"Baby, we can make another doctor's appointment," she says. "Maybe you need a prescription? Something to help you sleep?"

It's never been so much of an issue that I needed anything like that. I went to a therapist when I was younger to try and figure it out and she didn't think meds were necessary. She said it was probably a combination of stress and environment—meaning living in a funeral home was a huge contributing factor. She taught me some breathing exercises and reminded me that it was just a dream. As time went on, I had the dream less and less until it was almost completely out of my mind. And then, about three months ago it ramped back up and now it's almost every night.

My dad's voice carries down the hall and cuts through my thoughts. His tone is raised, and he sounds almost angry, which is out of character for him. I pause. "We're having dinner," he says. "Maybe if you'd like to call or use the contact form on the website."

I lean back in my seat and peer down the hall. My dad is standing with the front door open, his back to me, his frame rigid as a corpse. Someone else is in the entryway but I can't get a good look at whoever it is. I lean back a little more as my dad shifts his weight from one foot to the other. I get a glimpse of a tall, red-headed woman with a sharp, angular face, and a man with a shock of messy blond hair.

"It's urgent," the woman says.

"These things always are," my dad says.

The redheaded woman glances at me. I've never seen her before but there is a flicker of recognition in her eyes. The corner of her mouth draws up.

"Jonathan?" my mom calls.

"Tomorrow would be better," my dad says.

The blond man says something I can't make out.

"Have a good night," the redhead says as my dad closes the door a little more forcefully than is necessary.

He rejoins us at the table but sits quietly, his hands tented under his chin.

"What was that about?" I ask.

My dad looks down into his plate of rice. "People can't just show up whenever they feel like it." He shakes his head. "We have business hours for a reason."

"It was somebody needing funeral services?" I ask.

"They should use the contact form on the website if they need to get in touch or at least call." He sighs and runs his hands over his face. "This is why I keep thinking we need to separate the house from the business. We should have two separate spaces; that way people can't just show up at our home whenever they feel like it."

My mom clears her throat. "You know I don't want to do that," she says. "I don't think it's a good idea at all. Financially—it's too much."

"Are we hurting on money?" I ask, firmly stepping into grown folks business.

Mom and Dad both give me a that's-not-your-concern look and I immediately let it go.

"Besides," Mom says, nudging her plate forward like she's done with it. "Is it really that much of an issue? People only show up unannounced every once in a while. That's why I put the sign up on the sidewalk. Maybe I can put a sign on the front door?"

My dad shakes his head. "No, it's not that. It's not—" He stops and presses his lips together like he's trying to keep the rest of his words from spilling out. "It's fine. You're right. Maybe another sign would help." He forces a quick smile and picks at his food.

Mom stares at him in silence for a minute and I'm starting to feel awkward, so I clear my throat and eat another mouthful of noodles.

"What about hypnosis?" Mom says suddenly. "We haven't tried that."

"What?" my dad asks, confused.

"What?" I echo, equally confused.

"For Meka's dream," she says. "Maybe we can try hypnosis."

"The dream is an issue again?" my dad asks.

"No," I lie.

"Yes," my mom says firmly. "She said it changed. That there's more to it than there was before."

26

My dad shovels a spoonful of rice into his mouth and swallows. "I've read some things about hypnosis. I'm not sure it could work for bad dreams. Don't people usually go to hypnotists to uncover lost memories, though?" he asks. "I think I've heard of something like that before."

Mom looks down at her plate. "Maybe. I guess I'm not entirely sure how hypnotism actually works so maybe it's a bad idea but what I'm trying to say—" She stops short and sighs so heavily her shoulders roll forward. "Meka. I'd do anything to keep you from having that dream."

My dad gently touches my shoulder. "How about we eat in the front room? Watch a movie. Get our minds on something else."

"Sounds good to me," I say, scooping up my plate and heading to the living room as my parents hang back, whispering to each other. I know they're worried about me.

Lately, the dream—the nightmare—descends on me every time I close my eyes. The therapist had suggested that I have a subconscious fear of losing my mom, and that fear and anxiety are fueling the dream. I didn't agree. The thing that makes me afraid of losing my mom is the dream itself, but what can I do about bad dreams? I'm seventeen. I'm not a little kid with an overactive imagination. I feel silly complaining about it. I don't know how to tell them it's a big problem and I'm really struggling with it.

I settle into the couch and pick over my food as my parents join me and flip through the channels. We decide on *Young Frankenstein*. My dad protests but me and my mom out-vote him. I've seen it before. My film studies class did a monster flicks unit around Halloween and we worked our way through some classic monster movies. This is one of my favorites, with the Bela Lugosi version of *Dracula* coming in a strong second.

"Gene Wilder is so good in this," I say.

"I love him in *Willy Wonka*," my mom says.

"I like the new version," my dad chimes in. "The one with that boy who looks sick. What's his name? Tim Chalet?"

I have to slap my hand over my mouth to keep from spitting out my food.

My mom twists around in her seat and stares at him. "I know we're geriatric millennials but please tell me you're not talking about Timothée Chalamet?"

My dad shrugs. "Maybe?"

I file that away in my head under "things I'm gonna tell my friends about at school."

A half hour into the movie, and the TV screen freezes for a moment, then starts up again.

My dad huffs. "Here we go with the signal. Is the weather bad?"

A gust of wind rattles the house like it's answering his question. The lights flicker.

My mom raises her eyes to the ceiling. My dad looks toward the front door.

Another gust and the lights flicker out.

CHAPTER 3

NIGHTMARES AND NOAH

I dig through the junk drawer in the kitchen and find the flash-light. I click it on and shine it toward my parents, who are on their feet in the living room. My dad is staring at the lamp in the corner like it turned itself off on purpose.

"Is the whole block out?" I ask.

Mom goes to the window and peers out. "Looks like it."

"The generator should be on by now," my dad says. "I'll go check."

We can't afford to have the power go out for even a short period of time. The bodies in the freezer need to stay cold; otherwise, they'll start to decay faster than we'd like them to.

There's a rumble and an electrical hum, then all the lights and the TV come back on.

My dad sighs. "Oh, thank god."

"Why is the electrical in this house held together with bubble gum and duct tape?" I ask. "The wind isn't even that strong."

"It's an old house, baby," Mom says as she returns to her seat on the couch. "You know that."

The TV has reset itself and is now on the local news channel. A reporter is standing outside Barnes Hall on the Cornell campus.

"Vincent Hollowell, a professor of English literature here at Cornell, has been spotted for the first time in nearly ten years," the reporter says. "Hollowell sustained a near-fatal injury during a hike at Buttermilk Falls and was forced into early retirement nearly twenty-six years ago. Hollowell has become a bit of a recluse but has continued to be one of Ithaca's most influential benefactors, with sizable donations made to the city every year."

"What in the world?" my mom asks, leaning forward and staring at the TV as pictures of Professor Hollowell, his face covered by a mirrored face shield, the kind made popular when COVID-19 kicked off, flash across the screen. "I thought he was dead."

"Nearly dead," my dad says. "He was in the hospital for months. He was friends with my father. Pretty sure he went to see Hollowell in the hospital when all that first happened."

Silence swallows the room. My dad almost never talks about his own father. From what I understand, their relationship was complicated, with my dad refusing to even mention him most of the time. Grandpa Redwood was also a mortician and died before I was born but I trust my dad if he says the man was difficult. I picture my dad as a kid, looking to his dad for help and getting rejected by him. Kind of makes me want to stomp on the old man's grave.

"I swear I thought I heard someone say he died," Mom says. She laughs lightly.

"You probably have him mixed up with one of the other old rich dudes who run that school," I say.

"Money can buy you a lot of things in this town," my dad says. "Even a new lease on life, apparently. Hollowell has to be in his late seventies by now."

My mom turns to him and is about to say something else when she stops herself. She looks at my dad with a kind of concern that she usually reserves for the relatives of the recently deceased.

The picture on the TV freezes as the image of a missing woman flashes on the screen. Then the signal blinks out completely and a little hourglass appears under the words "No Signal."

"I think that's a wrap on movie night," my dad says.

"You seem really broken up about it," I say.

He dramatically puts his hand over his heart and pretends to cry. "I'm so sad I can't stand it."

I side-eye him as he pulls himself up off the couch and goes into the kitchen.

"I'm gonna go get ready for school tomorrow," I say. "I gotta do some laundry."

My mom presses her lips together. "You sure, baby? You barely touched your food."

"I'm fine," I say. "I'll eat later, if that's okay?"

Mom nods. "Sure, baby. I'll put your plate in the microwave."

I jog upstairs to grab my dirty clothes basket, then lug it down the butler's staircase that leads to the basement. We don't have an actual butler but that's what the narrow staircases in the back of old houses like ours are called. When I was a kid, I was terrified of them because they were dark and the narrow space smelled like damp wood and dust. They lead directly into the part of the house we use to prepare the corpses for burial. I didn't care about the bodies, but I was concerned that some kind of ghost was gonna snatch me if I used the back stairs. I'm not bothered anymore but ten years ago, when my parents first opened the Redwood Funeral Home, there was no amount of coaxing that would have convinced me to take them.

Now the butler's staircase is less of an obstacle and simply the fastest way to get to the laundry room. The basement itself is still and quiet as I drag my laundry down. Doesn't matter how many bodies are being prepped or taking up space in the walk-in refrigerator, there is always the distinct feeling that I am completely alone down here. Sometimes it's nice.

I throw my rumpled clothes into the washer, add some detergent, and hit the start button. I slide down and sit with my back against the washer as it rumbles to life.

There are only three windows in the basement. One is a narrow opening in prep room number one that we use for ventilation when things get a little too stuffy. The other two are at the top of the walls at either end of the hallway. When the setting sun filters through them it casts shadows along the dark gray linoleum in long, reaching tendrils. As I sit back, images from the dream threaten to creep from the back of my mind. I press my hands into the floor and clench my jaw so tight it hurts. I don't want to see those images while I'm awake, too.

I stand and wander into the main preparation room to try and clear my head. Prep room two is where we do the hair and makeup of our guests. It can hold two bodies at a time and tomorrow it will, but for now, the glinting steel tables are empty. I readjust the headrest on one of them. Mr. Chavez, a recently deceased grandfather of six whose mortal remains are lying in the refrigerator in the room next door, is only about five feet tall and his head won't need to be at the very top of the table.

After arranging the table, I pull open my mother's Craftsman 2000 tool cabinet that holds all her mortuary cosmetology tools. Everything is neatly organized—all the different shades of pigment arranged from dark to light in the top drawer alongside an assortment of brushes and palette knives. The next drawer down holds false eyelashes, lipsticks, mortuary wax, needle injectors, and wire. The bottom cabinets contain little jars of lacquer thinner for loosening up the mortuary makeup and Mom's secret weapon—Smithfield's Mortuary Spray Paint. Regular cosmetics are fine, but they can't be applied directly to the skin of a corpse. Deceased skin is way too dry to look natural under a layer of foundation meant for living, breathing people. Mortuary spray paint is usually applied over the finished makeup look to set it, but my mom uses it as a base. She applies it first, lets it dry, then goes to work creating a look that could rival any makeup artist. By my count, she's down to six cans of Smithfield's, and it usually takes a full can to do a single body, so I make a mental note to order another case and restock her cabinet.

In the hallway, my clothes are still spinning in the washer, and the shadowy silence of the basement is making me sleepy so I trudge back upstairs. I stop off in the kitchen to reheat my plate. As the plate turns in the microwave, I go to the fridge and am about to open it when my mom clears her throat. I almost break my ankle spinning around to find her face in the shadowy dark of the living room.

"Do not drink any of your dad's sweet tea," she says. "He made a whole pitcher and doesn't want to share."

I squint at her. The living room lights are off and she's got her face covered in a layer of light-colored cold cream. The muted glow from the microwave light is not helping her look any less nightmarish.

"Why are you sitting in the dark?" I ask. "You trying to give me a heart attack?"

"Never, baby," she says. "Your dad is having a stomach issue and he's using the bathroom in our room to handle it so I'm down here, away from the funk."

"Yikes," I say.

She sighs heavily and shakes her head. "That man needs a colonoscopy or something."

The microwave beeps and I take my food out.

"Can I eat in my room?" I ask.

She waves her hand. "Just don't leave the dishes up there."

"Okay," I say. "Night. Love you."

"Love you, baby," she says.

I retreat to my room at the top of the house. I set my food on the nightstand and stretch out across my bed. Over my head, window cards from the Broadway productions of *Sweeney Todd* and *Beetlejuice* are tacked on the slanted ceiling. Me and Noah had taken the FlixBus to the city to see a few shows.

I've pinned a bunch of photos between the other posters on my ceiling. One is of me and my mom when I was about seven, right before we moved in here. She's grinning and I'm grinning wider. She looks exactly the same now as she does in the picture. Meanwhile I'm taller, the baby fat that once plumped my cheeks has mostly gone away, my hair is longer.

Another photo, my favorite one, is of me and Noah. We were at Stewart Park with the lake in the background, our arms around each other, smiling like we didn't have a care in the world. Next to it, a picture of Noah and Caleb with me and Cipriana sitting on their respective shoulders. We'd all gone out to celebrate homecoming and one of our teachers had snapped the pic for us. Cipriana fell off Caleb's shoulders as soon as the picture was taken and broke her thumb. I laugh to myself. Poor Cip.

Noah's face is the one I hope to see when I close my eyes at night but I'm not that lucky. Lately, even when I stare at his picture, trying to burn it into my mind so that my subconscious or whatever it is that controls my dreams might have something better to take inspiration from, it never works. I still dream of my mom dying. The only thing that makes me feel better is that I don't need to dream about Noah. I can see him every day at school, or when we go for walks in the park or to the movies or when he comes over for dinner. I'd dated a girl in my freshman year for a month and a guy in my sophomore year for less than that. But with Noah, everything changed. Nobody sees me the way he does. My strange existence isn't so strange to him and that makes me feel like I don't have to change for him, or anyone else.

I take out my phone and am in the process of texting Noah when I think I would much rather hear his voice. I call him and he picks up on the second ring.

"Hey," he says groggily.

"Oh no. Were you asleep?"

"Nah."

"Liar."

He laughs lightly.

"I won't keep you up," I say. "I just wanted to say good night."

"Everything okay?" he asks. "You got that faraway sound in your voice."

I sigh. "Yeah."

"Didn't you just call me a liar? Look who's talking."

I smile. "Just, you know. Got a lot on my mind."

"The sleep thing?"

"Yeah." I try to hide how frustrated it makes me.

"The nightmare is keeping you from getting a good night's sleep," Noah says.

"Yeah, and you know, it's not even the fact that I've had it almost every night since my last birthday. It's like the dream makes me miss my mom even though she's right here." That is the truth I don't want to admit. The dream makes me think of what it would be like to be without my mom, and I hate it. It shakes me so bad sometimes I don't want to let her out of my sight. I've been trying to decide if it's fair for me to ask her to never ride in a car ever again. "It makes no sense and on top of that, it's changing."

"Really?" Noah asks, his gravelly voice ringing up a notch. "That's new, right?"

I sigh. "Yeah, and it just makes it more awful. Usually, I wake up right when my dad is crouched over my mom. It's like a bird's-eye view thing. But now—now I'm outside on the ground, staring up at the sky. And there's pain."

"Pain?" Noah asks.

"In my neck and in my chest and I'm screaming."

Noah is quiet for a moment. "I know we've talked about it before, but do you have any new ideas about what it means?"

"Not really, but I live in a house where dead people get carted around all day, every day. That's gotta have something to do with it, right?"

"But you had the dream when you were little," Noah says. "Before you started getting too involved with the dead people."

I huff. "Yeah. It started right before we moved here. It wasn't like this, though. It wasn't every night. I'm just—I have no idea what it's about."

"My grandma says dreams can be like messages," Noah says. "One time she had a dream about some fish and then boom, she found out my mom was pregnant with me."

"I've heard of stuff like that," I say.

"But do you believe it?"

I think for a moment. "I might? I don't know."

"I don't know if dreaming of fish means somebody's pregnant, but, like, sometimes maybe there's a deeper meaning behind it." Noah sighs. "My grandma also put Vicks on the bottom of my feet when I had a fever and she thought Robitussin could cure cancer so maybe she's not the most reliable source of information."

"Don't even talk about Grandma Peggy like that," I say, laughing. "Vicks works and Robitussin is the real deal."

"Yeah, okay," Noah chuckles. "It's all fun and games until you're eight and you get a cold. Now I have to explain why there's a piece of onion in my sock."

We laugh until we can't even form coherent sentences. When I finally get it together, I sigh. "Maybe if I could figure out what the dream is trying to tell me, I could get some sleep."

"I want that for you, Meeks. I really do," Noah says. My heart flutters a little when he calls me Meeks. "You come to school looking like you haven't slept in days," he continues. "And I know Cip and Caleb give you a hard time, but you need rest."

Cipriana and Caleb are not afraid to let me know when I look a mess. Since the dream started back up and it's affecting my sleep they keep telling me I look like a zombie, asking me if I'm a vampire since I like to stay up all night. A part of me thinks being an undead demon might actually be easier than being scared awake almost every single night and then walking around with this ache in my chest whenever I see my mom.

"If the nightmare is trying to tell me something is going to happen to my mom, I gotta figure it out." It sounds ridiculous but who has the same dream almost every night days or weeks at a time? It has to mean something. I wish I could pin it down and maybe do something about it.

"I love your mom," Noah says. "If there's anything I can do, please tell me."

"I will," I say.

"Hey," Noah says suddenly. "Can I ask you a question?"

"Depends on what it is," I tease.

"You ever see anything weird at your place? Like, I know you deal with bodies all the time but I mean . . . you ever see anything you can't explain?"

I laugh. "You've been watching too many ghost hunting shows."

Noah chuckles to himself. "That might be true, but I don't think I've ever asked you about anything like that before. I was reading this book about haunted places in Ithaca and thought I'd ask."

"I've never seen anything weird," I say. "Not here at least."

"Not there?" Noah asks. "But somewhere?"

"It was before we moved here," I say. "I woke up one night, I think I was maybe five? Could've been younger, but I swear I saw somebody outside my window. Somebody just standing there in the dark and his face was all messed up. His eyes were different colors and he just looked . . . wrong. I called for my mom and she came running but there wasn't anything there when she cut the light on."

"So it was, what?" Noah asks. "A ghost?"

"Probably not," I say. "Sorry to disappoint you but it was probably a creep."

"That's scarier than a ghost," Noah says.

"You're right about that," I say, laughing. "Listen, I'll let you go. See you tomorrow?"

"Yup," Noah says.

We stay quiet for a minute. We both have something to say but neither of us has worked up the courage to say it yet, and it feels like we're just waiting for the right time.

Noah laughs. "See you tomorrow."

"Okay."

I hang up and lie back. I'm such a coward, but I'm gonna say it. I know I will.

My phone buzzes as a text comes through from Noah—a single red heart.

CHAPTER 4

SITTING PRETTY

A knock at my door.

I turn toward it as it slowly creaks open.

"Mom?" I ask.

No answer.

My heart ticks up. There's a loud groan as the floorboard outside my room protests. Someone is standing on it. I swing my legs over the side of my bed and open my mouth to call for my mom again when my dad pokes his head in, but he's distracted, looking down at his phone as it lights up his face. I let out a long, slow breath. Noah's questions have me on edge.

"I hate to bother you," Dad says as he eyes the phone in my hand. "Who were you on the phone with? Noah?"

I nod. "Yeah. Just saying good night."

My dad's expression softens, and the corner of his mouth turns up. "Me and your mom used to talk all night when we were dating. We never wanted to be the first one to hang up. That's when we had landlines and we had to be tethered to the living room. You don't know nothing about that."

I laugh. "I know what a landline is, Dad. Give my generation some credit."

"Right," he says, straightening up. I notice he has on his official business suit—a charcoal two-piece with a white shirt underneath. "I was hoping you'd be up for a late-night pickup. I normally wouldn't ask, but your mom's exhausted. That stomach thing is really kicking her behind and we've just had a call about a guest."

I get up and search around in my various piles of clothes to find something to wear. "I'll get dressed. Be down in five?"

My dad nods and closes the door. I settle on a black sweatsuit. I probably won't have to talk to anyone so it's fine to wear my best nobody's-gonna-see-me outfit. I smooth out my hair, slip on a pair of sneakers, and meet my dad in the downstairs hallway.

Following him out back, I step into the frigid night air and wonder if I should have brought a jacket. I glance back at the house, then decide against it. My dad slips behind the wheel of the hearse and I slide into the passenger seat.

My mom has a Prius that she drives sometimes but I think all of us consider the hearse our main vehicle. I learned to drive in it which means I can basically drive anything because driving this thing is like driving a tank. Our 1957 Cadillac Superior Royal Crown hearse is an almost identical vehicle to the one they used in *Ghostbusters*. I've picked up my friends in it to go to the movies and on Halloween, we do a trunk-or-treat, handing candy out of the back. The car is old, but my dad has maintained every detail, from the sleek black exterior to the tan leather insides. It's his baby.

"Where are we going?" I ask. "Is the pickup in Ithaca?"

"It's about ten minutes from here." He sighs. "Another elderly guest. He had some kind of cardiac event. He's been gone a few hours. He had a DNR so he's probably in good shape."

A DNR. Do not resuscitate, a legal document that a person sets up before they die that says don't try to bring them back if they die. Sometimes when we pick up bodies where lifesaving measures were used they can be in rough shape—broken sternums or ribs from CPR, holes from tubes and needles, broken teeth from emergency intubation. It seems like this old guy, whoever he was, had had enough of this life.

"Should be a quick transfer," my dad continues. "Thanks for coming with me, Meka. I appreciate it."

I lean across the front seat and put my head on his shoulder. For all his strangeness, he's just a good guy. Our bonding activities might include picking up dead bodies in the middle of the night, but it's what works for us and I wouldn't want it any other way.

"You want me to go in and talk to the medical staff?" I ask. "I can get the paperwork and stuff."

He pauses, like he's considering it. "No, I—I think I can manage. They're waiting for us so hopefully it'll be fast. Sooner we get him into cold storage, the better."

I laugh a little.

"What's funny?" my dad asks.

"Nothing," I say. "Just casually talking about putting people in freezers. Not weird at all, right?"

"You worried about us being weird?" he asks.

I sigh. "Most of the time I don't care."

"And the other times?" he asks.

I shrug. "I don't know. I love what I do, I just—sometimes I think if I worked at Target or at the movies, people wouldn't have so much to say."

"Oh," my dad says softly.

"I don't want to work at those places, I'm just saying." I pause. What *am* I trying to say? "Other people don't get it. They think what we do is scary." I think of how many sideways glances I get from people at school just because they know that my family handles the funeral arrangements for their deceased loved ones. They avoid me like I'm the reaper or something.

My dad is quiet for a moment. "We are who we are," he says. "We come from a long line of people who take this work very seriously."

"I take it seriously too," I say.

"I know," my dad says. "But you don't have to. I want other things for you if this isn't the right fit."

"It is the right fit," I say. It is. But that doesn't mean that I don't wish there was some way to make people understand it better.

My dad reaches over and pats me on the leg. "You know, the people in our family—they did this work for so long, maybe it can end somewhere. Maybe you can be the first Redwood to beat the curse."

"Now we're cursed?" I ask, sitting straight up.

My dad chuckles to himself but it's sort of hollow sounding. "I'm joking," he says.

Ten minutes later my dad pulls the hearse up to the back door of a small senior living facility on the north side of town. Two night-nurses are waiting outside. I get out and open the rear door of the hearse while my dad talks to them.

"His family will be in touch in the morning," the nurse with the long blond hair says.

My dad nods as I pull the rolling floor out of the car, flipping down the loading ramp and making sure everything is secure. My dad disappears inside the building and a few minutes later returns pushing a gurney with an adult-size cardboard box on top of it. The top is open and tucked inside is a black plastic bag wrapping the remains of our new guest.

"Where's the lid?" I ask.

"They're out of them," my dad says.

The makeshift cardboard coffins usually come in two pieces and I've never had to load one without a top.

"Want me to cover it?" I ask. "I think there's an emergency blanket in the glove box."

"No," Dad says. "Let's just get him loaded up."

My dad wheels the gurney to the back of the car and I help him slide the box onto the ramp. We get the box and its contents into the rear of the hearse and my dad signs some paperwork with the blond nurse as I secure the temporary coffin. I climb into the rear compartment to make sure the lip of the rolling floor is flipped up, so the box doesn't slide off while we're driving. We've never had a body tumble over in the back of the car and I'd like to keep it that way.

"Appreciate your time," the nurse says.

"Right," Dad says. The nurse reaches for his hand to shake it and he does a weird half salute, then almost falls as he trips back toward the car. I smile to myself. I love my dad, but I think if you look next to the definition of "awkward" in the dictionary, you'd find a picture of him.

I'm about to get into the front seat when a loud cawing draws

44

my attention up to the pitch-black night sky. A half dozen ravens circle high overhead. I quickly get in and shut the door. My dad gets in too.

"That's over," he says, exhaling loudly. "Thank goodness. Your mom is so much better at this stuff than me."

"She is," I say, smiling.

My dad steers us back through downtown Ithaca. He avoids the city's cavernous potholes like they're land mines. Maybe it's because the hearse's suspension isn't great, maybe it's because our guest is in a drop-top coffin, but either way, he avoids as many as he can but he can't miss all of them. We bounce over a rut in the road and the bag inside the coffin rustles. I glance back making sure everything is still where it should be.

My dad reaches into his pocket and takes out his phone. "Can you text your mom and ask her to open the loading doors at the house?"

I reach for his phone but I fumble it and it disappears into the crevice of the front seat.

My dad grunts. "Why do they make the phones so slippery? It's ridiculous." He fishes around under his seat as he tries to keep his eyes on the road and his other hand on the wheel. Suddenly he sits bolt upright.

"What?" I ask. "Is it broken? Is the screen cracked?" I lean over and glance down between the seats. His phone is wedged in there but just below it is something else. It's a square corner of something—a book, a small flat box, I can't tell. A soft green light emanates from between the seats. "What's on your phone that's green?"

"What?" my dad asks but he says it so low I can barely hear him.

45

"Your phone," I say. "The lock screen, is it green?"

"Leave it," my dad says abruptly. "I'll get it when we're back at the house."

I stick my hand between the seats. "I can see it. It's right there." I grab the phone and my hand brushes the other object. There's a quick snap, like somebody popped a rubber band against my bare skin. I quickly withdraw my hand and examine my fingertips. I absolutely expect there to be blood.

"What is that?" I ask. My fingers are fine. No cut. No blood. Just an odd stinging sensation. I give my dad his phone. "There's something else under there. I thought it cut me."

My dad keeps his eyes forward as we pull to a stop at a red light. He reaches over and takes my hand, examining it closely.

"I thought something cut me," I repeat. "Or maybe, I don't know, burned me?" I look at the tips of my fingers. "It's the weirdest feeling."

I try to peer between the seats again as my dad lets go of my hand and readjusts himself in his seat. Now his jacket is covering the space between the seats.

"It's probably just something that slipped under the seat," my dad says. "Leave it."

Leave it.

He keeps saying that.

He'll probably use this as an excuse to detail the whole car himself, which he loves doing anyway, so I let it go.

Outside the foggy glass, the night is black. Little veins of crystalized condensation have begun to spread from the bottom of the passenger window, as if the temperature outside is plummeting. I press my forehead against the cold glass and shut my eyes.

I'm more tired than I realized. I let myself drift, my finger still throbbing in time with my heartbeat. We hit another pothole, and I hear the bag in the back shift again.

Slowly, our car comes to a stop. Behind my closed lids the glow of what is probably the stoplight presses in on me. It feels ominous . . . familiar. Like the dream.

"Meka," my dad says softly.

"Uh-huh," I murmur without opening my eyes.

My dad's breaths come in short, quick gasps.

I open my eyes.

We're at the intersection of East Court Street and North Aurora. St. Paul's sits on the corner, its familiar pride flag gently swaying in the biting breeze. A man in a safety vest is climbing out of a vehicle with bright green lettering on the side that reads Ithaca City Electrical Utility. He's putting orange cones on the road but waves us through.

"Dad, he's letting us go. We don't have to stop."

My dad doesn't say anything and he doesn't drive past the utility worker. He's looking straight ahead, eyes wide, his lips slightly parted.

I put my hand on his shoulder. "Dad?"

Then I realize, in the red glow of the stoplight, he's not looking ahead.

He is looking in the rearview mirror.

From the corner of my eye I register a brief movement, like a shadow moving across an already darkened space. A cold tremor rocks my body.

The black bag rustles again.

The person inside it is moving.

47

I turn my head even as everything in me screams not to.

The guest we just loaded into the back of the hearse is sitting straight up.

The head-end portion of the body bag has come partially unzipped. In the folds of the black plastic is a milky white eye and an open, gaping mouth.

"Meka," my dad whispers. "Don't panic. It's—"

The noise that comes out of my throat is less of a scream and more like a ragged tear. It rips through the inside of the car. My dad flinches so hard he hits his head on the low ceiling. I fumble with the lock and spill out onto the pavement at the intersection. The cold whips my face as I slip on the frost-covered pavement, trying to get enough traction to run. My dad stumbles out, rounds the front of the car, and grabs me by the shoulders.

"Meka! Meka, please calm down!"

"He—he *sat* up! He's not dead!"

"Yes, he is," my dad says. "He is dead. Meka, I need you to breathe."

I try to remember how to do that.

"Remember your training. Corpses do that sometimes." He holds on to me firmly as the panic begins to subside.

"My training?" I ask as I peer through the window of the hearse. The man is still sitting up, the black plastic body bag draped around him like a shroud.

The utility worker walks over, a look of concern stretched across his face.

"Everything okay?" he asks. He looks between me and my dad, then glances at the hearse. His eyes grow wide. "What the hell is happening in the back of your car?"

My dad tries to shoo the man away but he doesn't budge.

"I'm Jonathan Redwood and we're transporting a guest . . . a body . . . to the Redwood Funeral Home."

"He ain't dead!" the man says as his tone creeps up.

"I can assure you he is. This happens sometimes," my dad says, turning back to me. "You know this. It's happened before. In the prep room. I told you about it, remember?"

I search my memory for this and find it tucked away among other things I don't like to think about. Last year, during spring break, my dad had come up from the prep room looking more distressed than usual and told me and my mom that one of our guests had sat partially up during embalming. Not many things scare my dad but this had shaken him.

"That's all this is," my dad says in a flat, monotone kind of way. "An anomaly that is all too common in our business. Breathe, Meka. Just breathe."

I do and it helps. Some.

I can see our house from the intersection. I consider walking the rest of the way but my dad ushers me to the side of the car. The utility worker returns to his vehicle and I can tell by the way his face is lit up in the cab that he's on his phone.

My dad ducks halfway into our car and reaches over the seat to give the body a little shove. The corpse falls back and settles into the cardboard coffin.

"Let's get home," my dad says, giving my shoulder a little squeeze.

I sit backward in the front seat, keeping watch on the man in his body bag. I don't take my eyes off him until we wheel him out of the hearse and into cold storage in our basement. I double-check the door is locked.

My dad puts his arm around me and I allow myself to relax a little.

"So sorry about this," he says, but he was right. These things *do* happen. There have been lots of documented cases of corpses moving, even making sounds. My dad has seen bodies move on their own and when I think about it, so have I. Nothing like the horror show I just witnessed in the hearse but I'd seen an arm or leg twitch while I was doing a guest's makeup or hair. I'd seen the eyes or mouths of some of our guests open. Images of me supergluing Mrs. Lang's eyelids closed flood my brain.

"It's okay," I say. "It just scared me."

"Me too," my dad says. He's staring at the door to the cold storage room with a familiar kind of distance. Like he's thinking of something far away. "I'm so sorry."

"Dad," I say. "It's really okay." It is, but he's taking the incident much harder than I'd expected. He just looks so sad.

He gently takes my hand and examines it. "Is your finger okay?"

I'd forgotten about it. Seeing a dead body sit up in the back of your car kind of makes everything else irrelevant, I guess.

"It's fine," I say. "It doesn't even hurt anymore." There was a lingering tingly sensation, but no pain. "What was that under your seat anyway?"

My dad shrugs. "I'm not sure. Something must have slid out of my bag. I'll clean it out tomorrow. You should get some rest."

I give my dad a hug and head up to my room. I strip off my sweats and throw on some shorts and a T-shirt, cut out the lights, and crawl into bed. The nighttime is still and quiet. I hear my dad downstairs still, though. I expect him to trudge up the steps and past my room but instead, the back door opens. Its distinctive creak filters up to me and I sit up.

Pushing the curtain aside I peer out my window. I have a bird's-eye view of the rear driveway, the dumpster, and the garage. My dad is slinking across the drive and he goes to the driver's side of the hearse. He's got his work briefcase in his hand. He leans into the car and that strange green light filters out. Had he taken his phone to the car with him? I can't tell from my vantage point but a moment later, the light goes out and he shuts the door, returning to the house with his bag. He comes upstairs and pauses just outside my door. I can see his shadow in the faint glow of the hall light. It's quiet for a second, but I can tell he's there; then he continues into his room, shutting the door with a soft thud.

I grab my phone and google how often corpses sit up on their own. The answer that pops up . . . is none. The results say that a corpse fully sitting up is not something that happens—ever. Twitching extremities, yes. A deep sigh that's attributed to the buildup of gases inside a body, yes. But full-on seated corpses? According to Beyoncé's internet, that's not something that happens anywhere except right here at the Redwood Funeral Home.

CHAPTER 5

MOVIES

I sit at the lunch table the following day, resting my head against my forearms trying not to fall asleep completely. I'm exhausted. The dream had come again in the night and when it woke me at 4 AM, I decided to just stay up.

"Remember when we used to be able to take naps at school?" Cipriana asks as she scribbles something in her notebook and slurps Coke through a paper straw. "Those were the days. Bring a blanket and a stuffed animal and just curl up and go to sleep?" She almost swoons as she lets herself fall headfirst into the memory. "I'd give anything to go back to kindy."

"I want to know who decided teenagers don't need naps," Caleb chimes in. He clears his throat and pulls his mask up over his nose. "COVID came through and beat my ass a couple weeks ago and I'm still tired. I could really use some sleep right now, but Mr. Forrester says I have to make up all the work I missed. I deserve a nap, damnit. My lungs feel like they're gonna flip inside out every time I cough."

"That's awful," I say. "I'm sorry."

"And people keep asking me why I'm wearing a mask." Caleb rolls his eyes. "Next person that asks is gonna get the truth. I'm ugly and contagious. Mind your damn business!"

"You're not ugly," Cipriana says. "And I never wanna hear you say that about yourself ever again."

Caleb waves it off. "It's fine. Where's Noah? He said he was gonna help me out with this English assignment." He slaps a folder full of worksheets on the table. "Anybody know what a preposition is? Sounds like hemorrhoid cream."

"Umm, no," Cipriana says. "A preposition is a word or group of words that connects pronouns, nouns, or phrases to other words in a sentence."

Caleb looks at Cipriana with a blank expression on his face. "What did you just say to me?"

Cipriana rolls her eyes. "Get it together, please. You can't be half-assing it through every lesson."

Caleb slides his folder full of papers toward Cipriana. "Best friends help each other out."

Cipriana slides the folder right back to him. "This is me helping you. Do it yourself. Google is free."

Caleb scowls dramatically. "Where's Noah?" he asks. "He'll help me."

I scan the cafeteria and spot Noah as he waltzes in. More than a few heads turn to look at him, but he doesn't seem to notice as he zigzags through the crowd. He's not in his corpse attire and makeup but I don't know what it says about me that I like the way he looks both with or without it. He's tall, broad-shouldered, and his curly brown hair is always falling across his face in a way that makes something deep inside me twist up in the best way possible.

"Umm, I need you to calm down," Cipriana says as she grins at me. "We're in school, Meka."

"Shut up," I say, embarrassed that the way I'm feeling inside is so obvious to everyone around me.

Cip, still grinning, runs her tongue over her braces and clicks her teeth together. "It's okay. You don't have to act like you don't wanna eat him up right here in front of everybody. We get it."

The hot rush of embarrassment works its way up my neck and across my face as Noah slides into the seat next to me.

"Dang," Cipriana says. "Got your whole little fit on today, huh? Who you tryna impress?"

Noah turns and looks directly into my face. "Just one person." He kisses me gently on the cheek and nudges me with his shoulder. "Movies later?"

"Ohhh yes!" Caleb says. "There's this new horror movie out, what's it called?" He turns to Cipriana. "Help me out here."

"Hold on," I say. "You ran out of my house screaming the other day. Now you're tryna go see a scary movie?"

"I wasn't screaming," Caleb says. "I was yelling. There's a difference."

"I'm pretty sure you were screaming," Noah said. "And you almost got hit by a car."

"Whatever," Caleb says.

"I don't do horror," Cipriana says. "Y'all know this."

"Since when?" Caleb looks confused. "You're the one that makes us watch all those terrible ass horror movies. You know, the ones that go straight to streaming because they're so awful. What was that last one called? Killer Couch?"

"*Killer Sofa*," Cipriana corrects. "And that's why I like them. They're not actually scary. You want me to go get scared for real. No thanks."

Caleb rolls his eyes and turns to me. "Come on, Meka. You're not scared, are you? You'll go, right?"

"I can't," I say. "We've got, like, three guests to prep and I have to help."

Caleb's entire frame goes rigid.

"What's wrong?" I ask. "Having a flashback?"

"Damn, Caleb," Noah says. "I was wearing a costume. Nobody was actually dead. Please relax."

"We were in Meka's kitchen but there were dead bodies in the basement," Caleb said.

"It's a funeral home," Cipriana says. "What? You think the dead folks sit on the couch? At the dinner table?"

"Stop!" Caleb says a little too loudly. He quiets himself and hunches over his lunch. "It creeps me out when you call them *guests*."

"I mean, it sounds better than 'dead bodies,' right?" I ask.

Caleb looks like he's going to puke.

"Everybody dies, Caleb," says Cipriana.

Caleb huffs. "I know. Doesn't mean I wanna talk about it."

"You wanna hear something creepy?" I ask. Caleb is about to say no, and I'm about to tell him about the incident in the car but change my mind when I see how scared he already is. I decide not to torment him right at this moment. "This little girl came over for her grandma's funeral," I say, opting for the marginally less creepy story. "She drew a picture of herself holding hands with her dead grandma and then she drew a picture of me in a coffin."

Caleb and Cipriana look at me with their mouths slightly open. Noah blinks a few times and shakes his head.

"See," Caleb says. "Absolutely not. This is why we need to normalize punching little kids in the throat."

"Caleb!" Cipriana says. "Stop it!"

"No," Caleb says. "You draw me in a coffin, we're fighting. Baby or not. Two jabs to the esophagus."

I laugh so hard I almost choke.

Noah sets his hand on top of mine. "You sure you can't go? We could catch an early showing." He takes out his phone and looks up the movie times. "We could go and be done by six." He puts his phone away and leans closer to me so that his mouth is brushing my ear. "I can come to your house after, if you want. We could just hang out."

I grin at him and put my head on his shoulder.

"Are you two gonna gaze into each other's eyes all night?" Caleb asks. "Because if you are, you're uninvited."

"We'll all go," I say. Noah grins.

"Cip, you coming or not?" Caleb asks.

Cipriana hesitates.

"Suck it up!" Caleb says. "It's a zombie flick. I'll buy you a hot dog."

Cipriana's entire demeanor changes at the mention of food. "And a large soda?"

Caleb cocks his head to the side. "Do I look rich to you? A large soda and a hot dog is gonna be at least twenty bucks."

"I'm not a cheap date, thank you very much," Cipriana says. "What's it gonna be?"

56

Caleb crosses his arms over his chest. "Y'all see this? She's taking advantage of me and y'all just let her."

"Oh, I meant to tell you," Noah says as he traces circles on the back of my hand. "I have something for you. I'll give it to you later when we go back to your house."

"Like a present?" I ask.

Noah nods. "Nothing crazy, just something I made."

Cipriana sucks in a breath and the corners of her mouth turn down. "You made something for her with your own two hands? Like, you crafted that shit?"

Noah chuckles. "Yeah. So?"

Cipriana gazes down at the lunch table. "I can't even get this bum Peter to buy me McDonald's."

"Leave him!" Caleb shrieks, pounding his hand on the table like he's immediately had enough. "Who names their child 'Peter' anyway? Are we in biblical times?"

"My name is literally Noah," Noah says, holding back a laugh.

Caleb looks absolutely flabbergasted for a second before turning back to Cipriana. "You're too good for him and you deserve all the chicken nuggets, boo. A whole ten-piece."

"And a milkshake," Noah says.

"And a Filet-O-Fish," I add.

Cipriana's face twists up in disgust. "Okay, now y'all are going too far."

As the bell rings, Noah pulls me up and puts his arms around me. "Film studies?"

I nod. It's the only class we have together and I look forward to it every single day.

Cip and Caleb head off while me and Noah make our way to Mrs. Sheffield's class.

Film studies is run out of the old cafeteria in the C wing of Ithaca High. The sparkly new cafeteria is on the opposite side of the building and went up because the original space couldn't accommodate our universal lunch policy—all students, all grades, all at once. I sometimes wonder what genius thought having every single person in the school in one cafeteria at the same time was a good idea.

Noah and I get to class just before the bell sounds, and we take up our unofficial assigned seats. We always sit up front, close to the projector screen that hangs from the ceiling.

"Please don't let whatever we're watching today be as boring as *Nosferatu*," Sean Abrams, a super-senior, moans from the back row of seats.

Mrs. Sheffield doesn't even look up from her computer as she sits perched on the edge of a folding chair. "You need the credit this class will earn you, Mr. Abrams. I'm the only person willing to accommodate you. A little less complaining, a little more appreciation. *Nosferatu* is a classic."

Sean rolls his eyes and Noah just chuckles to himself as the rest of our class files in. We've only got about fifteen kids because Mrs. Sheffield is picky about who gets to take this class. Most students think it's just watching movies and messing around but there's more to it than that. Mrs. Sheffield expects reports and in-depth reviews for every film we see.

Mrs. Sheffield gets up and turns off the lights. It doesn't help much considering the entire east-facing wall is all windows with shades that barely work.

"Our film today will be *The Wizard of Oz* starring Judy Garland," Mrs. Sheffield says.

A murmur runs through our group.

"Mrs. Sheffield," one of my classmates, Hayley, says. "I've seen this. We've probably all seen it."

Mrs. Sheffield looks down her nose at Hayley, who quickly sits back. "Is that so? Well, tell me, then, who directed it? What kinds of revolutionary filmmaking techniques were pioneered during its production? What impact did it have on the studio or on its star actress? Are you aware that the 2005 film *War of the Worlds* took its cues from this film?"

"Huh?" Sean grunts from the back row. "The movie with Thomas Cruise?"

Noah twists around in his seat and stares at Sean. "Who's Thomas Cruise?"

"You know," Sean says. "He's in that vampire movie we watched, and he's always skydiving and flying planes and shit."

"Enough," Mrs. Sheffield says. She didn't raise her voice but the way she said it sounded a lot like shut-the-hell-up-Sean.

Noah turns back around and leans close. "He means Tom Cruise and I swear to god if he's serious when he said he thinks his name is Thomas, I'm gonna lose my mind."

"I mean, Tom is short for Thomas," I say. "And my dad thinks Timothée Chalamet's name is Tim Chalet."

Noah almost chokes trying to hold in his laughter. I want to join him but I think it might send Mrs. Sheffield over the edge. As she hits "Play" on the projector, I nestle in close to Noah. The sepia tones of the film's opening credits can't compete with the glare from the windows so I get up and go to the side of the room to see if there's anything I can do. I wouldn't mind just staying huddled up with Noah for the next hour and a half but if we can't see the movie, we can't prepare for the pop quiz Mrs. Sheffield is definitely going to spring on us.

I pull over a mobile whiteboard to try blocking out some of the light. It works a little but it's the sunlight from higher up that's the issue. I pull on the tangled cords that are meant to control the shades but they're so knotted, it barely does anything. As I'm studying the tangles, trying to decide if it's even worth trying to undo, I glance up. The courtyard outside the window is empty and covered in a light dusting of snow. Beyond it, the road is clear except for one car that's parked and one person standing on the sidewalk. They're bundled up so thoroughly I can't see their face but they're turned toward the window I'm looking out of. Whoever it is, is just off the car's rear bumper.

"Miss Redwood," Mrs. Sheffield says.

I turn to look at her. "Yes?"

"I appreciate you trying to help but you know it won't do any good," she says. "Please take your seat. We'll all just have to endure the glare."

I glance back outside to find that the person has disappeared.

When school lets out, I text my mom to tell her where I'm headed and me and Noah wait for Caleb to pull his car around. High above, in the cold, clear sky, ravens circle in a group of maybe a dozen or so. Their squawking echoes down and the other students look to me and then to the birds like it's my fault. Cipriana finally joins us, looking irritated.

"What's wrong?" I ask.

"Peter." She spits out his name like a curse word. "I invited him to come with us and he said he can't because he's going home to take a nap."

"Huh?" Noah asks, bewildered.

I grimace a little. "Cip, I love you. You know that. So I'm only being honest—"

"You don't need to say it," Cip says, holding up her hand. "It's a lie. I get it. I'm so sick of him."

"Dump him," Noah says. "You want me to tell him for you?"

Cipriana huffs. "No. It's fine. I'll get around to it eventually."

Maybe she will or maybe she'll keep making excuses for him like she always does but I've learned that some people have to do things in their own time. Cipriana is stubborn and thinks she can fix the dustiest boy on Ithaca High's lacrosse team. I just wonder how many more times she's gonna get her heart broken before she realizes that it's not her job to fix him.

Caleb pulls up and I take a long, slow breath. Caleb's car is, like, if somebody took seven different beaters and smashed them all together. I don't even know what make and model this Frankenstein of a car is because I'm pretty sure the body, doors, hood, and roof all come from different vehicles. I'm surprised it's even allowed to be on the road.

Caleb reaches over and rolls down the window . . . like, manually rolls it down. "Get in and don't slam the doors because the glass will drop down inside it."

"What does that even mean?" Noah asks.

"Exactly what I said," Caleb says.

Cipriana slides into the front passenger seat and me and Noah cram ourselves into the back. Noah's knees press into Cipriana's seat.

"Can you scoot up?" Noah asks.

Cipriana looks around for a handle on the side of the seat.

"Ain't no scooting up," Caleb says. "These seats don't move."

"We should take the hearse," I say. I'm only half joking.

"Over my dead body," Caleb says. "I bet it stinks in there."

"It stinks in *here*, Caleb," Noah says, annoyed. "It literally smells like open ass."

Caleb grins. "My gym bag is back there."

Noah and I exchange glances and then start to laugh as Cipriana pulls her shirt up over her nose.

Noah almost gags as he shoves Caleb's gym bag as far under the seat as it will go.

"Hurry up and drive so we can get some air circulating here," Cip says. "I feel like I can taste the funk."

As we turn out of the parking lot the car backfires and the sound, like a shotgun blast, ricochets through the interior. My heart jumps into my throat and Noah's eyes grow wide.

"When's the last time you had this thing looked at by a mechanic?" Noah asks.

"Who got money for that?" Caleb asks. "I make minimum wage at the animal shelter. I can barely afford gas."

Cipriana pulls her coat in around her. "Put the heat on, Caleb. I'm freezing."

"Heat only works once the car has been on for seventy-two minutes," Caleb says. "You know that. Why are y'all in here acting brand-new?"

Cipriana scowls.

"Just leave the heat off," Noah says. "Otherwise, it's gonna smell like roasted jock strap in here."

I almost gag.

"My god," Cipriana says. "Hurry up and get us to the movies so we can get out."

Ithaca's only movie theater that isn't for university students or

62

an indie place is in the shadowy remains of the Ithaca Mall. Like most malls, it's a collection of stores with weird hours and nothing anybody really wants. All the good places moved out of it and now the local hospital is taking over one of the wings for its admin department. There's an Auntie Anne's and there's a Claire's but besides the movie theater, that's about it.

We get our tickets from the kiosk and go in to find the place mostly abandoned. Two of our classmates are working the concession stand. The smell of popcorn and hot dogs that have been on rollers under the hot lights way too long wafts through the air.

Caleb buys Cipriana a large popcorn and a Coke. I buy Noah a tray of nachos and I grab a bag of Sour Patch Kids for myself. We find our seats in the middle of a mostly empty theater.

"Nobody is tryna see a zombie movie?" Caleb asks. "Cowards."

Two people are sitting in the back row and one more person is sitting close to the screen.

Cipriana and I sit between Noah and Caleb as a few other people trickle in.

The lights dim as Noah and I split both the nachos and the sour gummies as the previews roll. When the movie finally begins, Cipriana hides behind her hands as zombies get hacked to pieces by the cast of survivors.

"So gross," Cipriana whispers.

Noah interlaces his fingers with mine and I lean my head on his shoulder. It feels right for me and Noah to be snuggled up as we watch a zombie snack on somebody's brains. It's on brand for us. There's a sudden thud on the back of my seat.

I glance back. The two people from the rear of the theater had moved up and are now sitting directly behind us. Why sit directly behind us in a mostly empty theater? I turn my attention back to the screen, annoyed. I shove a handful of Sour Patch Kids in my mouth.

The theater is bathed in a hazy orange light as the survivors run from a horde of zombies on-screen. I lean on Noah's arm and he traces his fingers across my knee. Cipriana offers me the bag of popcorn and I shake my head but as I do, I catch a whiff of something. I peer into the bag. It's just popcorn, and I can smell the butter but there's something else. It's not coming from the bag.

My heart ticks up because I think I recognize the smell. It's subtle but unmistakable. It is the smell of human rot. I lean back and try to discreetly check myself. The smell can transfer to me— my clothes, my hair—if I'm close to a guest for an extended period of time. I'm super self-conscious about this so I almost never allow it to happen but there have been times when I forgot to cover my hair or wear an apron. I put my arm up and sniff the sleeves of my shirt. Nothing. My hair is slicked up so I can't tell if it's that.

I lean closer to Noah. "Do I smell funny to you?"

Noah peers at me in the dark. A devilish little grin pulls itself across his face and he puts his nose against the side of my neck, pressing his face into my skin. His lips trail along my jaw as he pulls back.

"You smell great," he says.

My heart is thudding but for a different reason now. "Good. I thought I smelled . . . something."

"Probably this nasty ass carpet they got in here," Noah whispers.

Another hard thump on my seat. This time Noah twists around.

"You wanna put your feet down?" he asks as he stares at the men sitting behind us.

One of the guys laughs but puts his foot on the floor.

I glance back again. They're both stocky and about my dad's age. One of them has bright blue eyes and blond hair. He looks familiar, but I can't place him. The other guy is wearing a beanie and keeps his gaze focused downward. You'd think they'd know how to act in a movie theater at their big ages, but I guess not.

The two men stay quiet for the rest of the movie but when the lights come up they don't stand. They mean mug us as we move toward the exit. Noah puts his arm around me and ushers Cipriana forward, away from the men, who just stare at us.

"Why the hell are old men so creepy?" Cipriana asks. She says it loud enough for them to hear but we're out the door before they can respond.

"You're not allowed to pick the movies anymore, Caleb," Noah says.

Caleb nods in agreement. "I'm taking that privilege away from my damn self because what the actual hell was that?"

"I liked the part where the two zombies fell in love," Cipriana says. "It's romantic."

"Romantic?" I ask. "Skin falling off. Breath probably funky as hell. But they're in love. That's the part you liked?"

"I don't even get why that was in there," Noah says, kissing me gently on the side of my face and gripping my hand in his. "It was random."

"Some of us need love too," Cipriana says. "Y'all two got it. Maybe leave some for the rest of us."

"I got love," Caleb says. "I'm about to make Jeremy from the basketball team my husband."

Cipriana whips her head around. "Do you even know him? Does he even know you?"

"No, but he will," Caleb says. "We're gonna get to know each other real well, real soon."

My phone buzzes in my pocket and I take it out to see a message from my dad.

DAD: Everything okay?
ME: Yup. Just got done at the movies. Some guys here were being rude.
DAD: Really?
ME: Yeah. No big deal. Omw home now.

Three little dots pop up on the screen like he's texting something else. My dad isn't big on texting and I'm actually a little surprised it's him on the phone and not my mom.

The dots disappear.

"Your dad?" Noah asks.

I nod. "We're expecting some new guests so he's probably just making sure I'll be back soon to help out."

"I don't know how you do it, Meka," Caleb says. "I really don't."

"I wanna know when you're gonna get over it," Noah asks. "Meka's been doing the same thing her whole life. It's not new."

"I'm never gonna get over it, actually," Caleb says in a snarky tone that gets under my skin a little.

"You should," I say.

We pile into the car and sit in awkward silence for a minute.

"Can I tell y'all something?" Caleb asks.

Silence again. Caleb isn't the ask-permission type. It's in his head and out his mouth, always.

"You're scaring me a little," Cipriana says. "You sound serious."

"I am," Caleb says. "You know my grandma died three years ago."

I do. Me and my family did the body. It was heartbreaking but my mom made sure Mrs. Henrietta Milley went out looking as gorgeous as she did in life. Caleb, however, didn't get a chance to see her because he was too afraid to look into her casket or come to the viewing. I reach up and put my hand on his shoulder.

"I know I give you a hard time about it, Meka," Caleb says. "I think it's my way of keeping it at a distance, you know? Like if I don't see it, or hear about it, then I don't have to think about the fact that people just up and die and that's it. It's all over."

Cipriana looks down into her lap and bites at her bottom lip. "You said you were serious and you weren't joking, huh? I'm so sorry, Caleb. I know you loved her a lot."

"It's okay, though," I cut in. "I get it. I promise I do."

Caleb twists around in the seat and stares at me with tears in his eyes. "You got to see her and I didn't because I was scared. Maybe a little part of me is mad about that."

I try to think of what to say to him. I can see the hurt in his face and I can hear it in his voice. I gently touch the side of his face.

"All the things me and my family do are for the living, Caleb," I say. "The dead don't care about hair and makeup or fancy coffins. All we're trying to do is make the goodbye as easy as possible for the people who get left behind because we have to keep going even when it feels like the whole world should just stop."

Cipriana dabs at her eyes and over my shoulder Noah sniffles.

"But it doesn't stop," Caleb says.

"It doesn't," I say. "So we keep going. We try to be happy and we go to the movies and we let our friends drive us around in a car that smells like you got a dead body in the back."

Caleb smiles even though his eyes are glassy.

"For real," Noah says. "If that's your gym bag smelling like that I think you need to go to the doctor or something. Are you using the deodorant with the chemicals?"

"I use the one made from a crystal that you gotta run under the tap," Caleb says.

Noah shakes his head. "Absolutely not. You need the aluminum, the bleach, all that because *damn*."

"Not too much on stinky-Caleb," Cipriana says.

"Love you guys," Caleb says.

"We love you too," I say. "You wanna help me move some bodies later? I think that's what my dad was texting me for."

Caleb's eyes grow wide.

"I'm joking," I say, squeezing his shoulder. "It's just jokes."

"Oh, I know," Caleb says, turning around and starting the car. "Because the day you catch me pushing bodies around is the day hell has officially frozen over."

We all laugh, breaking up some of the intensity of the very serious conversation we just had. Some part of me feels lighter. Noah covers my hand with his and kisses me on the cheek again. Caleb steers us out of the parking lot and around the back side of the mall. As we bump along the road, another car pulls behind us. Caleb glances in the rearview mirror.

"Damn," he says. "This guy is right on me."

I turn around and look into the car behind us. The blond man is behind the wheel. He revs his engine and his car comes perilously close to Caleb's rear bumper.

"Pull over and let him pass," I say.

Caleb brings the car to a crawl as he pushes it as far to the right as he can. The car behind us zooms around and flies past in a hail of dust.

"Annoying," says Cip.

I glance out and see if I can get the license plate but the car doesn't have one.

CHAPTER 6

A KISS BEFORE DYING

Caleb drops me and Noah off in front of Ithaca Falls, just a few blocks from my house. January in Ithaca brings with it a sometimes biting cold, made all the more intolerable by the gusty winds that roll off Cayuga Lake. The waterfalls are beautiful in the summer but in the winter, when the water freezes, the entire thing looks like it belongs on another planet. Tendrils of ice form on the face of the falls; giant icicles cling to the rocky facade. I've lived in Ithaca most of my life, walk past the falls every day, and it still stirs a sense of awe in me. A gust of wind snaps me out of my thoughts.

"Shiiiiit," I say through chattering teeth. "I love it here but maybe we should've had Caleb just take us back to my place."

Noah grabs my arm and pulls me onto the secluded path that leads to the base of the falls. The birch trees have long since lost their leaves, but their trunks are crowded together so tightly they offer a little shelter from the wind.

"This cold is disrespectful," I say. "I'm about to start wearing a snowsuit like when I was little."

Noah chuckles as he pulls me close and gazes up at a wall of stones that reaches high over our heads. People have written their names on the faces of the rocks, others have left messages.

"Have we put our initials on this?" Noah asks.

"No," I say.

Most of the graffiti is written in Sharpie or ink but Noah picks up a small rock and scratches our initials onto a stone.

"There," he says. "Perfect."

"That's gonna wash away when it rains or snows," I say.

Noah smiles. "That's okay. We'll know it was there. That's all that matters." He reaches up about a foot over his head and sets the rock on a small ledge.

It's a nice sentiment and Noah is really good at pointing out little stuff like that. It reminds me of my own job and how what I told Caleb was true—the things we do aren't permanent or lasting or meant to do anything other than make people feel better in the moment. This moment with Noah, our names etched on a rock that no one may ever know about except for us, is just like that. But it's okay. It still counts. It's still worth something. It still matters.

"Remember last summer when Caleb found a leech on his back after we went swimming over here?" I ask. We'd spent so many of our summer days at the natural pool near the base of the falls just hanging out and doing nothing. I was always a little too wary of weird stuff in the water to get all the way in, but Caleb and Noah didn't care.

Noah claps his hand over his mouth as he laughs. "I told him it was stuck on him and he just started screaming."

"We literally had to hold him down to get it off," I say. "He didn't go back in the rest of the summer."

"I don't blame him," Noah says. "But I'm gonna make him come back over here when it warms up. He's gotta get over it at some point."

"He's never going back in the water."

Noah's mouth twists into a sly grin. "We'll see. I bet I can convince him. Maybe we get what's-his-name to come out here too."

"Jeremy?" I ask. "What are you? A matchmaker?"

"Maybe," Noah says. "Just go with it, Meeks. Watch me work my magic. After I get them two together, I'm going to get Cip to break up with that bum Moses—"

"His name's Peter," I say, laughing.

"You know who I mean," Noah says.

We're both laughing so hard we fall all over each other. As I try to find my footing, Noah leans in close and kisses me. I want to stay in this moment forever but the wind whips across my face again and takes my breath away almost as much as Noah does.

"Cold?" he whispers against my lips.

"A little," I say.

"You're trembling," he says softly.

"That's not from the cold," I say.

He kisses me again and we could be in a blizzard for all I know. Nothing else really matters.

"We should get out of here before you freeze to death," Noah says.

"Let me," I say. "I just wanna stay here with you."

Noah scoops me up and trudges up the little hill. I hold fast to his neck, laughing, hoping he doesn't slip on the ice because if he falls, we're both done. I glance over his shoulder and see that someone has taken our place at the wall of stones and is gazing up at it. They're tucked inside a big brown coat and I can't see their face. This person's head is nearly level with the ledge where Noah had put our rock. Another gust of wind slaps me across the cheek and I squeal as Noah deposits me on the sidewalk, then grabs my hand and rushes me down the street. We trek toward my house with our heads bowed against the gusty air. As we turn onto East Court Street, Noah grins, little flecks of snow sticking in his dark brows and lashes.

"What's funny?" I ask.

Noah shrugs. "I just—it's just wild how this cold is about to make me run inside your house, dead bodies be damned."

A flurry of snow sweeps over us, and Noah grabs my arm, all but dragging me up the front steps of my house. A necklace of icicles hangs from the ebony trim of the roof two floors above, and Noah eyes them cautiously as I fish around in my bag for my key. I finally find it, but my fingers are stiff from the cold.

"Any day now, Meeks," Noah says as he bounces from one foot to the other. "I'm freezing my nuts off."

I fumble the key—not from the cold this time—but recover before Noah notices. Before I can put it in the lock, my mom pulls the front door open. She's dressed in a pair of wide-leg pants and a billowy gray blouse, her silk press perfectly coiffed, her winged eyeliner sharp. She jumps, letting out a little squeak.

Her gaze flits to Noah and her mouth turns up. "Noah, baby! Where you been hiding?" She lets go of me and pulls Noah into an embrace. He's so much taller than her that she looks like a little kid next to him.

"You're not busy are you?" Noah asks as he eyes the front room.

My mom pats his arm. "Don't worry. There's nobody in there

73

right now but we are expecting a . . . delivery." She turns to me. "I hate to have you working while you've got company, baby, but I'm gonna need your help later."

"No, I know," I say. "It's okay. Is it all right if we go upstairs?"

Mom looks Noah over from head to toe. "You know the rules."

"Ma'am, I'm not tryna end up on one of your little tables in the basement," Noah says.

Mom pats his shoulder. "Follow my rules and we won't have any issues, baby."

Noah looks like he wants to disappear into the ether, so I take him by the hand and retreat to my room, where I leave the door wide open and remind him that he can't sit on my bed. Mom's rules and mine too. Noah takes off his coat, cuts on the little heater in the corner and sits down right in front of it, rubbing his hands together. The baseboard heating in houses as old as mine isn't enough to contend with the central New York winters, so my mom put a space heater in each room for when the temperatures dip. I pull up music on my phone and connect it to my Bluetooth speaker. The soft guitar and haunting vocals drift out.

"You're obsessed with this man," Noah teases. "I guess a six-foot-something Irish dude really does it for you, huh?"

I laugh. "Hozier is a beautiful man. I can't even lie." I sit down next to Noah and put my head on his shoulder.

"Yeah, okay," Noah says, grinning. "The music's good." He closes his eyes and tilts his head back as the music plays. "What's this one talking about? It sounds kind of sad."

The music echoes in my room and I close my eyes too. "It's about feeling like there's this distance between two people," I say. "It's like your biggest fear is being unknown or misunderstood by somebody you care about."

I open my eyes and Noah is staring at me. His face very close to mine.

"You're listening to this song because it's beautiful, not because it feels true to you, right?" he asks.

I look away. Staring straight at him feels too vulnerable, too open. "Right."

He runs his hand down my arm and my skin feels like it's turned to fire under his touch. The rush of heat is almost too much. "I know you, Meeks," he says. "You don't ever have to worry about being unknown, at least not by me."

My face flushes hot and I feel like I can't quite catch my breath. "I know," I say. "You're not like Peter is with Cip."

Noah scowls. "Because my mom raised me better than that. I don't know what Peter's problem is, but Cip deserves better. All she has to do is say the word. I'll choke Peter out."

I raise an eyebrow in surprise. Noah isn't the fighting type. Protective, yes. Able to actually throw hands? I don't really know. I've never seen him do that.

"Okay, maybe not *choke*," Noah says. "Maybe just loudly remind him that he's trash." He lets the tips of his fingers trail along the side of my face and under my chin. "I'd never treat you like that. I can't even imagine it."

The warmth from the space heater and that little spark deep in the pit of my stomach is an overwhelming combination. I press a little closer to him and he presses right back. I imagine him kissing me. I imagine us doing much more than that but not here, not right now.

"Not gonna lie," Noah says, switching gears and giving me a little bit of a breather. "I thought there was gonna be a body laid out in that front room." Noah grimaces. "I am not prepared for that."

"You know I'd never bring you over if there's a viewing going on," I say.

"No, I know," Noah says, smiling shyly. "I'm trying to be better about it. I swear I am."

I chuckle and nudge him with my elbow. "Seems to be a theme. First Caleb, now you? Cip will be next."

"We all wanna support you, Meeks," Noah says. "But I don't think any of us are as cool with death as you are."

"Most people aren't," I say. "But I can't help it. It's the way I was raised."

"Growing up in a funeral home will do that to you, I guess," Noah says.

I get up, stretch my legs and sit on the edge of my bed. "You know, it's not like the guests are gonna stand up and come after you or something. I promise. The dead bodies, they stay in the coffin . . . most of the time." Images of the old man sitting up in the back of the hearse flood my mind.

Noah whips his head around and stares at me. "What do you mean 'most of the time'?"

I hesitate for a moment. "I kind of want to tell you something but I don't want to freak you out."

"It's too late for all that," Noah says, smiling. "I'm already freaked out so you might as well just tell me."

I sigh. "A man—a guest—sat up in the back of the hearse while my dad was driving the other night." I stop as Noah's face twists into a mask of shock and abject terror. "Sorry."

"No, it's—it's okay," he says through a forced smile. "I don't get how that's possible."

"It's usually something that happens during embalming," I say. "Sometimes there's a buildup of gas or fluid or sometimes something goes wrong. It happens but—" I pause. There is something about what happened that unsettles me. The whole thing was scary, yes, but this is something else, and grasping it is like grasping at smoke. It just slips away from me.

"But what?" Noah asks.

"I don't know," I say, frustrated. "It was just . . . weird."

"'Weird' is the understatement of the century," Noah says. "I'm just trying to think about what that must have been like for you and your dad." He blows out a long, slow breath. "I would have died on the spot. I would have ascended. You'd be dressing me up nice for my own funeral."

I slide back down onto the floor next to him and lean my head on his shoulder. "Didn't mean to freak you out."

"Don't even worry about it," Noah says.

"You let me tell you all my weird stories about dead bodies," I say. "I think that means you like me. A lot."

Noah drapes his arm over my shoulders. "I more than just like you. You know that, right?"

"I know," I say. We've been dating for over a year and we'd been friends since way before that. We're both right on the edge of taking things further but the nerves—my god—the nerves get us every time. "I feel the same way about you," I continue. "I just don't know what I'm supposed to say. I don't want to say the wrong thing or do the wrong thing. What if I ruin what we have?"

"Why would being a little more serious about how we feel ruin anything?" Noah asks gently as he traces my knuckles with his fingers.

I shrug. "I've heard people say when *that* word starts getting thrown around, things change and I don't want things to change."

Noah huffs. "I mean, I don't think we should say it if we don't mean it or if we're not sure."

I nod but I know how I feel. It's not about meaning it or not being sure. It's just the feeling of being so open that scares me a little. "We have time for that," I say. "That word—it's not going anywhere."

Noah smiles, then reaches into the pocket of his hoodie and pulls out something wrapped in blue tissue paper and sealed with a piece of clear tape. He sits it in my hand.

"Your present," he says.

I'd almost forgotten that Noah had promised me a gift. I tear open the paper like it's Christmas and find a small, beaded bracelet with a silver clasp coiled inside. On a wide flat bead in the center is an engraving, *M & N*.

"I made it," Noah says, taking the bracelet from me and fastening it around my wrist. "You like it?"

"I—I love it. You made this? For me?"

He nods and lets his gaze wander to the floor. "My mom's always making jewelry, you know. Bracelets and earrings, the dangly kind. I thought I'd try making something for you. I was gonna buy you one I saw at a shop on the Commons but this is better." He lifts my hand and sets it against his chest where his heart is racing. "I hope you know that I care about you a lot and even if we don't say it yet, I can feel it."

He leans in and kisses me softly, deeply. In his kiss is everything I think I could ever want. I gently twist my fingers in the curls at the back of his head.

"Meka! I need your help, baby!" my mom's voice cuts through the air as Noah reluctantly leans away from me.

"Her timing is terrible," he says, laughing. "You think she'd be mad if I tell her to wait a second?"

"I think you'd be wearing a toe tag in record time," I say.

I climb to my feet, pulling Noah up with me, and we go out into the hallway where I peer down the stairs to the first-floor landing.

"Dad's out back," Mom calls up. "Can you help?"

"On my way," I say. I turn back to Noah and squeeze his arm. "You just stay here, okay? I'll be right back."

"Trust me," he says. "I'll be right here. Don't even worry about it."

He heads back to my room and I go downstairs and out the back door.

The delivery is a ninety-six-year-old man who apparently died peacefully in his sleep at his assisted living facility. I help my dad load the man, shrouded in a black plastic body bag, onto a gurney and wheel him directly into the side door that leads to the basement. I park him in the refrigerator and check in with my mom, who has already positioned our other guest, Mr. Kelsey, the man who had sat up on his own in the back of the hearse, on the table in prep room two for hair and makeup.

Mr. Kelsey lies draped in a crisp white sheet, his upper torso exposed. The branches of a freshly stitched Y-shaped incision poke out from the top edge. This is a much more comforting sight than seeing him sitting up. He's dead. Whatever fluke had allowed him to prop himself up was over with.

"He doesn't need much work," my mom says as she buzzes around the room in her apron and elbow-length plastic gloves. "But we got in another guest who was in some kind of . . . accident."

"What kind of accident?" I ask.

My mom presses her mouth into a flat line. She doesn't need to say anything. Her silence tells me what kind of accident it is. A car accident.

I suck in a big breath and hold it in my chest. "How bad is it?"

"I haven't looked yet," Mom says. "But the hospital report is detailed enough for me to know it's going to be a mess."

I've seen so many types of injuries, but car accidents are so unpredictable. The effects can be gruesome. Images from my nightmare rush in like the tide and sweep me up in a wave of fear and anxiety. I grasp the edge of the steel table to steady myself.

My mom rushes up to me and puts her hand on my back. "Oh, baby. You okay? What is it?"

"The dream," I say.

My mom's face is a mask of concern. "It's triggering you like this? I don't like that."

"It's fine," I say. "I'm fine."

She nods even though I can tell she doesn't believe me at all. "Well, you don't have to be here for that one. I can handle it myself."

I stare down at Mr. Kelsey. "Probably a good idea."

Mom hugs me close and then nudges me toward the door. "Go back upstairs with Noah. He's scared to death of this place." She laughs. "But he's willing to face his fears to be with you. Must be love."

Must be.

I find Noah perched in front of the heater, every muscle in his body tensed.

"You good?" I ask as I sit down next to him.

"I'm better now." He interlaces his fingers with mine and his posture relaxes a little. "What were you doing? You wheeled that person into the basement, did you have to take them out of the body bag?"

"No," I say. "We'll do that later. But my mom just told me we got another guest, and it sounds like he was in a car accident. I won't be helping with anything except the wake on that one."

Noah's brow shoots up. "Really? Why?"

I stare into his face.

"Oh," he says quietly. "The nightmare. That makes sense."

I scoot over and lean against my bed. "It feels so real and then I wake up and there's always a moment, right before I remember that it was a dream, where I miss my mom so much it hurts." I clench my jaw to try and keep the tears at bay. "I hate it." I glance at the clock on my phone. I'll have to go to bed in a little while and there are only two options—an agonizing night of fighting my sleep until the very last moment, or dreaming of my mother's death.

Noah puts his hand on my leg. "I wish you could dream of me."

I sigh. "Trust me, I try."

"What's that mean?" Noah asks. He's grinning so hard I have to look away from him.

"Forget I said anything," I say, heat rising in my face.

"No, don't act all shy now," he says. "You try to dream of me? Do you look at my picture?"

I glance at the picture of us tacked above my bed. Noah follows my gaze and only smiles wider.

"Okay," I say. "Enough."

Noah holds up his hands in surrender. "I'm just giving you a hard time." He touches my hand. "I dream of you all the time."

I stare into his face. "And what are those dreams about?"

Now it's Noah's turn to be embarrassed. He chews at his bottom lip and then sighs. "We're a mess, you know that?"

"Oh, I know," I say. "But it's okay. I kinda like that about us."

Noah stays for dinner and my mom serves some kind of pasta she can't stomach, so she just watches us eat. When we're done, I walk Noah to the door as his mom pulls up outside. I step out onto the porch.

"Hey, Miss Cliff," I say as Noah's mom rolls down the window of her car and waves at me.

"Hey, hon. Where's your mama?"

"She's in the kitchen," I say. "Want me to get her?"

"No. Don't bother her. Just tell her I owe her coffee and a bookshop date. I'll call her later."

"Yes, ma'am," I say.

Noah slips his arm around me and pulls me close. I nestle against his chest as the cold creeps down my neck and across the bare skin of my arms.

"I love being this close to you, but I gotta get out of this cold," I say.

He kisses me. Really kisses me. He doesn't care that his mom is watching or that it's freezing outside. When he pulls away, I'm left breathless, and he has to nudge me back inside before pulling the door closed. He puts his hand on the glass, grinning his big, toothy smile. Then turns and hops in the car and they take off.

"Meka," my dad calls from the kitchen. "Do me a favor and run out to the shed and bring in another box of Smithfield's. Your mom wants all her stuff ready for prepping the guests tomorrow."

"Oh, she's gonna wait till tomorrow?"

"Yeah. She's tired. I'm cleaning up so she can get some rest."

That's fine with me. If we aren't going to prep any of the bodies tonight, though, I could have asked Noah to stay a little longer. I think about texting him and asking him to come back but change my mind.

Out the back door and across the wraparound driveway is a storage shed that used to be a single-car garage. It's the same hunter-green color as the house. My dad expanded it to house the hearse on one side and our overflow mortuary supplies on the other; jars of formalin cream, canisters of Vis-O-Guard gel, and boxes of Paulex powder and Lanol Care are neatly organized on shelves in the temperature-controlled storage area. I find a case of Smithfield's Mortuary Spray Paint and lift it off the shelf only to find it empty. There are a few more empty boxes on the shelf and two full ones. I'd noticed our supply in the prep room was low, but it looks like we're low on the overflow supplies too.

I scan the shelf from top to bottom. Maybe not everything is low. It looks like we have plenty of extra wax ligatures and there are lots of cases of embalming fluid, eye caps, and disinfectant. The only thing we seem to be getting low on is the Smithfield's. One full canister can do a body and there are fourteen canisters per case. I try to tally up the number of guests we've had since our last big supply order. It seems like we should have more spray paint, and I make a little note on my phone to check with Mom so that we don't run out.

I grab one of only two full cases of the Smithfield's and lock up. As I cross the driveway the dark descends around me like a shade and the cold is numbing, but something makes me stop.

From the far side of the house—a sound, like air escaping a tire but in quick short bursts. I know the sound. I set the case of Smithfield's down on the step and move toward the side of the house. The little window in the prep room is open and the light inside is on.

Three more quick hisses.

It's the smell that pulls it all together. The flowery rose scent of mortuary spray paint. The sound is a Smithfield's nozzle being depressed. I hear the sound almost every day, but I've never heard it from outside the house before. The little curtain covering the prep room window is drawn, obscuring the figure inside.

I don't need to see inside to know what's going on. My parents must have started the prep of the car crash victim early, but I wonder if maybe he's already been embalmed. That happens sometimes. Guests come in from other funeral homes after they've been prepped to get the signature Redwood Funeral Home hair and makeup. The thought makes me oddly proud.

I leave my mom to her work and grab the box of supplies off the step, then duck back into the warmth of the house. I stow the Smithfield's in the hall, then go to my room. I get under my covers and text Noah.

ME: Wish you could have stayed longer.

Noah responds almost immediately.

NOAH: We're just pulling up to my house now. My mom is dead tired but I could walk back if you want me to?

I think for a minute. I'd like that but it's getting late and he'd have to walk back home in the freezing cold. He doesn't have a license, so he doesn't drive. He says he prefers walking or a bike anyway but bikes are no good in the Ithaca winters.

ME: No, it's okay. What are you about to do?
NOAH: I'm gonna order some food and knock out probably.
ME: You just had dinner at my house!
NOAH: I'm still hungry! Don't judge me Meeks.

I laugh.

ME: Not judging. See you tomorrow? Maybe we can get
lunch or something?
NOAH: Yup. It's a date.
ME: Enjoy your late-night snack.

Noah texts me three pink hearts.

I lie still in the dark, listening to the sounds of my house. The knocking of the baseboard heat kicking up, the quiet hum of the space heater, and somewhere outside the cawing of a raven.

That night, for the first time in months, I don't dream at all. No nightmares, no good dreams either. Just blackness behind my lids.

CHAPTER 7

LOSS

Lots of people prefer wake services be held on Sunday mornings. That means Saturdays are usually prep days or private viewing days, but this particular Saturday is different. We don't have anyone scheduled till Monday. As a habit, I'm up at eight but instead of slipping into a black or gray pantsuit, I throw on some sweats and decide to get ahead of the game. I set up the front room and call the local police department to confirm an escort to Kings Cemetery for the guests who are being interred there next week. When the front room is prepped and the phone calls are done, I sit down at the desk in my dad's office to reorder supplies.

The room used to be a walk-in pantry, but he converted it into an office so that he isn't ordering embalming equipment at our dining room table. His desk is neatly organized with stacks of labeled file folders, billing worksheets, and pens and pencils stuffed into a plastic cup. I get comfy in his chair and take out my phone to text Noah.

ME: Guess what?

I wait a few seconds for him to respond. The clock in the upper right of the screen says it's nine thirty.

ME: I didn't have the dream last night. I didn't have any dreams. Weird, right?

My mom sets down a stack of papers and I notice her nails are pale pink today and so is her blouse.

"Could you look through these and make sure our obits are in there for the week?" she asks.

"Yup," I say, pulling the stack of newspapers toward me. We submit all our guests' obituaries to the local paper and even though most people prefer digital copies, families sometimes like to keep the paper copies as mementos.

"If you're doing some ordering," Mom says, "please add a new set of straps for the body lift. The other set is stretched out and we need to replace them ASAP. I cannot be responsible for dropping somebody's granddaddy on the floor."

"You want me to order more Smithfield's too?" I ask.

Mom glances at the computer screen. "We can always use more, right?"

"I mean yeah, always, but have you been out to the storage shed? We're down to two extra cases. I brought one inside because we were running low downstairs."

She straightens up and gazes toward the back door. "I thought we had four extra boxes."

"Nope. But there's some empty boxes out there, maybe they got miscounted."

Mom sighs. "Can you add twelve new cases to the cart and see how quickly we can get them here?"

"Twelve?" I ask. "That seems like a lot."

"It is. But supply chain issues are slowing things down. I thought we had more but . . ." She trails off, then shakes her head. "It's my fault. I should have been better prepared."

"It's okay," I say. "I can do the order and I think we have enough to cover the guests we already have scheduled."

I click across the screen and open the supply ordering app. I scroll through, looking for the Smithfield's logo when something catches my eye. We order so frequently from the site that the products we've previously ordered scroll on a ticker across the bottom of the screen.

Hunter's Mortuary wax—3 cases—last ordered
November 6—Want to reorder? Click here to add to cart!

As the words tick by, I expect to see our last order of Smithfield's from back in November but instead I see something else.

Smithfield's Mortuary Spray Paint—2 cases—last ordered
January 5—Want to reorder? Click here to add to cart!

"We just ordered some two weeks ago." I look at the screen again to make sure I'm seeing the quantity and dates correctly. "That can't be right, can it? I didn't even see that shipment come in. We definitely don't have that much extra out in the shed. That's, like, two cans every day. We haven't had that many guests."

"We've had a lot of guests, baby," Mom says, peering over my shoulder at the screen. "Maybe my count was off last time I did inventory." She sucks her teeth and shakes her head. "No. I don't usually make mistakes like that. My inventory is always on point." She narrows her eyes at the screen. "Let me ask your father. Either we have a stash somewhere I don't know about or somebody's stealing it from us."

"Thieves like dead body paint?" I ask. "Weird."

Of all the places to try and rip off, a funeral home wouldn't have been at the top of my list. Mom looks genuinely confused as she continues to study the computer screen.

"I'll just order the straps for now, and then we can double-check with Dad later," I say.

Mom shakes her head. "Babe!" she calls down the hall. "Did you order more Smithfield's?"

"What?" my dad calls back. "I don't think so. Maybe. Give me a minute."

My mom's brow furrows. "You said you didn't see the shipment come in? And it's not in the shed?"

I shake my head. "Nope."

"I don't like being so low," she says. "How soon can we get a new shipment here?"

I click through a few fields and check the "expedited shipping" box to get an idea of how long it might be.

"Looks like, if we order today, it'll take ten days to get here."

Mom chews at her bottom lip. "We have six guests scheduled to come through in the next ten days."

"Oh, okay, so we're good?" I ask. "There are fourteen cans in each case and a few more downstairs. That should be plenty."

Mom still looks worried, but she shrugs. "Your father

isn't allowed to do the ordering anymore. Let's get that order in ASAP."

"I'll do it right now," I say.

Mom kisses me on top of the head and goes out of the room. Before I start the new order, I thumb through the newspapers to check the obituaries. Mrs. Lang's is in there and so is Mr. Kelsey's. Names and dates are correct and then, near the bottom of the page, I see an obituary for an older woman by the name Margaret Lindsey Hayes. I'm drawn to the name because it sounds vaguely familiar. Sometimes I come across someone I know—a teacher or even a classmate. I read through her obituary.

Margaret Lindsey Hayes, lifelong resident of Ithaca, passed away on January 5, 2025, from natural causes. She is survived by her son, Mark Douglas Hayes, and her daughter, Marie Hayes. She is preceded in death by her beloved husband, Dr. Albert Hayes. Funeral services will be held at St. Anthony's on January 10 at 6 PM. In lieu of flowers, the family requests donations be made to the Celiac Disease Foundation, an organization Mr. and Mrs. Hayes felt strongly about.

It occurs to me that this is the obituary for the wife of my mom's doctor. I look over it again, reading one part aloud.

"Preceded in death by her beloved husband, Dr. Albert Hayes."

Doctor Albert Hayes.

"Hey, Mom," I call. "Isn't that doctor you're seeing named Albert Hayes? The one for your stomach?"

I search the page for his name. Maybe they died close together, from an accident or something, but I don't find anything.

The doorbell rings. A little stab of panic ripples through me as my mom bobs past the office door.

"Is there a service today?" I'd prepped for the upcoming ones, but if somebody is here for a service now, it means I forgot to do something.

"No," Mom calls. "I'm not expecting anybody. Let me see who this is and what they want. I was really looking forward to some peace and quiet today."

I pick up my phone. Still nothing from Noah.

A sudden, agonized cry splits the air.

If anybody else had heard it, they might have jumped out of their skin, but I've heard cries like it so many times it doesn't faze me at first. That's the noise you're supposed to make in a funeral home.

It's the sound of grief exiting the body.

"Oh god," my mother's voice sounds among the audible sadness.

I stand.

My dad hurries past the open office door. For some reason, I feel like I can't move. The crying—no—the wailing builds on itself until it's a frenzied cacophony of gasps and choking sobs. A few moments later my dad staggers into the office doorway, his eyes wide, lips slightly parted. He grasps the doorframe like he can't stand up on his own.

"Dad?" I ask. "You okay?"

He only looks at me like he's trying to memorize something about me.

"Meka, baby," my dad says. "Come here."

My mom calls me baby. To her, I'm always her baby. But my dad almost never calls me that. A rock falls into the pit of my stomach and the shock wave ripples outward through every limb.

I step toward him but it feels like I'm moving through quick-sand. He reaches out and pulls me close, crushing me to his chest so hard we stumble out into the hallway. As we find our footing, I catch a glimpse of the person who'd been wailing so mournfully.

It's Miss Cliff. Noah's mom.

Her eyes are puffy and red. Her sandy hair is pulled into a messy bun on top of her head. She's in her pajamas—a pair of tattered sweats and an oversize T-shirt—all bundled inside her big winter coat. House shoes, no socks. She's not like my mom, who is always done up, but I've never seen her in pajamas. She looks like she just got out of bed. She clutches a tissue to her mouth like she's trying to keep in the terrible sounds. My mom turns to me and her bottom lip is trembling.

"Miss Cliff?" I ask from the confines of my father's arms. "What happened? Are you okay?"

She doesn't look at me. She keeps her eyes locked on my mom. "I—I can—I had to—I can tell her—"

"No," my mom whispers. "I'll do it."

Mom comes toward me with her arms out and suddenly everything changes. Her strides are long and slow. The clock in the hall sounds like it's ticking at half time. Ravens have gathered on the outside perch and their caws are long and lingering. Even the frantic beating of my own heart seems slower.

"What is it? What's wrong?" It's my voice, but I feel like it's coming from somewhere outside myself. It's muffled and unnatural. When my mom reaches me, she cups my face in her hands.

"I need you to listen to me," she says. "Meka? Do you hear me?"

I can hear Miss Cliff's sobs. My dad's ragged breathing sounds like he's desperately trying to keep some terrible sound from clawing its way up his throat. My mom takes me by the arms, holds me firm as she speaks softly to me.

"Meka, baby, something has happened."

"Okay," I say, my gaze flitting to Miss Cliff again. "Is Miss Cliff okay?" I step back and am about to go to Miss Cliff to put my arms around her, but my mom stops me. My dad puts his hand on my back. He's trembling.

"Miss Cliff and Noah went home after they left our house last night," Mom says. "At some point Noah must have gotten hungry and he had some food brought to the house and—"

"I know," I say. "He told me he was ordering food." My heart is beating so hard it hurts. "Where's Noah?"

Nobody says anything but the silence is loud. It cuts through my brain like a knife.

"*Where's Noah?*" I repeat. Maybe they didn't hear me. Maybe I'm not saying it clearly. "We're going to lunch. I'm gonna pay because he paid last time. So, where is he?" I look out the open front door. Maybe if I can ignore what my gut is telling me . . . if I can just push it away right now . . .

"Baby," Mom says, her voice a strained whisper. "Miss Cliff found him late last night."

"Found him?" I ask.

I can't breathe.

"Yes. He was outside." My mom takes a deep breath. "He must

93

have gone out to grab the food he ordered. It was icy. He slipped and hit his head. Meka, baby, he—he didn't make it."

Miss Cliff cries out again, and this time, the sound seeps into my head, into my bones. It curls around my heart and for a split second, I think I might be having a heart attack.

"Didn't make what?" I ask. "What do you mean?"

My mom shakes her head. "Baby, I don't know how to tell you this." She tightens her grip on me. "Baby, Noah is gone."

CHAPTER 8

THE LONGEST GOODBYE

"*Gone where?*" I scream. I can't understand.

"Meka," Mom says softly. "Noah died."

I'm not hearing her right. Those words don't make sense. "No." I try to pull out of my mom's grasp, but she won't let me go. "No. No. No!" My voice creeps up with each denial until I am screaming at the top of my lungs. "NO!"

Blood rushes in my ears, my heart beats furiously as it starts to shatter into a million pieces. I shove her away from me. I don't want to be touched. I take out my phone and call Noah. His ringtone echoes through the hall. Miss Cliff pulls his phone out of her pocket and holds it in front of her. A picture of Noah and me with our arms around each other on the carousel at Stewart Park. "Meeks" flashes across the screen.

"No!" I shout. I scream. I wail.

"Baby, please," my mom sobs. "Baby, listen to me."

My mom is holding me up now because my body isn't doing

what I need it to do. I can't breathe or see or hear. I want to disappear but suddenly, I shake free from my mom and run to the front door.

"Oh, Meka," Miss Cliff says as I brush past her. "Meka, sweetie. Please don't go."

I run out into the street. A car lays on its horn and the blaring noise sounds like it's a mile away. The car swerves around me and turns off my street. The biting cold numbs my skin, but it can't reach deep enough to numb the agony.

Noah.

My Noah.

Gone.

I stare up at the gray midmorning sky. Somewhere there is wailing, shouting, my dad's hands on me, pulling me inside. I can't hear him over the rush in my ears and I want to tell whoever is screaming to shut up. Then I realize it's me.

The terrible sound is coming from me.

Two days pass in a haze of tears and ragged screams. My throat is sore from it. My eyes are bloodshot, the lids swollen. I can't eat. I barely get out of bed. Caleb and Cipriana come by, but my mom sends them away. They call me and when I don't answer, they text.

CALEB: Meka. I love you. I'm here if you need me. I'm so sorry. Please call me.
CIPRIANA: I can't believe this Meka. I know you're hurting. We love you.

I read the messages but don't respond. I just can't. It makes no sense that I have to continue on without Noah. How is that going to work? We're supposed to be at the movies and meeting up between classes. We're supposed to be working up the nerve to say all the things we're feeling and now it's too late. There is no time left.

The third day after Noah died—when I realize this is how all my days will be tallied from now on and feel like my chest is going to cave in—I hear a car pull around the side of the house. When I go to the window, Miss Cliff climbs out of the passenger side of the hearse.

I'm downstairs and out the back door before I can think. My bare feet against the freezing concrete is a shock to my system. Everything is more intense than it had been . . . before. The cold more biting, the lights brighter, the sound and silence both overwhelming.

My dad slips across the ice as he wraps me up. "Meka, get inside. You can't see this."

"He's here?" I ask. "You brought him here?"

I stare at the hearse. A plain brown coffin made of cardboard sits in the back. It's the same kind of box we've picked up hundreds of guests in over the years but now, Noah is in there.

I push past my dad and fling myself into the glass, pressing my hands and face against it. I let the grief envelop me because there is no stopping it anyway. I sob against the car as my dad tries to comfort me but there is no comfort to be had.

I cry until my face is numb from the cold. My bare feet are probably frostbitten, but it doesn't matter. Nothing matters. My mom comes out and steers me inside. She parks me on the couch in the playroom.

"Stay here," she says sternly. "I'll be right back."

She disappears and I sit as still as I can, trying to hold the broken pieces of myself together. When the tears ebb, I step out into the hallway. Through the glass in the back door, I watch my mom and dad load the cardboard coffin onto a gurney and push it toward the basement entrance. I quickly cut through the kitchen and slink down the butler's stairs, running directly into my mom.

"You're not slick," she says. "What are you doing?"

"I—I need to see him," I sob.

She stares into my face, then takes my hands in hers. "I'm told there was a small injury to his face from when he fell." She takes a deep, wavering breath. "Even still, I think you should wait until he's been prepared. Let Dad get him ready, let me get him dressed."

I gaze into the preparation room. The table is empty but soon Noah's body will be on it. It's too much to think about, too much to feel. My legs go out from under me, and I collapse into a heap on the floor. My mom curls up next to me and holds me as I weep. She says nothing and I'm glad. I don't want to hear that it's going to be okay because it's not. I cry until there are no more tears left.

I don't see Noah this night. Instead, I retreat to my room and bury myself in blankets in hopes of avoiding the terrible reality that Noah's body lies cold and empty a few floors below me.

As hard as I try, I cannot avoid sleep. I stay awake as long as my body will allow and when I can't fight it anymore, the nightmare floods my mind. I see my mother's broken body on the pavement, the hazy orange light, and I hear the song on the radio. Then I'm in pain, lying on the pavement, looking up at the stars.

I wake with a start just as the sun is warming the sky and for a moment, I am so relieved to be awake that I almost smile. Then Noah's absence falls down around me and my heart breaks all over again. All this time, I'd been so worried that the dream meant something terrible for my mother but now it's Noah who is gone. I should have asked Noah to stay longer that night. I should have told him to come back, but I didn't and now I'll have to live without him for the rest of my life. Whether sleeping or waking, I'm sad and suffocating. It's not fair.

"Meka," my mom says. She's there suddenly, wearing a black blouse tucked into her jeans, her hair pulled back in a sleek bun at the base of her neck. Her skin is ashen and she looks like she hasn't slept. I so rarely see her this way, I'm taken aback.

"Baby," she begins. "I wanted to tell you that your dad and I worked through the night. Noah is prepped. You can see him whenever you're ready."

I stare up at her from my seat on the bed. She looks broken. I wonder if I look broken too.

"Why is this happening?" I ask. "Why him?" The tears come in a flood and my mom sits on the bed next to me, holding me like I'm a piece of glass, like she's afraid I might break. A part of me already has.

"I don't have an answer, baby," she says softly. "I wish I could tell you why these things happen, but I can't. Sometimes the people we love are ripped away from us and it's impossible to understand." She rubs my back and traces her fingers along the side of my face. "I know it hurts and I wish I could take this pain away from you." She sighs and I melt into her. "I love you," she says. "I will be right here with you every step of the way. Even when it hurts. I got you. Understand?"

I nod and try my best to gather myself. "When is the—the funeral?"

She sighs again. "Miss Cliff doesn't want a big thing. She

wants to do a private memorial tomorrow evening. We'll do the main service here and then she wants a brief graveside ceremony."

"Tomorrow?" I ask. "No. That's—that's too soon."

Mom puts her hand firmly on my shoulder. "Baby, no amount of time will make you ready for this. If it's tomorrow, next week, next year—you will never be ready but we have to move through it." She squeezes my hand, then goes to my dresser to pull out clean clothes for me. "I want you to shower, brush your teeth. You have to take care of yourself, even if it feels like a chore. It won't actually make things better, but it might make you feel a little more human."

"I don't want to be human," I say. "I want to be something that can't feel anything. I want to be numb."

Mom comes back over and stands in front of me. She gently takes my face in her hands. "Please don't say that, Meka. This feeling," she touches my chest, right over my heart, "the sadness, is only possible because of the way you love and care for other people. It's what makes life worth anything at all, even when we grieve, *that* is an act of love."

"Then why does it hurt like this?" I ask. I don't know if I'm expecting a real answer or not.

My mom kisses me gently on the forehead. "It will get better. You will grow around the grief, I promise."

She believes she is telling me the truth but I know that's not the only option. I've seen people so broken by grief that I don't think there is any growing around it for them.

I shower, get myself together, and surprisingly, feel at least a little more real. I stand at the top of the basement steps trying to prepare myself to see Noah. My mom offers to come down with me, but I want to see him alone.

I descend the stairs slowly and stand just outside the preparation room. Through the small window in the door, I can see the coffin—a sleek mahogany model with an almond velvet interior. The head end is open. I'd once helped a family pick the exact same coffin for their teenage daughter. I want to throw up. I swallow hard, pushing the nausea down, and step into the room.

The smell of rose-scented Smithfield's hangs in the air. Normally the smell doesn't bother me but knowing that it's in the air because Noah had been prepped in here makes me want to be sick. My mom has covered her tool chest with a sheet and put away anything she used to get Noah ready. I'm grateful. I can't handle seeing those tools right now.

I approach the casket and Noah's upper torso comes into view. I cannot look at his face. Not yet. Instead, I focus on the silver buttons on his black suit jacket and the way his hands lie across his belly. The little scar on his left thumb where he'd cut himself on a piece of glass at Buttermilk Falls the summer before is visible. The silver ring he always wears on his pinkie is missing, though.

I have stood next to more caskets than I can count and I've never been as afraid to look upon the person lying inside as I am in this moment. Maybe it's because I wasn't connected to those other people. When I looked at them in the caskets, they weren't people I'd spent so much time with it was impossible to tally the days. They weren't people I had laughed and cried with, people I'd loved. I swallow hard, grit my teeth, and let my gaze wander to Noah's face.

He lies with his eyes closed, his lips slightly parted. The bridge of his nose and plains of his cheeks are freckled. His tan skin is still supple, not dry, or unnatural looking at all. In the bright light of the prep room, I can clearly see where my mother has used her immense skill to camouflage a defect over his left cheek. Nobody else would notice it. The color matching is perfect and the texture of the mortuary wax is just a little smoother than his normal skin. She even painted on freckles. I think of him falling and striking his face on something that gouged out a piece of his cheek. I wonder if he had tried to call out and couldn't. Had there been time for that or was it just over in the blink of an eye? I grip the edge of the coffin, fighting the urge to scream. I reach in to hold his hand. As soon as our fingers touch, I rear back. He is cold and stiff.

My heart drops into the pit of my stomach. "I'm sorry," I sob. I retake my position at his side and grasp his hands. "I—I'm not afraid of being here with you. Please, Noah. Please don't leave me."

But he's already gone.

I know that. I can feel it.

I take off the bracelet he'd given me and fasten it around his wrist.

"You keep this for me," I say through a torrent of tears. "Wait for me, okay? Please wait for me. I'll see you when I get there."

I don't know what happens when we die. I don't know if he can wait for me somewhere beyond this life, but it gives me the only shred of hope I can cling to right now. This can't be all there is. I lean into the casket and kiss him gently on the forehead. I let my lips linger on his cold skin knowing this will be the last time. It hurts so much I think I might break apart and then . . . Noah sighs.

I jerk back, tripping over my own feet and landing hard on the floor. I scramble back, pressing myself into the wall. I can't see Noah's body from where I am on the floor but I stare at the edge of his casket. Maybe he'll sit up and I'll wake up and all of this will be a nightmare.

The door to the prep room groans open and my mom sticks her head in.

"Baby, what in the world—"

"He breathed!" I say, scrambling to my feet.

Mom comes in and takes me by the arm. "What are you talking about?"

"I leaned into the coffin to kiss him one last time and—and—he sighed."

Mom glances at the casket and then back to me. She gently guides me back to Noah's side and we peer down at him.

"Baby, Noah is gone," she says softly. "The stress you've been under, the grieving, it's a lot to hold all at once. Sometimes we see and hear the things we wish were real."

"I just—I thought I heard him take a breath when I kissed him." I try to take stock of myself. Am I hallucinating? Am I really so broken in this moment that I'm imagining things? I shake my head and Mom leads me out of the prep room.

I spend the rest of the day and evening in my room. The image of Noah in his casket is burned into my mind and it will not allow me to replace it with another memory of him. I want to think of him the way he was when he sat in my room and put that bracelet on me, or the way he looked at me when we almost said that we loved each other. We thought we had more time and now there is none left. The image that will be forever associated with him will be of him lying in that coffin and I hate it.

A motor turns over outside. The hearse's engine has a very distinct kick to it, because despite my dad's meticulous upkeep of the car, it's still sixty years old and is probably coming to the end of its long life. At least it got sixty years. Noah only got seventeen.

I move to the window to see what's going on. I can just make out the silhouette of my dad in the driver's seat. The curtains that hang from the rear windows of the hearse are drawn. He carefully backs out of the drive and takes off.

"Hey, baby," my mom says. She's there with a to-go bag from Simeon's restaurant. She holds it up. "Best mac-n-cheese in Ithaca. Not in the world. I think my mac-n-cheese holds that title but I know this one's your fave." She sits the bag on the bedside table.

"I just saw Dad leave," I say. "Where's he going?"

"Oh, he's got something to do on campus. Some last-minute thing."

"He took the hearse," I say.

Her gaze flits to the window. "Huh. I don't know, baby. You know he likes driving that thing around even when it's not necessary because he thinks it means people won't try to talk to him. God forbid." She sits next to me and drapes her arm around me. "That man has been all over the place these last few days. I think we all have."

The knot in my throat threatens to choke me. I stare at my mom, and it occurs to me that, once again, she looks not quite her usual level of put together. Her skin is dull and her makeup is a little cakey, something she considers almost criminal. But it's not just that. There's something else about her that's off.

"You okay?" I ask.

She smiles at me. "I look a mess, don't I?"

"No. Never."

"You don't have to lie, baby." She smiles. "I ran out of my favorite foundation and picked up this one from Walgreens. It should be illegal to sell this stuff to people. I look like a clown."

"You look great," I say.

"I said don't lie." She nudges me playfully.

I force a quick smile but I can't stop looking at her face. I know this strange feeling but it takes me a moment to place it and when I do, it still doesn't sit right. I feel like I'm looking at one of our guests. But my mom's fine. She's right here. This isn't the nightmare and still . . . it's not like I'm looking at a dead person but it's as if that spark that makes us who we are is dimmer in her than it normally is. I don't like it at all. Is this what happens when people we care about die? A little piece of us goes with them? If that's true I wonder how hollow I must look right now.

"What do you need from me?" she asks. "I know nothing can make you feel better and part of this process is sitting with the pain for a while but how can I help? What can I do?"

She puts her hand in mine.

"I just need you next to me tomorrow because I don't know how I'm gonna do it." That is the honest truth. I can't fathom how I'm supposed to sit and look at Noah in his casket as we say our final goodbyes. It doesn't seem real. "We were supposed to have more time. We were gonna do so many things. We had all these plans, and now he's just gone. It's not fair."

My mom turns and gazes out the window. "You're right, baby. You're right."

Tears pour down my face in endless rivers. A part of me wishes they'd sweep me away, drown out all the hurt and emptiness. "You won't seal the casket until I see him one more time, right?" I ask.

My mom shakes her head. "No, baby. I won't."

The next day, I sit in the back of the viewing room, in the last row of folding chairs. I keep my gaze glued to the hardwood floor beneath my shoes as my dad wheels Noah's casket in and positions it at the front of the room between two flower arrangements sent over by Bool's. The girl who works the front desk at the shop, Amya, had history class with Noah last year and sent over the flowers free of charge. My mom opens a folding stand and props a large printout of Noah's yearbook photo on it. His grin is way too cheesy; it looks like he's about to bust out laughing. He told me that the school photographer hadn't told him where to look so he just smiled as wide as he could and hoped for the best. She sets smaller framed photos of him on a table near the front, the same ones I'd had pinned on my ceiling and a few of him and his mom together. I look away from the photos.

The collar of my dress suddenly feels too tight, like it's choking me. My mom picked it out—a long black sheath dress with a belt around the waist, black stockings, black shoes. How plain and sad it looks makes me think of Noah. He loved to dress. Cip and Caleb were always giving him a hard time about how put together he was. He was a lot like my mom in that way, always dressed to impress even when the only person he was trying to impress was me. My throat tightens up. Is everything going to remind me of him from now until forever? How am I supposed to live like that, with this horrible ache always threatening to take me down?

Miss Cliff arrives with a few of Noah's extended family members, and she hugs me as she passes by to her seat at the front. Noah's dad passed away when he was little, and his mom only has one older sister and a few cousins. They all file in, dressed in black and draped in sadness. Miss Cliff gives me a quick smile and I'm taken aback. She's sad, obviously, but the smile is convincing. Like it's not hard for her to twist her mouth up and feign happiness at seeing me. I feel like I'll never smile again, and Noah was my boyfriend; I loved him but Noah was Miss Cliff's only child. I thought she'd be a complete wreck, but she settles into her seat and even manages a small chuckle at something one of her family members says.

My parents take up their places at the back of the room. Someone gets up to speak, and I quickly move to my mom's side.

"The casket's not open," I say. "Miss Cliff said she wanted it open."

My mom squeezes my arm. "She changed her mind. It's too hard for her right now."

"What?" I ask, my heart thudding in my chest. "No. I—I thought I was gonna get to see him one more time."

"Meka—" my dad begins.

Something takes over me—grief, delirium from too little sleep, I can't say—but the next thing I know I'm marching up the center aisle with only one thing in my mind—I need to see Noah. I grip the handle and pull up on the casket lid as startled gasps and groans erupt behind me.

"Meka!" My mother is suddenly at my side, pulling me away. "Don't do this, baby. Please."

I tug on the lid, but it still won't budge. The casket is sealed—something we usually don't do before the service is over in case anyone needs to see their deceased loved one one last time. I am that person now. I need to see Noah.

"Why is it sealed?" I ask as my mom and dad struggle to pull me away. "You said you wouldn't seal it! I need to see him! Please! I can't see him one more time?"

My mother shakes her head as my dad bites back tears.

"Mom!" I scream, my voice breaking under the weight of my grief. "Mom, please!"

"I'm sorry it has to be this way," my dad sobs.

"Meka," Miss Cliff says softly.

I shake free from my mother's grip and kneel in front of Miss Cliff. I put my head in her lap and she gently puts her hands on my head.

"I'm sorry—I'm sorry." I know I'm in the wrong. I know I'm making a scene but I'm not in control of myself and I don't know what else to do.

"It's going to be okay, Meka," Miss Cliff says, giving me that genuine smile again. "You have to be strong. We'll get through this."

"I—I don't want to be strong!" I snap. "I can't do this! He can't be dead! Bring him back! Bring him back now! Please!" As if she could do that. As if that is in her power.

"Meka," my mom says softly. "Please don't do this."

I stand, embarrassed, and flee to my room. I've seen people act a fool at a funeral. I've seen people try to climb into the casket. I even saw a woman try to follow her deceased mother into the open grave by just jumping in like she was diving into a pool. I never thought I'd be the one showing out in front of a bunch of grieving people. The shame I feel is heavy but by the time I've composed myself the service is over.

My mom comes to my room and tells me I should stay here while the coffin is transported to the Ithaca City Cemetery, just a few blocks from my house but I'm out the door before she can finish what she's saying. I'm going. I can't let Noah make this last trip alone.

The hearse leads the way with Miss Cliff and Noah's family riding in a blacked-out sedan behind it. I ride in the hearse, squeezed in beside my mom. I put my hand on the casket, picturing Noah resting inside it. My mind is scattered to a million places. As we exit the car, the cold is nothing compared to the sting of grief.

We gather outside the Cliff family's crypt. Noah's great-great-great-grandfather had been a Cornell alumnus. When he died, his daughter enshrined him in a tomb cut into the rolling hills of the Ithaca City Cemetery. Now Noah will lie beside him and the other members of the Cliff family for eternity.

As the casket is deposited inside a narrow hollow in the crypt, I can't get a handle on what I'm seeing. The boy I love is being sealed behind a wall right in front of me. I'll never see his face or feel him close to me again.

When all is said and done, Miss Cliff hugs me and says she'll be around to check on me. She leaves with her family and while my mom and dad offer to stay, I tell them to go. After everyone clears out, I sit in the snow in front of the crypt and let the cold numb me. I lean against the decorative stones, wishing for all of this to be some terrible nightmare that I can wake up from.

As I lean against the side of the crypt, movement draws my attention up a sloping hill that leads to the upper portion of the cemetery. A person is standing at the precipice. I hadn't seen any other vehicles in the small lot next to the cemetery. It didn't look like there was another service happening today. But this person is dressed all in black and maybe their coat is too big or they've got some kind of blanket draped around them but they almost look like they're wearing a cloak.

The cold wind whips my face, and I shut my eyes.

When I reopen them, the person has moved to stand beside a pillar adorning one of the mausoleums up there. They lean against it and I can't tell if they're looking in my direction or not. In the blustery wind and swirling snow, it's hard to make out the details of their face. I want to yell at them to go away. I want to be alone but who am I to run off somebody visiting their deceased loved ones? Isn't that why I'm here too?

A gathering of ravens squawks high over my head and the cold becomes too much for the thin sweater I'd put on. I stand, brush the snow off my clothes and walk home, feeling more alone than I ever have.

I go around the back of the house, not wanting to walk past the front room where Noah's picture is probably still propped up. The hearse is gone again and as I open the back door, something catches my attention. A brown paper bag sits open in the top of the dumpster out back. Something inside, some kind of fabric, spills out over the edge. My eyes water as the frigid wind wraps me up again, but I step closer to the dumpster. The fabric is a jacket or maybe a black sweater, I can't tell.

"Meka?" My mom spots me through the glass and comes rushing out. "You're going to get hypothermia being out there with no coat." I let her take me inside and she rubs my arms trying to push some warmth back into them. "Why don't you go get out of those clothes, I'll make you something to eat, and we can just watch a movie or something?"

I nod and she keeps her eyes on me as I trudge upstairs to my room. I put on a pair of sweats and ball up my dress before shoving it into the back of my closet. I never want to see it again. I switch on the space heater and sit down in front of it to warm myself only to find myself crying a minute later because the last time I was in that spot, Noah was next to me.

This is how it goes. Noah is gone and I have to find a way to live. It feels like everything should stop, like I should be able to pause the world around me, but it doesn't work like that.

CHAPTER 9

TIME MARCHES ON

SIX WEEKS LATER

I wonder what it's like to be a recluse. That is sort of what I've become. Leaving the house still feels like it takes a lot of effort so most days I just stay inside. I haven't taken much time to reach out to my friends. The cold still clings to everything. An alternating series of thaws and refreezing has left Ithaca a frigid icy mess.

Miss Cliff has joined me in my avoid-people-when-possible thinking. She moved to a house in South Hill and keeps mostly to herself. I've seen her once in the six weeks after Noah's death, and the encounter left me shaken.

I was in a bookstore, humoring my mom's request to get out of the house, when I saw Miss Cliff bob past the window. I ran out to say hi, called her name twice, but she was on the phone. She was smiling, laughing, saying something into the phone and then chuckling again as she disappeared into the co-op next door. She must not have heard me or she ignored me on purpose, and either way, it was weird seeing her so jovial, so unaffected.

My mom says she hasn't been in touch with her and gently reminds me that Miss Cliff has very recently lost her only child. Whatever she is doing to keep herself sane is allowed even if that means finding things to be happy about. I immediately feel terrible for being so judgmental. It's just that one of the last things she said to me was that she'd check up on me and she hasn't. Noah is gone and now it seems like she is too.

I still feel like an exposed nerve. Noah's loss is just as fresh in my mind as the day it happened, and I am struggling every single day. Everything is still too bright, too loud. I can't eat the food me and Noah used to eat. I can't listen to the songs Noah always sang along to. More than once, I've picked up my phone and actually called or texted him and the realization that he won't answer brings me so low I feel like I'm drowning.

I had hoped the grief would work some kind of magic in my brain, that it would let me dream of Noah, but I'm not that lucky. In fact, the opposite ends up happening. The nightmare has become more vivid in all its awfulness.

One night, almost two months after Noah's death, the nightmare plays in my mind as soon as my head hits the pillow—me in the back seat of our car, the familiar but strange song on the radio, Mom in the passenger seat, Dad driving. A flash—my mom's body crumpled on the pavement as my dad crouches over her. His face stuck in a horrible gaping scream. And then, for the second time since my birthday, there's something else—something new. A bright light overhead, a small room, and a flash of something silver. I awake, sitting bolt upright. A layer of sweat blankets my entire body. My T-shirt sticks to my back and my shorts cling to my legs. I swing my feet over the side of my bed and press them into the chilly floorboards. I try to focus on the cold as I catch my breath. I've been hoping for a change in my nightmare, a shift to something else—anything else. This scene is new, but not any better. These images come with the same feeling of terror and helplessness as the rest of the nightmare. I glance at my phone. It's three in the morning and there's a text from Caleb.

CALEB: Love you, boo. Just wanted to tell you that.

I text him back for the first time in weeks.

ME: Love you back.

I make a promise to myself that I will call him and Cip the next afternoon and make plans to get together. I've continued the school year virtually because I can't stand to be at Ithaca High, walking the halls where Noah and I spent so much time, but that means I haven't seen Caleb or Cipriana either. I miss them and my mom has been urging me to get out of the house more anyway. I know she's right. I have to find a way to keep moving forward but a part of me feels like that means leaving Noah behind and I don't want to do that.

I move to the window and crack it open. The cold March air creeps in like an unseen hand and wraps itself around me. It helps clear my head a little, but as I breathe in the crisp late-winter air, something accompanies the chilly draft inside—the faint scent of roses.

I grab a hoodie and slip into the hallway. The pipes knock and creak as they struggle to push hot air through the baseboard heaters. Down the hall, my parents' bedroom door sits ajar. The pale light from the hallway seeps in enough for me to see that neither of them are in bed. I take the back staircase down to the first floor and stop to listen. All I hear is the boiler kicking up, the *tap tap tap* of the air trapped in the pipes, and the ticking of the grandfather clock. There's a rustling near the back door and I stifle a scream before I realize it's just one of my dad's ravens, come to scoop up what's left of the seeds he'd left them. Its body is like a shadow as it crowds the little glass window, then flies off. A heavy, unsettling silence fills the house.

I grab a glass of water and am about to head back upstairs when I realize there's a light on somewhere in the basement. Not the main hallway light but something bright enough to faintly illuminate the wall by the back staircase. Easing myself onto the steps I hold my breath and listen. The distinct sound of air hissing out of a can wafts up.

Prepping a body at three in the morning?

We don't do that unless it's an emergency and those situations are always really obvious because my parents start running around the house, making calls, and ultimately, I'm roped into calling some poor family member at two in the morning to ask if they have personal items for the deceased and pictures of them when they were alive for reference. Emergency situations are pure chaos. This is not that.

The hallway is cast in shadow and a thready light streams from the crack under the door of the prep room. I approach on tiptoe. My mom's voice filters out in a whisper.

"Why would you get a different brand?" She sounds annoyed but hearing her pose the question tells me she isn't by herself in there.

"It's cheaper," my dad says. "We go through so much I thought we could save a little money."

"Right. And now look." She huffs. "We can skimp on some things but not this."

"I know," my dad says. "You're right. Forgive me?"

"Nothing to forgive," says my mom as all the irritation goes out of her voice. "It's okay. It's just that the work has to be flawless and in order for that to happen, I need the right supplies. I really don't know how much more—"

"Please," my dad says softly. "Please don't say that."

I hover outside the door, confused. My dad rarely goes in the prep room when we're doing makeup. He doesn't know the difference between cobalt blue and lapis. He probably couldn't shade match someone's skin color if his life depended on it.

I step close enough to look through the window only to find it blocked by some kind of makeshift curtain. I hear the air hiss again. They are definitely prepping a body in there, and I wonder how awful it has to be to have them doing the work in secret in the middle of the night. I stand still, barely breathing, and listen, my ear almost touching the door.

"We've been using Smithfield's since the beginning," my mom says. "Nothing even comes close. It's okay, though," my mom continues. "We have more Smithfield's on the way. We'll just dump this other stuff in the trash." She sighs. "I'm worried."

"I know," my dad says, dropping his voice even lower. "I haven't heard anything. Nothing has changed. I think we're in the clear."

"And if we're not?" my mom asks. "What then?"

Worried about the knockoff Smithfield's? I know how seriously we take our work so it doesn't surprise me but Mom sounds genuinely upset. I'm guessing my dad won't cut that specific corner ever again. I leave them to figure it out and make my way back to my room as quietly as possible.

My room is now the approximate temperature of the inside of one of our walk-in freezers. A gust of wind blows a swirling mist of powdery snow inside. I grab the window and slam it closed when something draws my attention—movement next to the dumpster. I peer into the dark expecting to see some racoons, maybe a possum. Instead, I glimpse the shadowy outline of a person pressed against the side of the garage. Maybe my mom is right. Maybe somebody *has* been pilfering our supplies. I shove the window back open.

"I can see you!" I shout as the cold blasts me in the face again. "Get the hell outta here!"

The figure doesn't budge.

"Oh, you think it's a game?" I quickly slip on a pair of boots and scramble out into the hallway and down the main stairs.

My mom and dad are coming up from the basement just as I'm barreling out the back door.

"Meka!" my dad shouts. "What is going on?"

"Somebody's tryna break into the supply shed!" I holler as I careen down the back steps and onto the part of the driveway that wraps around the back of the house. My feet nearly slip out from under me as I skid to a stop. "Come out so I can put my boot up your—"

"Meka!" my mom yells. "Bring your narrow behind in the house right now!"

I stand still, staring into the dark where the figure had been, my breath pumping out of me in billowing white clouds. It is cold and silent and there is no one here.

"Meka!" my mom shrieks again.

I turn and stomp up the back steps as my mom slams the door and locks it.

"Have you lost your entire mind?" she asks, looking me over from head to toe. "You were gonna fight an intruder with your bare hands? In pajamas and snow boots?"

"I'm calling public safety," my dad yells from his office. "You sure there was someone there?"

"Positive!" I yell back. "Lucky I didn't catch them. I'm ready to fight."

Mom crosses her arms over her chest. "When's the last time you fought somebody, Meka?"

"Probably fourth grade," I say. "And it wasn't really a fight as much as a shoving match but still, I'm ready."

Me and my mom stare at each other for a few seconds in complete silence. She breaks first, descending into a fit of laughter. I smile too. I actually smile and find something funny—even if it's because somebody is trying to rob us—for the first time since Noah died.

My dad comes back out into the hall, a puzzled look on his face. "Why are we laughing? I thought somebody was robbing us."

As my mom waves her hand, I notice that three of her nails are broken off.

"What happened to you?" I ask.

She follows my gaze, then tucks her hand into her pocket. "Don't look at it. You know I hate it when my nails aren't done. They came off when we were transferring one of our new guests onto the prep table."

"So that's what you two were doing downstairs just now?" I ask.

My dad sits on the bottom step. "Just trying to get ahead. I have a bunch of meetings this week on campus so work might get backed up if I come home late."

"Oh, okay. I could've helped," I say.

"It's fine. Really." Mom sighs and leans her head on my shoulder. "I love seeing you laugh, baby."

She's wearing one of her fancy plush robes with the matching head scarf. The smell of Smithfield's wafting off her is overpowering.

"Mom," I say, leaning away from her. "You're gonna have to wash that robe on hot. You were prepping in that?"

Mom glances down the length of her body and cinches the belt around her waist. "Emergency situation. But you're right. This robe is probably going in the trash. I wasn't even thinking."

When public safety arrives, they look around but find nothing other than some indistinct tracks in the snow. Whoever it was is long gone by now. The locks and windows on the shed are intact so there isn't much else they can do aside from taking our statements and asking us to call them if anything else happens.

My parents go off to their room and sleep hunts me as I lie in my bed, listening for any sign that someone is outside. I evade sleep as long as I possibly can but eventually my lids close on their own, and as the world fades away, the nightmare tears through my brain.

The inside of the car appears, the gauzy orange light, my mom crumpled on the ground. Then everything changes and I'm sitting somewhere, a bright light overhead, flash of silver. This time it is defined enough for me to make out what it is—the edge of a preparation table, similar to the ones we have in the basement only this one isn't ours. This one has a rounded lip while the ones we have are more angular. My dad stands at the head of the table draped in black, holding something in his bloodstained hands— a book.

I jolt awake, my body drenched in sweat, my muscles tense and aching. I kick away the blankets and lie staring at the ceiling. The dream is changing again. Grief has seeped in and screwed everything up. I can't dream of Noah, but my mind can conjure images of my dad standing in a prep room holding a book? I want to scream.

The next morning, I make the short walk to Ithaca Falls and stand at the entrance to the surrounding park. The early morning air is frigid, but I'm bundled up enough to blot out most of the cold. I try not to get my hopes up, but as I duck off the street and down the narrow path that leads to the rock wall at the base of the falls, I let myself hope it's still there.

Please still be there. Please.

When I find the place where Noah had drawn our initials on the rock, it's blank. Melting snow has erased Noah's handwriting. I put my hand on the wall and hang my head. I miss him so much it hurts. It's like there's a hole in my chest. The feeling stirs something else in me—the memory of the dream. It's the same feelings—loss, emptiness, and longing.

Behind me, the quick snap of a stick draws my attention. I whip around and scan the empty pathway. There's nothing but the thick tangle of trunks and branches stripped bare. There is a rustling of leaves in the windless cold. A stab of panic ripples through me. Most of the wild animals in Ithaca are not much to worry about—deer, foxes, possums, that sort of thing—but every once in a while I'll hear that somebody caught a black bear digging through their trash. But it's winter and they should be hibernating. With my luck, I feel like the one bear that decided not to knock out for the winter would be here, ready to tear me apart. I suddenly want to be anywhere but in the secluded enclave at the foot of the falls.

Just then, I hear a loud screech, the call of a bird . . . a raven. It circles overhead once, twice, then lands on a branch just opposite me. It tucks its wings against its body and its gaze darts around before landing squarely on me. It sticks out its neck and squawks once, then again, and then lowers its head and begins making a low, almost guttural sound, like a person clearing their throat.

"Hey," a voice crackles as the wind whips past me.

I spin around, expecting to see that someone has walked up on me while I wasn't paying attention.

"Hey," the voice says again. "Get . . . out . . . get . . . out."

The voice is coming out of the raven.

I blink. I'm losing my mind. I need help. The grief is too much and I'm losing my mind and I need to go to a hospital.

The raven fluffs out its feathers and beats its wings hard against its body.

"Get . . . out." The voice is nearly human, but not. It's like a voice that comes out of a toy.

The bird lifts off the branch and ascends into the sky.

I readjust my hood, shove my hands into my pockets, and head toward the street. I need to get home. I need to tell my mom what I just saw and maybe I need to be sedated or something. I step out of the enclave and onto the path that leads up to the road. I glance back in the direction of the falls, halfway expecting to see the raven again but then I see . . . something else. A figure is standing just off the main path in the shadow of the surrounding trees. They're dressed in a black parka with a fur-lined hood pulled tight around their face, hands in their pockets, with dark pants and boots.

I quickly try to calculate how fast I can get up the rest of the path and into the road where there might be other people around, but this person is too close.

They take a step toward me.

"Sorry," I say, stepping back. I don't know what for but I'm trying to let them know I'm not a threat.

The person slowly removes their gloved hand from their pocket and extends it toward me. I stumble back, then make a break for it. I sprint up the rest of the path, scramble up the embankment and onto the sidewalk where the road is quiet and mostly empty. My heart hammers in my chest as I glance back. The person is still just standing there.

"Calm the hell down," I whisper to myself. This is a public place. A literal tourist attraction in the summer. Even in the winter people come here all the time.

I turn away from the figure and continue up Lake Street, walking as fast as I can. I feel stupid for being so jumpy and wondering if I'm gonna need therapy to deal with what are clearly hallucinations brought on by my grief. I'm pretty sure it has something to do with being back in that place where Noah and I had stood together not so long ago.

I head down the hill, veering into the street when the snow berms block the way. Halfway to the bottom, I realize that my footsteps aren't the only ones crunching across the icy terrain. I push down my hood and glance back over my shoulder. Not close enough for them to reach out and touch me but close enough for me to hear their boots on the snow, is the figure in the black parka.

CHAPTER 10

THE INCIDENT AT KATE'S

I stop. So does the figure.

I take two steps forward. So does the figure.

I pick up the pace—and so does the figure behind me.

I take off, my sneakers skidding across the tightly packed snow. I stumble down University Avenue and near the bottom of the hill I hang a left and enter the gates of Ithaca City Cemetery. Spinning around I throw my fists up in front of me and let out some weird combination of a scream and a grunt. An older woman in a red coat and black beanie walking a fluffy brown dog stops on the sidewalk, shoots me the bird, then continues down the street. The person in the black parka is gone and I am alone in the cemetery, just steps from where Noah lies entombed.

I haven't set foot inside the cemetery since Noah's funeral. I've been up to the gate, but I couldn't go in. It was like my body stopped functioning at the entrance. I could see the Cliff family tomb from there and that was enough for me. But the fear of somebody who's probably just trying to get home from class or work has pushed me over that barrier that separates the living from the dead.

The Cliff tomb, with its intricate red-and-black brick pattern, stands stark against a blanket of white snow. I still cannot bring myself to walk up to it, but someone else has. Snow has been cleared away from the tomb's entrance and a pathway of overlapping footprints leads up to the door. A wreath of white roses, their petals curled and yellowing, lies against it. A brown teddy bear with a heart on its chest sits like a sentry at the entrance. There is suddenly a buzzing at the back of my head. A wave of dizziness washes over me. I feel like I might faint.

I tilt my head up and look at the sky. "I miss you, Noah," I say as a knot claws its way up my throat. "So much." It hurts too much to stay any longer. "I'm sorry," I say. "I'm sorry, Noah. I—I can't do this."

I glance at the tomb one more time, then leave the cemetery and walk the rest of the way home. The shame I feel is just as stifling as the sadness. I'm a coward for not being able to stay with Noah in that cemetery and I'm so mad at myself for it I want to scream.

At home, I climb the front steps and go inside. I lean against the front door, wondering when things will get better or if they even can. I turn and flip the dead bolt on the door and as I glance through the glass in the direction of the cemetery, I see the figure in the black parka standing at the end of my street.

The front door is bolted but I still feel like that's not enough. I glance down at the latch. It's engaged; I can see it sticking into the doorframe. I jiggle the knob, then take stock of what I have close to me—a coat rack, my dad's walking stick that may or may not be just a random stick he found on one of his walks, and a small but weighty rock we use to keep the door propped open in the summer. Funeral homes aren't in need of deadly weapons. Most of the people that come here are already dead. I pick up the rock and grip it so hard my knuckles audibly pop as I peer back outside. The figure is gone.

"Meka," my mom says.

I jump, dropping the rock which misses my toe by an inch.

Mom puts her hand on my shoulder. "You all right, baby?"

"I—yeah, I'm fine," I say as I attempt to get my heart to slow down a little. I suck in a chest full of air and let it hiss out. "You scared me."

"I did?" she asks, looking puzzled. She glances past me, out the window in the front door.

"There was somebody following me," I say. "I think." I'm still not sure and I guess it could have been nothing.

My dad walks into the hallway from the kitchen. "I heard a bang. What was that?"

"I dropped the door-propping rock," I say.

"Why were you holding it?" my dad asks as he bites into a half of a ham sandwich.

"She said somebody was following her," my mom says. She quickly moves to the door and peers out. She double-checks the lock.

"I was gonna clock whoever it was with the rock," I say.

My dad joins Mom at the door. "I don't see anybody," he says. "You sure somebody was out there? What did they look like?"

"I—I don't know," I say. "I couldn't see their face. They had on a big winter coat."

"Why would anybody want to follow you home?" my mom asks.

"I—I don't *know*." I try to figure out how to explain but I start to doubt the whole thing myself. It's possible somebody was behind me, walking the same direction as me. That doesn't mean they were following me.

"Meka, baby," my mom begins.

"Please don't," I say quickly.

My mom presses her hand down on her hip and tilts her head to the side. "Excuse me?"

I shake my head. "No. Mom, listen. I know you're about to say you're worried and that I need sleep. You're not wrong, at all. But I can't really do anything about it right now."

"If it's causing you to hallucinate—" she begins.

"I didn't imagine it," I say, but I don't know if that's true.

"Okay," Mom says gently. "Or maybe you're feeling paranoid. Whatever the issue is, lack of sleep could be to blame for all of it."

"Whoever it was is gone," my dad says.

"Good," I say. "See? No big deal."

My mom looks at me like she wants to say it *is* a big deal and that she's not going to let it go, so I just avoid her gaze and hope she'll leave it alone. I turn to my dad.

"Dad," I begin hesitantly. "Please don't judge me when I ask you this but—" I stop. I don't even want to ask because I know it sounds impossible. "Can—can ravens talk?"

My mom's eyes widen. "Baby. Get in the car. We're going to the doctor's office and we're gonna get you some help. It's gonna be okay, I promise."

"Hold on," my dad says. "Obviously, we can go to the doctor if you need to, Meka, but yes, ravens can talk."

"What?" my mom asks, before I get a chance to.

"Ravens are highly intelligent," my dad says. His eyes are alight, and I can tell he's about to launch into telling me some obscure facts about ravens. "They have the cognitive abilities of a seven-year-old child. They use tools, they can reason and solve problems. They can mimic human speech like a parrot."

I sigh. Okay. I'm not losing it completely.

"Simple stuff mostly," Dad continues. "Maybe two or three words. Not full-on sentences. And it's not quite independent thought, just mimicry, but still an astonishing feat. They're incredible creatures."

My mom covers her mouth with her hand. She'd never shame him for what he likes but it can be a little intense sometimes.

My dad tilts his head and looks at me. "Why do you ask?"

"There was a raven by the falls," I say. "It said 'hey.' Then it said 'get out' right before I saw the person in the coat."

My dad doesn't smile now. His mouth actually turns down into a sort of scowl. "It did?"

"Yeah," I say.

My dad looks thoughtful as he glances at the perch where his ravens usually congregate.

"Interesting," my dad says. "But it would have had to hear someone say those words before it could repeat them."

"It was quiet," I say. "Nobody said anything."

"Not that you heard, anyway," says my dad. He thinks for a minute. "It probably picked it up from someone nearby. Strange but not impossible." He smiles gently. "Why don't you and your mom order a pizza or something. Relax a little. I need to pack."

"You're leaving?" I ask.

He nods and looks at his sandwich like he doesn't want to take another bite. "Business. We might have a new supplier for our bulk orders of trocars and eye caps. They're using some new alloy which makes them cheaper without skimping on the quality. It's really remarkable."

"I've never seen anybody so hyped about trocars," my mom says, kissing him on the cheek and rubbing his arm.

A trocar is a long, sharp instrument used in the embalming process. It goes in the lower abdomen and helps access and drain built-up fluids and gas, replacing them with embalming fluid. There are different makes and models and my dad has his favorites.

"I'll be upstairs if you need me," Dad says. "And keep the doors locked. Just in case."

I touch the lock to make sure it's bolted.

"Where do you want pizza from?" my mom asks.

"Let's do Ned's," I say, happy to move on from the subject of my imaginary stalker.

"You got it," Mom says, giving me a little nudge in the shoulder. "They have this great gluten-free, no-cheese option."

I scrunch up my nose. "What's it made out of? Cardboard? Is it even pizza if there's no cheese?"

Mom rolls her eyes and shoos me into the living room. Upstairs, there's a loud bang and then the sound of my dad cursing.

My mom sighs. "Help your father, please."

I jog upstairs to find my dad struggling with his suitcase as he wrestles it from the closet next to my room.

"I got it," I say, grabbing the handle and yanking it out into the hall.

"Thanks," my dad says. He pulls a tissue out of his pocket

and dabs at his forehead. "I was just going to do a carry-on but I need the bigger one this time in case I want to bring back samples."

"TSA is gonna let you on a flight with a bunch of trocars in this thing?" I ask. "I feel like that's going to land you on the no-fly list."

My dad chuckles to himself. "Hasn't been a problem before."

I grab the handle of his bag but my grip slips and it tips over, popping open. A jumble of clothing falls out. I reach for it to shove it back inside but a smell emanating from the bundle of black clothing wafts into my face. It's smoky, like the smell that sometimes drifts out of our wood-burning fireplace when it's windy outside.

I cover my mouth with my hand. "Dad, what is that smell?"

Flustered, my dad shoves the thick black cloth, which I'm not even sure is clothing now, into the suitcase and zips it closed.

"Sorry," Dad says. "I was moving some of Grandpa Redwood's stuff around and I must have gotten some of his things mixed up with mine."

A second mention of Grandpa Redwood in the span of a few months when I can count on one hand the number of times my dad had ever spoken about him before strikes me as odd.

"What was Grandpa Redwood doing? Dancing around a firepit? This thing smells like smoke."

He shrugs. "Maybe? Morticians have probably been caught doing stranger things than that, right?"

"Have they?" I ask. "I'm gonna need you to elaborate. Immediately."

I expect him to laugh but instead he just looks a little sad.

"I feel like I should tell you more about him," Dad says.

I'm caught all the way off guard. "What?" I ask. "Now?"

"Well, only, you know, if you want," Dad says, stumbling over his words. "I know I don't talk about him much. The kind of person he was—I don't know—I feel like I should say something."

"Uh, Dad," I say gently. "Are you okay? We do not have to talk about the man if you don't want to. I'm perfectly fine never knowing a single other thing about him if you don't want to tell me."

My dad gives a stiff laugh. "No, you're right, I just thought . . . it's silly." He pulls the suitcase into his room and glances at his watch. "I'm going to pack so I can get out of here on time. Help your mom while I'm gone and double-check the supply order I put in, okay?"

He kisses me on the top of my head and nudges me toward the stairs.

The smoky smell still lingers in the hall as I make my way back downstairs. I catch my mom in the kitchen.

"Mom," I say quietly. "Is Dad okay?"

"As far as I know," she says. "Why?"

"He was talking about Grandpa Redwood," I say. "He was being weird. Like he wanted to tell me something about him but then changed his mind."

Mom looks a little concerned but then smiles. "I'm sure it's nothing. Maybe he's feeling a little sentimental?"

"I thought they didn't like each other," I say.

"It's more complicated than that," Mom says. "But if he isn't ready to bring it up I won't either. I can't even say I know all the details."

"All the details of what?" I ask. "Like, what happened between them?"

My mom gives a quick nod and pretends to look for something in the fridge, knowing good and well she doesn't eat most of the stuff in there. "I'm sure he's fine," she says.

I don't really believe her and now it seems like they're both keeping something from me. I leave it alone for now but that strange smell is still stuck in my nose and my gut is telling me something is off.

In the late afternoon, my dad takes a Lyft to the airport and I'm about ready to sink into the couch for the evening when my mom starts gathering up her purse and putting on her shoes.

"Come on," she says. "Let's get out of the house for a little bit." She stands in front of the mirror in the hallway and checks her lipstick, gently dabbing at the corners of her mouth. Her hair is pulled into a bun at the base of her neck and she smooths it down, unnecessarily because not a single hair is out of place anyway.

"Where we going?" I ask.

"I need to get a few things from Kate's."

I don't even pretend to hide my disappointment. "I thought we would go to H&M or something. Kate's? That place is for old ladies."

"You telling me I look old?" she asks.

"No," I say quickly, as my life flashes before my eyes. "Absolutely not. I'm just—I didn't know you shop there. Nothing you wear looks like it comes from there."

She smiles. "Good. I get everything altered. That's the trick to making anything look good—get it tailored to fit you in just the right way." She sticks out her leg and gives a little turn. She's got on a pair of jeans and a chunky black sweater. "I even get my jeans tailored. Been doing it for years."

"If you say so," I say. I've never had anything tailored in my life but my mom makes it seem like it's the key to unlocking the secrets of the universe. Noah got his clothes tailored sometimes too. He was so tall and lanky, nothing ever really fit him right until he got it taken in or let out.

An ache grips my chest like a vise. This is the part I hate. These little moments where he appears so clear in my mind that it takes my breath away. I grab my coat and my phone and head out the door with my mom.

Kate's is run out of a historic building on the Commons, a street lined with shops and restaurants in the heart of Ithaca. In the fall the Apple Harvest Festival takes it over and local vendors sell everything from apple cider doughnuts and funnel cakes to handmade scarves. Noah and I used to go every year. Again, the thought of him makes my heart feel like it's being torn in half, like all the careful stitching I'd done to try and mend it is coming undone, but I try to smile. I try to remember that this is a happy memory and that I get to keep those too.

I slip into Kate's on my mom's heel and try to ground myself again. The store is bright, the music is soft; it smells like air freshener and freshly oiled wood.

"Hey, Kassie," the clerk says to my mom.

"Hey," Mom says back, smiling at the young woman behind the counter.

"You guys are on a first-name basis?" I ask. "The situation is more serious than I thought."

"Oh, hush," Mom says. "Rachel, this is my daughter, Meka. Meka, this is Rachel."

Rachel reaches over the counter to shake my hand. Her jet-black hair is pulled back so tight it's drawing the corners of her eyes up. Her thick black eyeliner is sharpened to a deadly point.

"Nice to meet you," she says, smiling a little too hard.

"Same," I say.

My mom immediately goes to a rack full of dresses and starts thumbing through.

"Do you have this in a twelve?" my mom asks, holding up a long black dress with little white polka dots scattered across it.

"Let me check," Rachel says. She disappears into a back room and returns a moment later with the dress in my mom's size. "Changing room's open," she says.

"Be right back," Mom says to me.

I nod and she takes the dress from Rachel and disappears behind a curtain in a little alcove at the rear of the store.

Rachel returns to her post at the register and I wander the shop. I look through the racks of sweaters and overcoats. At the rear of the shop is a display with hand-beaded bracelets and I touch my wrist where the bracelet Noah had given me used to be.

"Mom?" I ask.

She pokes her head out from the dressing room. "You okay, baby?"

We exchange a glance that says no, I'm not okay.

"Okay, give me one second," she says as she disappears behind the curtain.

The bell over the door dings as someone else enters the shop. I don't turn around. I'm just trying to keep my legs from going out from under me when there's a sharp intake of breath from behind me.

I instinctively turn my head toward the sound. A man has

entered the shop and is standing in front of Rachel. Her eyes are wide and I'm wondering why she's suddenly dropped the big smile she had for me and my mom. She's not even looking at the dude's face. Her gaze is directed toward the counter where the man's hand is resting. In it is a knife.

"Hey, Mr. Lions," Rachel says in a strained voice. "I—I haven't seen you in a long time."

The man huffs. "I'm on the goddamn sidewalk every day. Do you know how cold it is at night?"

His clothes are worn, he's got on two, maybe three, layers of coats or sweaters, I can't really tell. His boots are laceless and his facial hair is long and unkempt. He grips the knife so hard his hand begins to tremble. I realize that I've seen him around. He's always holed up in some doorway on the Commons and I think I've even seen him at Stewart Park a few times.

"I can call someone for you," Rachel says. She takes a step back, reaching for the phone.

The man slams his fist onto the counter.

"Who can you call?" he asks. "Who is gonna help me? When I'm dead they can come get me just like the others."

Rachel holds her hands in front of her. "Please, Mr. Lions."

"They're gonna get me!" the man shouts. "They're gonna cut me up in little pieces!"

There are suddenly hands on me and my mom is silently pulling me into the changing room. She puts her hand over my mouth and shows me her phone—she's dialed 911 and is holding the phone close to her ear.

The dress she'd been trying on is draped from her shoulders, like she was in the process of changing out of it when she grabbed me. Her back is to the floor-length mirror hanging at the rear of the fitting room. In the reflection is a jagged scar running almost the full length of her spine, ending just below her shoulder blades.

"We need help at Kate's on the Commons," my mom whispers into the phone. "There's a man with a knife."

There's a loud bang and Rachel yelps. I almost step out of the fitting room but my mom grabs me by my jacket and presses her finger to her lips in a plea for silence.

"Ma'am?" the 911 operator's voice echoes through the phone. "Ma'am. We're on the way. Just hold tight."

Heavy footsteps approach the rear of the shop. I stop breathing. My mom hangs up the phone and I feel like we've lost our lifeline. The bell on the shop door dings again.

I hope that means Rachel got out because it looks like me and Mom aren't gonna be so lucky. I push my mom behind me and her dress slips down a little farther, revealing another scar on her chest that snakes up from her sternum and branches out to the left. She follows my gaze and quickly readjusts her clothing. She gestures to the curtain and makes a pounding motion with her fist.

We're gonna jump him? I silently mouth to her.

She nods.

He has a knife! I wordlessly scream at her.

She turns and slips her hand into her purse and pulls out a small cylindrical container that says Pepper Spray in bold letters on the side.

Maybe we have a chance or maybe this dude knifes us to death in the dressing room of Kate's. For a moment I think about how down I'd been right after Noah died. I'm still down but I'm not feeling like I want to join him anymore. I'd be lying if I said the thought hadn't crossed my mind and I'd had to talk to a grief counselor about that too. But no. I didn't want to die, I just didn't want to be so hopelessly sad anymore. And now, right now, I don't much feel like dying either.

I'm fully prepared to go upside this man's head with a mirror, a can of pepper spray, and the wrath of a girl stuck in a changing room with her half-naked mother when suddenly there is a flurry of footsteps. It sounds like somebody is running full speed from the front of the shop to the back. There's a muffled yelp, a loud thud, and a crash of glass. The man's hand suddenly appears under the curtain, limp and flecked with blood, the knife nowhere to be seen. More footsteps and then the bell on the front door dings again. I grab the pepper spray and yank the curtain open to find the man semiconscious on the floor. The display table with bracelets is busted and lying in pieces.

"End . . . of . . . days," the man mumbles. "Little . . . tiny . . . pieces."

I glance toward the front of the store and see Rachel standing out on the sidewalk among a gathering of onlookers, none of whom came in to help us. My mom grabs her stuff and I pull her through the store and out the front door. Outside, she quickly puts on her coat.

"I called the police," Rachel says.

"So did I," my mom says.

Rachel nods. "Are you guys okay? I'm so sorry I just ran outside, I thought he was gonna stab me!"

"It's okay," my mom says.

"Actually, not okay," I grumble to myself.

Rachel descends into a fit of tears as the police and the Ithaca Department of Public Safety escort the man out to a car. As they're getting him situated, the knife falls out of his pocket and hits the ground with a soft thud.

"Nobody searched him?" one of the officers asks.

Another officer shrugs like he either doesn't know or doesn't care. He picks up the knife and tests its weight in his hand.

"Ha!" he huffs. "It's fake. Made of plastic or somethin'."

"That doesn't make any of us feel better," my mom says angrily. She turns away from the officers and sighs. "They need to worry about why he doesn't have a place to sleep and stop trying to just throw everybody in jail."

Rachel leans in close to us. "Did y'all see the person who ran in there and punched Mr. Lions? They came outta nowhere."

I almost pull out my phone to send a text to Cipriana and Caleb to tell them the wildest shit imaginable just happened when a police officer comes over to take our official statements.

When we're done, we're told that Ithaca PD will probably get in touch with us soon and that we should be expecting a call or a visit from them. Rachel lets my mom in the store to change back into her clothes and then locks up and calls it a day. Me and my mom head home, stopping to pick up our pizza along the way.

Mom goes on and on about how the city needs to allocate more resources for unhoused people and she's also pretty worried about Rachel but my mind is stuck on the fact that Ithaca apparently has its own superhero now.

CHAPTER 11

STRANGERS COME TO CALL

"Double-check the locks," my mom says when we get home.

"Mom, that man is locked up for the night, maybe longer," I say. "He is not coming here to get us."

Mom isn't convinced. "Lock everything up anyway. If it isn't good ol' Mr. Lions, it might be whoever was stealing supplies out of the shed or whoever it was that was following you from the falls."

When I tally up the people who may or may not be out to get us, I'm surprised that the number is so high. I do what she says, checking the locks on the doors before settling down in the living room with our pizza and a plan to watch some old movie Mom picked out for us.

"Are we gonna tell Dad about what happened at Kate's?" I ask.

Mom hesitates for a moment. "Yes, but not till he gets home. I don't want to worry him while he's working. We're okay, we're safe. I'll fill him in when he gets back."

I stake out a spot in the corner of the couch while my mom goes to change.

"Mom," I call up to her from the living room. "What's the dude from the movie's name? I want to look him up."

I hear her groan. "Meka, baby, you know who Bruce Willis is. Come on now. You're making me feel old."

I know exactly who Bruce Willis is, but I can't resist giving her a hard time about it. I find the movie just as she returns to the living room in a black sweatsuit and fuzzy black slippers. Her hair is in a bun on top of her head and her face is covered in a thick, white face cream.

"Trying something new?" I ask.

My mom's skin care routine is too complicated for me to follow. It's got at least ten steps and she never puts it off. No matter how tired she is or how late she stays up, she tells me the key to her perfect complexion is never skipping a single day or a single step.

Mom gently touches the side of her face and some of the cream comes off on her fingertips. She rubs it into the back of her hand. "It's supposed to keep the skin hydrated so it's nice and plump."

"What's it called?" I ask. "Maybe I can try some."

She smiles. "You don't need it, baby. You're perfect."

"My blackheads say different," I sigh. "What's this movie about?"

"Bruce Willis plays an undertaker," she says. "It's right up our alley. You want popcorn?"

"No, I'm good, but Mom?"

She starts the movie and the opening credits begin to roll.

"Yes, baby?" she says without turning to look at me.

"When I was in the fitting room with you, I saw, well, I don't wanna make you uncomfortable but—"

"The scars," she says.

I try to replay the entirety of my life's memories back in that moment. I don't remember ever seeing the scars on my mom's back and chest. We'd been to the beach a few times but only because I had begged and begged for us to go. She was firmly against it but finally agreed after my dad assured her it would be fun. I'm pretty sure she had been wearing a suit but what I remember was the mint green kaftan she'd worn and how she'd painted her nails to match it. I don't remember seeing the scars then. She never wears anything low cut enough for me to see clear down to her sternum or the full length of her back so I try to think if I would have noticed at all.

"I got them a long time ago," she says softly. "I'm very self-conscious about them."

I suddenly feel like bringing it up is overstepping. "We don't have to talk about it," I say, gently touching her hand. "I'm sorry. I shouldn't have said anything."

"No, it's fine." She smiles and squeezes my hand. "I try really hard to keep myself up. I try to keep myself together. The scars aren't ugly. It's not about that. They're a part of me, but they *are* a reminder that I don't have control over every single aspect of my life—my appearance—and I don't like that."

I thread her words through the needle of knowing exactly what kind of person she is. It might sound vain to somebody who doesn't know her but *I* know her—and this isn't about vanity. She says things like "keep myself up" and "keep myself together." It's about control and I have to believe it has everything to do with being around death every day of her life.

"You said they're a part of you," I say, trying to think of something to tell her that really matters. "So that means they're beautiful."

She blinks twice in quick succession, then grabs my hand and holds it tight.

"What did I do to deserve you, huh?"

"Must have been something really good because I'm, like, the perfect daughter."

"Can I tell you something?" she asks.

I look into her face. I can't tell if this is going to be something serious or not.

"Sure," I say.

She pulls the collar of her sweatshirt up under her chin, being careful not to let her face cream touch the black fabric. "Sometimes, I have your father use some of our—supplies—to cover the scars."

I laugh, but then I stop. She's not joking. She's not laughing. She is waiting.

She lowers her head. The face cream covers every inch of her face, even her upper eyelids, but a thin strip of skin is visible just under her lower lid. With her makeup removed, the skin is dull, almost ashen.

"You mean the mortuary supplies?" I ask

She watches me intently. When I look down, she pats my knee.

"Sorry," she says. "I know it's a little weird."

"It's okay," I say. Is it? I don't know.

"I can make the injuries—the scars—on my chest almost disappear completely," she says. "Your dad isn't as good at doing the makeup as I am." She laughs a little. "The mortuary makeup lasts a long time and then I don't have to think about them as much."

"It works just as good on your skin?" I ask.

She nods. "My skin is always a little . . . dry. So it works fine."

"That makes sense, I guess," I say. "If you need help or something—"

"No," she says quickly, patting my knee again. "No, baby. Your dad and I can handle it. I just wanted to tell you because, well, I don't know. I just thought you should know."

I grab her hand and squeeze it. "Get under a blanket with me," I say. "Your hands are freezing."

She pulls a big fluffy blanket off the back of the couch and we snuggle under it and watch our movie.

I hope I'll dream of the knife-wielding man. I hope the terror I felt would be enough to carve out a new space in my head, but the incident isn't enough to keep the song, the car, my mother's broken body out of my mind. It *does* change the details in the dream. When Noah died, the table had come into view and the strange book; now there is more. There is a window, rain outside it, the rhythmic pattering of the droplets, but buried with that is something else . . . words. Not a song. Not a conversation, just words. I grasp at them when I wake up, trying to remember what they were, but it's pointless.

My dad returns from his trip three days later and is so horrified when my mom tells him what happened at Kate's that he just sits on the couch with his head in hands for a solid ten minutes.

"You should have called me," he says. "I would have come home right away."

"We're fine," my mom assures him. "Really. And it turns out the knife wasn't even real. It was plastic."

"Is that supposed to make me feel better?" he asks with a ring of genuine sincerity.

"Yes?" I offer. "I mean, maybe. I don't know."

"Mr. Lions needs more help than what he's getting," Mom says.

"Of course that's what you're worried about," Dad says. "And you're a saint for it but my god, Kassie, you could have been—" He stops short.

Mom turns her face away from him and stares out the living room window.

"You could have been hurt," my dad continues.

"Or killed," I chime in. I'd meant to say it in my head but it just kind of slips out.

Dad's face goes ashen.

"He was talking about the end times and saying somebody was gonna cut him into pieces," I say quickly, trying to put the conversation back on track.

My dad lifts his head and swallows. "What?"

I nod. "Even after he got dropped he was mumbling about 'little tiny pieces.'"

My dad looks like he's about to say something but changes his mind. He stands and puts his arms around me. "I'm just glad you're both okay."

I hug him back. "We're good, Dad. And I wasn't going to let anything happen to Mom either. Believe me."

My dad straightens up and gently grasps my shoulder. "Love you."

"Love you too," I say.

The look in his eyes wrecks me. He's cloaked in sadness again but it's more than that, it's despair. I recognize it because it rides shotgun with a lot of people who've come through the house grieving their loved ones.

My dad breaks from me and heads toward the stairs. "Kassie, I need to speak with you alone when you've got a minute." He treks upstairs and my mom sighs.

"We should have told him earlier," I say.

Mom shakes her head. "No. It would have stressed him out too much. Don't worry. I'll go talk to him."

She disappears up the stairs and I cut on the TV. A few minutes later I hear a sound I've rarely heard in my entire life—my parents arguing.

I mute the TV. Their muffled voices filter down through the floor. I can't hear exactly what they're saying but they're going back and forth, my dad's voice low and almost frantic, my mom's tone higher, more measured.

I consider unmuting the TV and ignoring them but there's a pit in my stomach, a feeling in my gut that makes me get up and slip into the back staircase. I make my way up, avoiding the boards that creak. At the top, I peer down the hall and catch a glimpse of my mom pacing inside her room as my dad sits on the edge of their bed. I duck back, concealing myself on the landing, peeking out just enough to see them both.

"They went back on their word," my dad says.

"You don't know that for sure," Mom says. "Let's not jump to any conclusions."

My dad stands and runs his hands over the top of his head. "I know how difficult it is. I know that more than anyone but they could put us all at risk. I can't believe they'd put us in jeopardy this way."

Mom gently puts her hand on my dad's shoulder. "Is it really so hard to believe? You said it yourself; we understand more than most."

All of this over some trocars and eye caps? That's what my dad's trip was for. I thought they were arguing about what happened to me and my mom at Kate's but this is something else. It sounds business related.

"What about Meka," my dad says. "Is she—"

"She's okay," my mom says. "For now."

"I have to go," my dad says. "I have to make sure everything is still intact or there is going to be a serious problem. Especially after what happened the other night." He sighs heavily.

"Are you sure this is all connected?" my mom asks.

"It has to be," Dad says.

He sounds afraid and I'm not sure what that means. Are we in some kind of financial trouble? People die every day so it's not like there's a shortage of business. I step back into the stairwell and the board creaks under my weight.

"Shit."

"Meka?" my mom calls.

I'm halfway to the bottom of the stairs when I hear footsteps emerging from my parents' room. I hit the first-floor landing running, and race back to the couch. I dive-bomb into the corner and pull out my phone just as my mom emerges from the back stairwell.

"You guys okay?" I ask, trying not to reveal that my heart is backflipping in my chest. "I thought you were arguing."

"Arguing?" my mom asks. "No. Just having a discussion. Not a discussion you heard any parts of, right?"

"Huh?" I know I sound like the worst liar on the planet. "I can't tell what you're saying from down here."

"What about from the back staircase?" she asks.

"Not from there either," I say.

"Yeah, okay," she says, a knowing smirk on her lips. "Grown folks business, Meka."

"Yes, ma'am," I say.

The doorbell rings and I bolt off the couch to answer it, avoiding my mom's pointed gaze. I yank open the front door to find Gerald, our regular delivery guy. He shoves a clipboard at me.

"You know the drill," Gerald says. "Signatures on the yellow and the pink copies. Where's your mother? How's she doin'?"

I sign for the delivery and hand the clipboard back to him. "She's in the living room," I say. "She's fine. She and my dad are great." Gerald never asks about my dad but always seems interested in my mom. I always have to remind him that if he looks at her in a way she doesn't like, I'll happily add him to the list of guests in the freezer.

"Hey, Gerald," my mom says as she appears in the hall behind me. "How's it goin'?"

"Better now that I've seen your gorgeous smiling face," Gerald replies. "I've been delivering to you for what? Ten years now? You've got the same gorgeous face as you did the first time I saw you."

Gerald is pushing sixty and has a tuft of hair growing out of his left nostril. He's not bald but it'd probably be a better look than the squirrel-pelt toupee he insists on wearing every time he shows up here. If it's one thing dudes like him have, it's the audacity.

"You're too kind, Gerald," Mom says.

Gerald practically skips back to his truck and my mom laughs as my dad rejoins us in the front entryway. When Gerald hauls in three boxes of Smithfield's and some other smaller packages, he spots my dad and literally scowls.

"Gerald," Dad says.

"Mr. Redwood," Gerald replies in a weirdly formal tone.

My dad bites back a smile, then disappears into the kitchen without another word.

"How's your wife?" my mom asks as Gerald nudges the boxes off his hand truck.

I whip my head around. "You have a wife?"

Gerald looks at me quizzically. "Unfortunately."

I'm literally struck silent. This man acts like my mom is the rising sun and the whole time he has a wife? And . . . who would want to marry him? I have too many questions and because I don't really care about Gerald's feelings, I'm about to put every one of them to him but my mom puts her hand on my arm.

"See you next time," my mom says.

Gerald gives her a little nod and goes on his way.

"Man, he's annoying," I say.

My mom chuckles to herself and eyes the boxes of supplies. "Will you put this stuff away for me?" she asks.

"Only if you promise me that I can knock Gerald out if he ever makes you uncomfortable," I say.

Mom rolls her eyes and laughs. "Fine. But don't kill him. I don't wanna have to see that man naked on a prep table for any reason."

The thought of it makes me want to throw up so I try to push that horrifying image out of my head and get to work putting away the supplies as my mom starts dinner. I take the smaller packages downstairs and put them away. Mom's got some new shades of eyeshadows and a few new lipsticks. I stack up three new cans of Lanol Care, a hydrating spray that works really well on dead skin, and a new brush set.

In the front entryway I grab a box of Smithfield's and haul it through the house and out the back door. I sit the box in the snow and unlock the supply shed. Inside, I rearrange the shelf, tossing a few empty boxes out and making room for the new shipment. I make a mental note of how much we have, and while I still think the numbers are lower than they should be, neither Mom or Dad brought it back up.

I run back to the house to grab the other boxes as my dad is heading out the front door.

As he pulls it open he almost runs into a group of people standing on the porch. I hadn't even heard the bell.

"Jonathan," one of the men says.

My dad says nothing but when he glances back at me, the look on his face is unmistakable . . . it is fear.

"Dad?" I call out.

"If we could have a moment of your time," another man says.

There are three of them and they're all similarly dressed—dark pants, button shirts, long dark overcoats. I think it's some of the same people who came to the door during dinner that night before Noah . . . before Noah died . . . but I can't be sure.

"What do you want from me?" Dad asks.

It's a strange thing to ask a prospective client. They want funeral services. That's the only thing that it could be.

"A choice needs to be made," one of the men says.

My dad's posture stiffens and he grips the doorknob with his right hand.

"The incident in front of St. Paul's—" one of the men begins.

"Not here," Dad says, cutting the other man off. "Let me get my things."

"Jonathan," Mom's voice rings out as she steps into the hall. "Who—" She stops abruptly and turns and steps back into the kitchen. "We're having guests for dinner?" she calls in a sickly sweet tone. "I can make extra."

"No," Dad says firmly. "I'm going out. I'll be back before dinner's done."

"Everything okay?" I ask, eyeing the people on the porch.

He hesitates for a moment. "Yes."

It's a lie if I've ever heard one.

"Love you," I say as I hoist up another box.

"Love you," he says. "Do me a favor and take care of your mother."

I start to laugh but he doesn't even crack a smile. Without another word, he leaves with the visitors and I hear a car rev its engine, then take off.

CHAPTER 12

AN UNEXPECTED GUEST

I stick my head in the kitchen. "What is going on?" I ask. "Do you know those people?"

My mom ties her apron tightly at her back. She seems flustered. "I've seen them before."

She's not answering my question but I can't understand why. "The way you're acting is weird and the way Dad is acting is weird," I say. "You know that, right?"

"Can you put away the rest of those boxes?" Mom asks, brushing off my concerns. "I need your help in here."

I sigh. "Does it involve me getting to taste whatever you're cooking?"

"Maybe," she says.

She doesn't have to tell me twice. I pick up both boxes from the hall and even though I feel like my forearm is about to snap, I lug them out to the supply shed.

The sun is setting and the temperature is about to plummet.

I'm so busy thinking about how good it's going to feel to crawl under my blankets and cut on the space heater as I set the boxes in the snow that, at first, I don't realize I'm unlocking the padlock . . . again.

I'd already opened it when I brought out the first box and I don't remember relocking it. I had more boxes to bring out so I wouldn't have locked it anyway. It's something I do so often maybe I did it out of habit. I quickly set the boxes inside the shed and lock it back up.

A rustling from the area of the dumpster draws my attention. The air is biting but the frigid chill that runs through me isn't from the weather.

"Somebody there?" I ask. I kick myself for asking. Watch it be Mr. Lions who jumps out and finishes what he started at Kate's. "I'll beat the brakes off you," I say. Again, not having been in a fight in years, I'm not confident that I wouldn't get my ass whooped but I say it anyway.

I step into the snow to try and peer around the dumpster but as I do, something catches my eye. There is a piece of paper sitting on the back step. I must have walked right over it when I came out. I approach the paper, whatever it is, like it's a snake in the grass, like it's dangerous. It's sitting right in the center of the step, free from snow as if it fell out of the sky.

The beating of wings and rush of black feathers swoops past my face and I stumble back. A raven lands in my dad's bird feeder and pecks at the remnants of broken sunflower seeds before taking to the air again.

My heart is in my throat.

It's not a piece of paper, but an envelope—with my name scrawled across the front. I look over my shoulder. I know someone is standing there. I can feel it. I snatch the paper and stumble inside, slamming the door shut and locking it.

"What is going on?" Mom calls from the kitchen. "Why are you slamming doors?"

I peer through the glass but I don't see anything or anyone. I back into the kitchen as the panicked feeling falls away from me.

"I—I unlocked the shed, but when I went back out it was locked again and I heard a noise."

Mom looks up from peeling potatoes. "What?"

I don't know what to say. Maybe I'm still shook from what happened at Kate's or how strange both my mom and dad were acting. I don't know, but something just doesn't feel right.

"What's that?" Mom asks, her gaze flitting to my hand.

I stare down at my hand like the fingers clenching the envelope aren't mine.

"It was sitting on the back step," I say. "It has my name on it."

There's a muffled thud from somewhere outside. Mom raises her chin and tilts her head like she's listening.

"The wind is kicking up out there," she says. She scrapes the potato peeler down the side of a russet and lets the skin fall into a bag in the sink. "Meka, baby, you got me worried. What's in the envelope?"

I examine the writing again, then tear it open. There's no letter inside but there is something. I tip up the open envelope and let whatever it is fall into my hand.

It's a bracelet.

I set it on the kitchen counter and back away as if it might suddenly come alive and strike out at me. The mixture of horror and confusion coursing through me is a potent mix. It makes my head dizzy.

"Meka," my mom says. "What is it?"

I stare down at the bracelet. "No. No, this can't be real. Why would somebody do this? Why would somebody leave this here for me?"

My mom turns around and pushes her hand down on her hip. "Meka, please. What is going on?"

"That's—that's my bracelet," I stammer. My mouth is dry, and the words don't come out right.

"Okay?" my mom asks. "Did you lose it somewhere?"

"No," I say. Now my voice sounds far away like it doesn't belong to me. "I put it on Noah right before the funeral. He—he was buried with it."

"Meka," my mom says. She's got a look in her eyes like she pities me. "Meka, that—that just can't be."

"It is," I say softly, knowing how impossible it sounds. "I would know it anywhere. He—he gave this to me and then I put it on him." I pick it up. "Now it's here. How?"

"Baby," my mom says.

I shake my head. I don't want to be told that I'm losing my mind or that I haven't slept or that I'm hallucinating. This isn't a similar bracelet. It's the *exact* same one. I pass it back and forth between my hands, holding it close to my face so I can see all the small details. The silver clasp is the same. The wide flat bead with our initials engraved is the same.

"This bracelet was on Noah when we buried him so why is it sitting on the back step in an envelope with my name on it?" I ask, as if there is an answer that would satisfy me.

I pick up the torn envelope and study the handwriting on the front. If I didn't know any better I would say that I almost recognize it . . .

"Meka," my mother says more forcefully this time. "Whatever you think this is, it just can't be. It . . ." she trails off, shaking her head. She turns around and starts peeling potatoes again.

"What? So we're not going to try to figure out what this is or why it's here?" I ask. "Nobody knew about this except me and Noah. He—he died before I could show it off and I wanted him to have it when we buried him."

Tears sting my eyes and a knot claws its way up my throat. I grip the edge of the counter and stare at the bracelet.

"Mom," I say.

She doesn't answer me. She just keeps peeling the damn potatoes. Something inside me breaks open.

"Mom! Please listen to me! I'm not crazy! We have to—"

My mom gasps and stumbles away from the sink, clutching her hand against her chest. She drops the potato peeler on the counter and grabs a dish rag, wrapping it around her hand.

"I'm sorry," I say rushing to her side. "You cut yourself? Is it bad?"

My mom presses the rag tight. She peeks under it and her eyes grow wide with fear. "I—I might need stitches."

"Oh no," I say, feeling like it's my fault for distracting her. "Let me see. Maybe it's not too bad." I reach for the cloth but she yanks her hand away.

"No," she says. "Don't look at it." She scoots past me and heads toward the stairs. "Do me a favor and call your dad. Tell him to come home right now."

She bounds up the stairs and I take out my phone. My hand is trembling so bad I almost fumble it. I call my dad. His voicemail picks up immediately and I hang up. I text him.

ME: I need to talk to you. Mom cut her hand and we gotta go to the hospital. Please pick up the phone.

All I can do is stare at the bracelet. *How the hell is this here?*

I take it to the sink where the little light under the cabinet is brightest. I hold it there, examining it. I'm even more sure that it's the same bracelet and not just a similar one but I know that's not right. Somebody knew about the bracelet. Somebody put a replica on my porch. I shake my head. That scenario makes even less sense than anything else.

"Mom," I call out. "Let's go to the urgent care. They do stitches there."

I set the bracelet on the counter and glance down into the sink. There, among the peeled potato skins, is a chunk of skin. My stomach turns over. My mom is definitely going to need to go to the hospital. Half of her damn finger is lying in the sink. Can it be reattached? That's only if the whole thing's cut off, right? I don't know, but a part of me feels like I need to snatch the piece of flesh up and put it on ice. As I consider doing this, I see the discarded potato peeler lying next to the sink where my mom had dropped it. The plastic handle is broken at the tip and the blades are dull. How my mom had managed to cut off such a huge part of her own finger with it is beyond me. I look at the little piece of flesh again. Something about it makes me pause. There is no blood. The chunk of skin is neatly flayed off and curled at the edges almost like . . .

My heart nearly stops.

No.

That can't be right. Too much is happening all at once and my mind is playing tricks on me. Still . . .

I grasp the potato peeler and poke at the little piece of skin and finally, unable to resist testing my theory any longer, I pick it up with my bare hand. I press it between my thumb and forefinger. It's soft, moldable . . . like wax.

Mortuary wax.

My phone vibrates on the counter and I almost jump out of my skin. I pick it up, hitting the green button.

"Dad!" Silence echoes on the line. "Dad?" I pull the phone away from my ear and stare at the screen.

It's not my dad's number that's there. It is a name and number that I haven't deleted from my phone because it still hurts too much and there it is, right alongside a picture of his beautiful, smiling face.

Noah.

I press the phone to my ear. "Who—who is this?"

"Meeks," a painfully familiar voice says.

My blood turns to ice in my veins. The room tilts. Am I awake or am I dreaming? I can't tell.

"Noah?" I ask, the words made of nothing more than bated breath.

"Get out of the house," he says. "Now."

Above me, there's a loud thud and I think I hear my mom's muffled voice. I stare at the phone in my hand. The call has ended. Whoever it was hung up. A sudden and overwhelming sense of terror washes over me. I move toward the back stairs but I feel like my body is moving in slow motion.

"Mom?" I call out as I reach the top of the stairs and go down the hall to her room. "Mom, we gotta get out of here. Something is happening! Somebody just called me from Noah's number and—"

I'm stopped short as I enter my mom's room and stand just

outside her bathroom. She is standing by her sink, her hand still wrapped in a towel—and a man is standing in front of her with his back to me.

He's dressed in dark clothing and is holding something in his hand. A knife. Not the fake plastic kind Mr. Lions had threatened Rachel with in Kate's. This one looks like something a hunter would use to carve up a wild animal. The curved blade is as long as my forearm and serrated on one edge. It glints in the glaring white light of the bathroom as the man looms over my mom.

"It's all over," the man says. "This is all done now."

I look to my mom, expecting to find her terrified but she is stoic.

"Get out of my house," she says firmly.

"No," the man says. "No one is going anywhere."

He takes a step toward her and without thinking, I launch myself directly at him. I wrap my arms around his head and neck, squeezing as tight as I can, clawing at his face. My finger finds something soft and I press into it. I think it's his eye. He screams and thrashes around wildly, slamming his back against the bathroom door, knocking the wind out of me. I tumble to the floor and roll onto my back gasping for air. The man glowers at me. His eyes are a piercing blue and his messy blond hair hangs over his forehead.

I know him.

"You—you were there at the movie theater," I stammer.

"I don't want to have to kill you too," he says.

I scramble to my feet and retreat toward the bedroom door as the man advances on me.

"Just leave!" I scream at him. "We won't tell anybody! Just go! Please!"

The man says nothing as he takes another step toward me and raises the knife.

"Mom!" I scream. "Run!"

I brace myself. This is going to hurt.

From behind me, somewhere down the hall, there is the pounding of footsteps—running.

Someone in a black coat with the hood up pushes past me, sending me careening into the wall. They slam into the guy with the hunting knife and they both tumble into the bathroom. My mom shrieks as I struggle to regain my footing. I rush to the bathroom. The stranger has the man with the knife by the back of his coat and they are grappling on the floor as my mom tries to get out of the way.

I reach in to grab her, when suddenly the man with the knife wriggles out of his coat, delivering a swift kick to the stranger's ribs, before turning on my mom. I get another good look at him and something is off . . . he is all wrong.

His arms are different lengths and his right forearm below the elbow is a different color and texture than the skin of his bicep on that same side. A row of thick black stitching encircles his arm just below the elbow joint. The right hand is bigger and is missing its middle digit.

The man raises his arm and brings the knife down into my mom's left shoulder. He grips the handle with both hands, dragging it down with the full weight of his body, separating the skin from the bone.

I scream but my mom doesn't. She just stands there looking

down at the wound, her mouth hanging open. The person in the black jacket hops up and grabs the man with the knife in a bear hug. The knife dislodges from my mom's shoulder and the man wielding it flips it around in his palm and plants it in the upper thigh of the man in the black coat.

The room feels like it's tilting. My vision goes double, then refocuses. The knife-wielding man yanks the weapon from the other guy's thigh and looks at the blade.

"More secrets," the man says. He suddenly turns and with a closed fist punches me directly in the face.

I fall back and my head smacks against the hardwood floor. I lie there as the man steps over me and then sprints out of the room. I hear him on the stairs and a few seconds later, the front door bangs open. Then my mother's voice sounds and the room around me fades in and out.

"Meka!" she shouts. She leans over me, her face a mask of concern.

She should be crying, right? She's gotta be in pain. I look at her shoulder and see that it is almost completely separated at the joint. The tendons, muscle, and bone are visible.

"Mom," I say, but it doesn't come out right. The pain flashing in the back of my head blurs every thought, every word. "Put— put pressure on—on your shoulder."

"Do you need to?" another voice asks.

"No," my mom says.

"Oh, right," says the other voice. "No . . . blood."

No blood.

I'm missing something. Of course there's blood. It's every-where. I'm probably lying in a pool of it. My mom's shoulder is hanging off and this other person got stabbed in the leg so there must be blood. I look at the bathroom floor. No. Not there. Maybe in the bedroom? I twist my neck to try and see if there is blood in my mom's room but no, there isn't any there either. I try to sit up but the person in the black jacket holds me still.

"Don't move, Meeks," they say. "You hit your head."

I—I know this voice. My brain doesn't work right so the word that comes out can't be true but it comes out all the same.

"Noah."

The figure reaches up and pulls the hood away from their head. Noah stares down at me.

Everything goes black.

CHAPTER 13

A REVELATION

The nightmare rushes in all at once. I'm sitting in the back seat of the car. Or maybe I'm lying down. Dad is always driving and Mom is always sitting in the passenger seat. A song I can't make out the words to plays on the radio. My father's cries split the air. I'm suddenly in a prep room, staring up at the edge of a steel table. My father stands very still at the head of it. He's wearing all black, like a shadow has fashioned itself into a robe and draped around him. His bloody hands are busy. He's writing in a book and he's murmuring something to himself. The words are unclear and there is a strange rhythmic quality to them. I've never been in this part of the nightmare before. I have some vague awareness that I *am* dreaming but I can't wake up.

My father writes in the book with a pen and he glances up, looking at the prep table. His expression is sadness and fear all in one. He suddenly rushes toward me; I cry out as he lifts me up and holds me close to him. I scream and thrash as my gaze darts wildly around the room. I have a fleeting glimpse of the prep table . . . and the person on it.

It is my mother. My dad pushes my head down and I gasp, breathing in the smell . . . that smell . . . like smoke.

I try to open my eyes but everything hurts. My skull feels like it's been cracked open.

I'm alone. At least that's how it feels. I start to panic. Where's my mom? And Noah—no. Noah is dead.

"She's okay," my mom says. "But I need your help over here."

Confusion settles over me. I force my eyes open and find myself staring up at the ceiling of the prep room in my basement. Pain rockets up my neck and straight into my temple. I reach up to press my hand to it to try and stem the pain. A balled-up black jacket is tucked under my head and I'm on the floor. I glance toward the door but have to quickly shut my eyes to keep the room from spinning.

"Meka, lie still," my mom says. "Try not to move. It's okay, baby."

"You sure she's good?" a voice asks. "Should we take her to the hospital?"

I sit bolt upright, turning my head, trying to ignore the pain.

My mom is sitting on the prep table; a white sheet is draped around her leaving only her horribly injured left shoulder exposed. She is dragging a suture through the skin to repair the wound and Noah is standing beside her, holding an open jar of mortuary wax.

I scream.

The sound roars out of me like a freight train. I scramble to my feet and leap toward the door only to find that it's been barricaded—the other prep table and my mom's rolling cabinet of supplies have been dragged in front of it. I push the table but the wheel locks are on. I kick around under it to disengage them with no luck.

"Meka," my mom says firmly.

I don't turn around. This is a dream. My nightmare has seeped into the real world somehow.

"Meka!" my mom snaps and I stop, my heart and head pounding. "This is not going to be an easy conversation," she continues. "But we need to have it right now because something is very, very wrong."

I turn slowly around, and it takes everything in me not to start screaming again. My mom's shoulder is nearly detached from its socket but there is no blood. The smell of formaldehyde lingers in the air. It's tempered by a light floral scent. My gaze flits to Noah.

Noah. My Noah.

He stands as still as a statue, staring at me.

"Somebody tell me what is going on right now because I think I'm losing my mind," I say as I fight off a wave of dizziness.

"You're not," my mom says. "I'm here. So is Noah. You're not losing it."

My knees buckle and I start to head for the floor but Noah is there, grabbing hold of me and lifting me up. I want to put my arms around him but I scramble away from him instead.

The hurt on his face cuts through me.

"Meeks," he says, his dark eyes sad and pleading. There is a large defect in his cheek. Bits of unpainted mortuary wax are laid over it.

"Are we dead?" I ask.

That has to be it. That guy in the bathroom killed us and now

Noah is here to usher us into whatever comes next. The little girl at Mrs. Lang's funeral was a psychic or something. She drew me inside a coffin and now look at me. Dead.

"*You're* not dead," my mom says as she places another suture in her shoulder. "As for me and Noah . . . we're somewhere in between."

Noah glances at her and then back to me. "Meeks, you need to sit down."

My name from his lips is the thing I missed most and now I have it back and all I want to do is run away. Noah reaches out and gently nudges me toward the empty prep table near the door. I sit down on it and grip my hands together tightly in front of me. Noah stands close but not too close, almost like he can sense that I'm perilously close to freaking out.

"Tell me what this is," I say. "Tell me right now before I start screaming again."

My mom lowers her head. "I don't even know where to start."

"At the beginning," I say. "Tell me everything."

"The beginning," she repeats. "That's the worst part."

I glance at Noah, still completely unsure of what I'm really looking at. It can't be him. Noah is gone and I have spent the past couple months trying to accept that terrible truth. But as my gaze meets his there is the sense that yes, this is Noah. My Noah. I want to reach out and grab his hand but I can't. Not yet.

My mom readjusts herself on the prep table. "There was an accident when you were little. You were seven and we were driving home from the city. We wanted to leave in the afternoon but we got caught up and didn't start driving until maybe ten at night."

A creeping dread pulls itself over me. I almost don't want to hear whatever she's going to say next. I consider interrupting her, telling her to stop, but I don't.

"A storm had come through and the roads were slick," she continues. "The last hour into Ithaca is all winding roads. You know that. Some of them were washed out."

She opens and closes her mouth several times like she's trying to get the words out but can't. I sit silently, unmoving, afraid to even breathe.

"We came around a blind corner and a truck swerved into our lane—" She stops abruptly. Her eyes have that faraway look of remembering something painful. "Your father—he—he saved me."

"Saved you?" I ask.

My mom swings her legs over the edge of the prep table. The terrible injury on her shoulder isn't completely stitched up yet and as the sheet slips, the scars on her chest are visible again. "You have to understand something, and I don't even know how to explain, but . . . your father—he was born with a very unique ability, something passed down to him through the generations of his family. When someone dies . . ." She trails off before beginning again. "When someone dies, he can reanimate them. He can bring them back."

"I don't—I don't get it." I'm trying to put the pieces together, but nothing makes sense. "When you say Dad saved you, what does that mean?"

Mom clenches her jaw so hard I can hear her teeth click together. She looks completely defeated. "Please don't be angry with him. He didn't—he just—he couldn't figure out how to go forward without me."

I stare at her trembling frame, her wound.

"He brought me back from the dead," she says. "He brought me back, but I am not the same as I was before."

I turn to Noah and he lowers his gaze. "He brought me back, too."

My head feels like it's detached from my body, like I'm floating away.

"I wanted to tell you so many times," my mom says. "Especially when you started having the dream."

The dream. It wasn't a dream at all. It was a memory.

"How could you let me think I was just dreaming?" I ask, suddenly hurt and angry. "I feel like I've been losing my mind and you—you let it happen?"

My mom gets off the table, clutching her arm. "How could I? I'm telling you now and it still seems like you can't believe it. Was I supposed to tell you this when you were little? You couldn't understand it then—"

"I can't understand it now!" I say angrily. I look her over and it feels like my nightmare has come true. Losing her was my biggest fear and now it seems like I *did* lose her that rainy night all those years ago.

"Your father brought me back because he couldn't see his life or yours without me," she says. "I sometimes wonder if maybe it was a mistake."

Now the tears come in a flood. "It's a mistake to have you here with me?"

"Look at me," my mom says. "Look at what I have to do to keep myself from rotting away right in front of you."

Everything clicks into place—her elaborate skin care routine, her perfect makeup, her perfect hair, even her wardrobe. I knew it was never about the vanity of it, but I never expected this.

"But you have the perfect setup for maintaining yourself," Noah says.

His voice startles me. It's not that I forgot he was there, but it feels so much like the room is empty.

"Your job is making dead people look alive," he continues. "And Mr. Redwood is an undertaker. You two are, like, the perfect couple to keep this whole thing up."

My mom smiles and I have to remind myself that I'm talking to two people who should be dead. Still . . . her smile makes me feel more at ease.

"You're right," Mom says. "And Jonathan has helped me maintain myself all these years. I couldn't have done it without him."

"I'm sorry," I say, suddenly feeling frantic again. "What are we talking about here? What is this? I don't understand. Reanimation?" I'm dizzy again and I grip the edge of the prep table.

"If I'm being one hundred percent honest," my mom says, "I don't fully understand it either." She sighs and shakes her head. "Call your father. He can explain it better."

"I did," I say. "I tried to call him right before I came up and found you in the bathroom. I texted him too."

My mom goes to the tray stationed next to the prep table and retrieves her phone. She makes a call, fumbling with it, as her arm still isn't working properly, then just stares at the phone. "Pick up," she whispers. "Pick up, please." When my dad's outgoing voicemail message echoes out of the phone, she hangs up. "Something isn't right."

"You think it has something to do with the guy who attacked you?" Noah asks.

My mom nods. "It has to."

"I recognized him," I say.

My mom's eyes widen. "What do you mean?"

"Him and another guy were sitting behind me and Noah at the movies right before—" I stop myself and turn to Noah. "That was the day before you died."

"Meeks," Noah says, his voice a whisper. "I'm so sorry."

My mom looks like she's going to crumple in on herself, like something heavy just sat squarely on her shoulders. "They've been watching us. They always are but now more than ever."

"Who is *they*?" I ask.

My mom walks up to me and lifts her right arm as her left dangles at her side. I cannot help but look into the gaping wound. The bone of her clavicle and the rounded head of the humerus are visible. The muscle is showing but it's no longer pink beneath the skin, more of a gray color. The wound is dry. No hint of blood or fluid of any kind. I swallow hard.

"I don't know who *they* are," my mom says quietly, like she's telling me a terrible secret. "But ever since those people came to the door right before Noah died, your dad has been on edge. It's like he's been dreading something that he can't even bring himself to talk about . . . even to me."

"What do they want?" Noah asks.

"They want Jonathan," my mom says. "We have to get ahold of him right now." She steps toward the door and I get up and move in front of her.

"You can't go anywhere like that," I say, pointing to her

shoulder. "Not if you're trying to convince people you're not . . . well, you know what I mean. Let me at least try to fix it."

She hesitates for a moment and then positions herself back on the prep table. I turn to Noah.

"I might need your help," I say.

He nods and I hold out my hand to him.

Death is my life.

I remind myself that I've never had a problem being around dead bodies before. Why should this be any different? Even as I pose the question to myself I realize how unhinged it sounds. I think of the drawing the little girl made in the playroom as her grandmother lay in a coffin in the front room of the house.

She can be dead and I can be alive. It's okay.

Noah slips his hand into mine. His skin is cold as ice but I'm starting to feel like I don't care.

CHAPTER 14

TERRIBLE TRUTHS

I examine the edges of my mom's wound as I pull on a pair of sterile gloves and hang an apron around my waist. Noah stands near me.

"Should we just staple the edges closed?" I ask. "The cut was clean. No jagged edges."

"No," she says. "Wounds don't heal and I don't want to walk around with a bunch of staples. We have to stitch the layers closed one by one with the nylon thread. You have to recreate the internal structures, if that makes sense?"

"The wounds never heal?" I ask in disbelief. "Ever?"

She shakes her head. "No. Every papercut, every nick or scrape I've had in the last ten years is covered under mortuary wax and paint and Smithfield's." She touches the branch of the scar on her chest. "Even these. They're not really scars." She picks at the marks and painted mortuary wax peels off in little flecks.

There is nothing but sadness in her tone. I touch her undamaged shoulder and gently press my forehead against hers.

"I love you," I say.

"I love you more," she says. "And I'm sorry you have to be here to see this."

"Better me than, well, who else could do it?" I ask.

Mom shakes her head and the wound on her shoulder opens itself up like a gaping mouth. "I guess you're right. Still, it shouldn't be you."

I cut away the ragged stitches she'd made as she had tried to repair herself. The holes where the needle had looped through her skin don't close.

"Noah, can you hand me a curved needle and the thread from the top drawer of that cabinet?" I ask.

Noah finds the supplies and hands them to me. I begin to stitch the innermost layers of her tissue closed and realize there's a problem.

"The shoulder bone is dislocated," I say. "The skin won't come together cleanly."

"We can pop it back in," my mom says. "Put your hand here." She presses my palm to the curve of her neck just above where the injury begins. "Hold it steady."

She reaches down and grabs her left arm with her right hand. She yanks it up in one smooth motion and the joint pops into place with a loud *crack*.

"Does that hurt?" I ask, feeling a little queasy.

"Not at all," my mom says. "Nothing does."

"Nothing?" I ask.

She shakes her head. "Meka, baby. I—I'm so sorry. I know how all of this must sound."

I feel like I'm teetering on the edge of a chasm. If I stumble, I'll fall into it, into confusion so thick I don't think I'll be able to pull myself out. I can't let that happen.

"I was always so worried I was gonna lose you," I say. "Sometimes, even though you were right in front of me, I felt like I already had." It was that strange feeling of not being able to sense when she was in the room with me. Like when she'd been sitting in the dark in the living room or the way she'd just kind of appear out of nowhere sometimes. And when she sat with me on my bed and I looked at her and felt like that spark that makes us human wasn't the same in her. Now I know why and it doesn't make me feel better. It scares me.

My mom puts her hand on top of mine, and I notice the missing chunk of her finger is filled in with mortuary wax.

She sighs. "You knew, somewhere deep down inside, that it was true."

"But you're not gone," I say. "You're right here with me."

She turns her head and smiles but the look in her eyes says *yes, but at what cost?*

I stitch her shoulder together, layer by layer, then fill in some of the visible divots with mortuary wax. She directs me to use the Smithfield's to prep her skin and another layer on top to set the wax.

"Wait," I say. "Is this why our supplies were off?"

My mom grimaces. "Yes. I miscalculated how much I'd need and then we got some new guests. It all just snowballed."

I'm starting to think of how much she has had to keep to herself. How many secrets she was juggling just to keep up appearances. I'm exhausted just thinking about it.

When we're done, the wounds look like maybe she'd been out

in the sun a little too long, the strap of a bra or swimsuit leaving a slightly less brown strip of skin down the front of her shoulder. She hops off the table and goes to her phone, dialing my dad again. He still doesn't pick up.

"Let's get Noah patched up and then we'll figure out where Dad is," Mom says. "He went with those people. We need to try and track them down."

"Don't you think that's dangerous?" I ask, as Noah lies down on the prep table and my mom rummages around in the repurposed tool cabinet. "These people came here to kill us."

"Not us," my mom says. "Me."

"They know what you are?" I ask. "Wait. If they know what you are, they know you can't be killed, right?"

"Maybe not killed," Mom says. "At least not in the way you're thinking. We can be destroyed but it would take . . . a lot."

"What's that mean?" Noah asks.

"It would involve complete dismemberment," Mom says. "Our body parts scattered to the ends of the earth, maybe burned to ashes."

I gasp and my stomach turns over.

"Sorry," she says. "I don't mean to be so blunt but that's what it would take and I think that's what they were aiming to do. And they saw Noah. Whoever they are, they know about him now too."

"And that guy who was here, the blond one," I say. "He's like you two."

My mom looks confused.

"You didn't see his arm?" I ask. "It looked like it didn't even belong to him. And when we were in the movie theater, I thought I smelled something rotting. I thought it was just the smell from the prep room stuck to my clothes but now I'm pretty sure it was him."

"I was too busy looking at the knife," Mom says. "But if that's true . . ." she trails off, then huffs. "We need to find your dad."

I stare down at Noah as he looks back up at me. The dent in his cheek is noticeable and needs to be repatched. My mom moves to his side and assesses his leg injury.

"This can be easily fixed," she says as she pulls back the torn pieces of his pant leg. The assailant's knife had made a mess of his leg but again, there was no blood, just the ragged edges of a nasty wound. "But you'll need to maintain it," Mom continues. "I'll show you how. It's tedious and because you don't have the benefit of living in a funeral home, it'll be a little trickier for you. You have to dress the area with formaldehyde, cover up the scent, resew it if need be. Mortuary wax goes on top, then makeup to match your skin tone. Smithfield's at every step of the process."

"How long do I have to do all that?" Noah asks.

My mom stares at him and something breaks in her expression. She frowns. Her eyes are sad and shadowy. "Forever."

Noah shifts and returns his gaze to me.

"I can help you," I say. "You could come live with us if it would be easier." I glance at my mom but her expression doesn't change.

Noah reaches up and puts his hand on mine. A swell of grief washes over me. I had missed him so much and even though he's here with me now, I still feel like I've lost something I can't get back. I gently touch his face, letting my fingers move over the defect on his cheek. My hand buzzes, not painfully, but enough to make me hesitate for a moment. Images of him lying in his coffin push their way to the front of my mind. I pull my hand back and inhale shakily.

"It's just me," Noah says.

"I know," I say. "It's just—"

"This is all weird as hell," Noah says. "I'm literally back from the dead. It's not right and I don't expect you to just be okay. I know I'm not."

"You're not?" I ask.

Noah shakes his head. "How could I be?" He looks down the length of his body as my mom makes quick work of repairing the wound in his leg.

Watching her put Noah back together makes me wonder how many times she's used these techniques on herself.

"Just lie still," I say to Noah. "I'll fix this." I gently touch his face again, and he closes his eyes.

I start by scraping off the wax that is discolored and dried out. Removing it reveals a defect the size of my fist that goes right down to the bone. He must have fallen hard into something the night he died, and I wonder if it was the injury that killed him or if it had knocked him out and he'd frozen to death outside his house. A shudder runs through me and I try to put my thoughts elsewhere. The tissue beneath the mortuary wax is gray and stiff but nowhere near as decayed as the muscle and tendons under my mom's skin.

"Use a brush to paint the wound with formaldehyde," my mom says. "Then spray a layer of Smithfield's before you lay the wax down."

I do as she says and the smell of the preservative makes me want to gag. I brush the interior of the wound, then spray it with Smithfield's. The rosy scent of the spray wafts into my face. I then fill the defect with fresh mortuary wax and mold it to fit the confines of Noah's face.

"Smile for me," I say.

Noah's eyes open slowly. "Anything you say."

A familiar flutter invades the pit of my stomach. He smiles and I have to tear my gaze away from his beautiful eyes to assess the wax and make sure it looks natural.

"Looks good," I say.

Noah lets his face relax but the faint remnants of the smile linger. I match a foundation to the suntanned hues of his skin and cover the wax, using a small brush. I finish it off with another layer of Smithfield's and Noah sits up. My mom hands him a small mirror and he gazes at his reflection. I don't know if I expect him to smile or what, but I'm worried when his shoulders slump and he pushes the mirror back toward my mom.

He reaches out and takes my hand in his. "Thanks."

"Of course," I say. "Anything you need me to do, I got you."

Noah lifts his head, and his gaze meets mine. For just a fraction of a second, things between us are the way they were before.

"I'm worried about your father," Mom says. "I need to get ahold of him right now."

"What about my mom?" Noah asks.

"What about her?" Mom asks.

Noah's brows push together in concern. "If these people are coming after us, after people who know what we are, that includes my mom."

Panic floods my mom's expression. Her frame goes rigid. "Call her."

Noah pulls out his phone and calls his mom. A moment later he hangs up. "She's not answering."

My mom opens and closes her hands as she stares down at the floor. "Okay," she says softly. "Okay. I just need to think."

"We have to get to Dad and we have to check on Miss Cliff,"

I say. "We're going to go upstairs. We'll go check on Noah's mom. Then we find Dad. Sound like a plan?"

My mom nods and I think she's happy someone else is making decisions right now. All of this has shaken her and she's not alone. I feel like I'm going to lose my mind at any moment as I watch my deceased mom and my recently deceased boyfriend walking and talking together.

"Should we call the police?" Noah asks.

"And tell them what?" my mom asks. "Baby, I think they would lock *us* up just for wasting their time. They won't believe us."

"So we're on our own?" I ask. "Nobody can help us?"

"We have to figure this out," my mom says. "Just us."

We move the second prep table and supply chest away from the door. Noah palms a heavy glass vase that normally holds fresh flowers and my mom balls up her fists. I don't think any of us can withstand another attack and I damn sure am not tryna fight a knife-wielding man with a vase and my bare fists.

"If that dude with the knife is still out there, we are not prepared to fight him," I say. "Did you see the size of his knife?"

Noah huffs and grasps the vase tighter. "I'll knock him out."

"I'm sure he's gone but we're being cautious," my mom says.

"If he can't really hurt us, why are we so worried?" Noah asks.

Mom hesitates and then glances back at me. "He can't hurt us, but he can injure our physical bodies. You saw what the knife did. Injuries mean more maintenance and more maintenance means it's harder to look alive. We don't want that."

Noah nods and I grip his arm as Mom slowly opens the door and peers into the hallway. I try to crane my neck to look out, too, but accidentally bump into her, forcing her to step out into the hall.

"We're gonna die," Noah says.

Mom shakes her head. "We can't."

"I can," I say.

Noah's face is suddenly serious again. "Over my dead body."

"Literally," I say.

My mom squeezes my arm and gives me a stiff smile as she signals for us to follow her. We trail her cautiously down the hall. I feel like my senses are on ten. All the little noises that are usually comforting to me are making my skin crawl now—the knocking of the old pipes, the flush of air in the vents. The hall lights cast eerie shadows, creating an ominous atmosphere that only compounds my fear. Noah, though trying hard to maintain a brave facade, can't entirely conceal the worry etched across his face.

We make our way upstairs, my mom in the lead, me and Noah following close behind, his hand resting gently on my back. A sweep of the first floor turns up nothing and once we've checked the upper floor, me and Noah lock everything up while my mom changes her clothes. A few moments later she comes back downstairs, dressed in a black sweatsuit and a pair of sneakers. I almost never see her dressed so casually and I have to stop myself from giving her a hard time about it. We have way bigger things to worry about right now including the fact that she and Noah are basically reanimated corpses. I grab a coat and shrug into it.

Noah runs downstairs and grabs the coat he left in the prep room. When he returns to the first floor, my heart leaps into my throat. He's wearing the black coat with a fur-lined hood.

"That was you at the waterfall," I say. "You were following me?"

My mom shoots Noah a dagger of a glance and his eyes grow wide.

"I'm sorry!" he says. "Don't be mad!"

"You were supposed to lie low," my mom says. "That's how it works when you're trying to convince people you're dead."

"I know," Noah says. "I know, but I—I couldn't stand being away from Meka. I just wanted to see her."

"You were stalking me?" I ask.

"Yes," Noah says with zero hesitation. "And I don't regret it because if I hadn't been watching you, that guy in the old lady store on the Commons would have got both of you."

"That was you too?" I ask.

"What do you mean 'old lady store'?" my mom asks, her brows arching clear up to her hairline.

"Sorry," Noah says to my mom again, before turning to me. "Sorry."

"Old lady?" my mom asks again.

"Mom," I say. "I don't think it's the right time for that question."

She presses her mouth into a tight line. "Fine."

Mom grabs her keys and we head out the back door and pile into her car. The evening air is biting and I rub my hands together furiously as my mom starts the car. The AC is blasting.

"I'm gonna get frostbite in here," I say.

"Sorry," Mom says as she dials down the cold air. "It's better this way. Fresh mortuary wax tends to run in the heat."

She holds up her hand and wiggles her newly repaired finger.

CHAPTER 15

EVERYTHING IS FINE

Noah's mom moved to a place in South Hill right after Noah died; well, after I thought he died. When we pull up to her place, a small bungalow-style house surrounded by trees and a high fence, a light is on inside.

"Just wait here a minute," Noah says as he opens the door and gets out.

He goes to the front door and rings the bell.

"I have a terrible feeling Miss Cliff knew Noah wasn't following the rules," my mom says.

"I'm still confused on how it even happened," I say. "Miss Cliff asked Dad to do this? How did she even know he *could* do something like that?"

"Your dad saw how she was grieving," Mom says as she rests her head back on the seat. "He saw how *you* were grieving. He couldn't let it go. Maybe he should have. I don't know. I can't imagine losing you the way Noah's mom lost him. A freak accident that should have meant a twisted ankle, not a death." She takes a deep breath. "So he offered her a chance to bring him back but he also told her there would be rules."

"What rules?" I ask.

"Your dad has only ever reanimated me and Noah," Mom says. "But Grandpa Redwood, that man used his gift much more frequently."

"You serious?" I ask. Maybe that's why him and Dad fell out. I can't imagine my dad doing this strange work if he didn't feel like it was absolutely necessary.

"Grandpa Redwood set out some guidelines for the newly reanimated," Mom says. "When someone is reanimated, they have a choice to make—fake your death immediately and live in anonymity, maybe reinvent yourself at some future date or . . ." she trails off, a faraway look in her eyes.

"Or what?" I ask.

"Or you make it seem like you never died at all," Mom says. "You keep on living, or at least pretending to live. You can't go on that way forever, though. At some point you have to die. And because our bodies don't change from the point of death, it's really about keeping up this endless ruse." She stares into the dark outside the car. "It's exhausting and over time it gets harder and harder to do."

"That's what you were gonna do?" I ask. "You're supposed to look ten years older than you do. What happens when you're a hundred and you look thirty?"

"It's a strange problem to have," Mom says. "Dangerous too."

I'm about to press her for more information when the door to Miss Cliff's house opens and Miss Cliff steps onto the porch. Noah hugs her and then waves to us, signaling for us to get out of the car. I follow my mom up the front steps. She and Miss Cliff exchange glances.

"You mad at me, Kassie?" Miss Cliff asks.

"Let's go inside," my mom says.

"Meka, sweetie, it's so good to see you!" Miss Cliff says as she sweeps me into a hug.

I hug her back but the tension between her and my mom is thick. We all go inside and me and Noah sit on the couch in the front room while my mom remains standing.

"Hungry?" Miss Cliff asks. "I can put something on the stove."

My mom glances at me.

"Mom," Noah says. "You know it doesn't work like that."

Miss Cliff huffs. "Just give it time. Your body is still recovering."

"Maxine," my mom says firmly. "We've been over this. There is no recovering. There is no healing. Eating your home-cooked meals isn't going to happen."

I stare at my mom. She has a list of food allergies a mile long and again, I try to think of how many times I've paid close enough attention to what she actually eats. Could it really have been nothing all this time?

"He can eat a little something," Miss Cliff says. "I've seen him."

"I didn't want to upset you," Noah says quickly. "You didn't see what I had to do afterward, though." Noah turns to me. "The food just rots in my stomach. I have to get it out . . . manually."

"What does that even mean?" I ask.

"You don't wanna know," Noah says. "But maybe I had to get creative with a vacuum cleaner."

"Please god, tell me you mean by sticking an attachment down your throat," I say.

"Where else would I have—" Noah stops short. "Oh. Yeah, no. Not like that."

I breathe deep. My mom is covering her mouth. This is serious and I just said something entirely unserious.

"Sorry," I say.

"You can't just pretend that things aren't different now," my mom says, refocusing on Miss Cliff. "You can't just act like everything is normal. You put Noah in danger if you do."

Miss Cliff huffs, rolling her eyes. "You don't get to say that to me, Kassie. You're a damn hypocrite!"

I get up off the couch. "Miss Cliff, I love you. You know that, but please, don't talk to my mom that way."

Miss Cliff is trembling as her gaze moves from me to Noah and then back to my mom. She suddenly begins to cry and my mom shakes her head.

"Maxine, we don't have time for this," Mom says bluntly. "You're upset but you have to get it together for yourself and for Noah."

"I'm trying!" Miss Cliff says. She collapses into a chair at the dining room table and my mom sits beside her.

"There's been a funeral," my mom says, measuring her words carefully. "Everyone thinks Noah is dead. That's the path you chose, and you have to accept it."

"But he's not dead," Miss Cliff sobs. "He's right here. He's fine. He just needs to go back to the way things were before."

Noah stares into his lap.

"Maxine," Mom says, her voice taking on the tone of a mother talking to a child. "Noah is dead. Nothing is the same and it never will be again."

Noah takes me by the hand and pulls me toward the back hall. "We're gonna let you two talk for a minute," Noah says to my mom and Miss Cliff.

He leads me to a small room off the main hall. When we're inside he shuts the door and flips on the light. I'm struck silent as the room lights up. There's a desk with a laptop sitting closed on top. A bed that's made up, a laundry basket, a closet full of his clothes, even a few posters of his favorite bands. It's completely normal and for some reason, I feel like it shouldn't be.

"She put all this together," Noah says as he looks around. "You heard her. She keeps telling me that things are going to be okay, that everything will go back to normal if I just give it time."

"I don't think that's true," I say. "How can things ever be normal?"

Noah sits on the edge of his bed and takes off his coat. "I'm worried about her. She thinks I'm gonna go back to school. She keeps trying to feed me." He laughs in a nervous, uncomfortable way. He touches the hole in the leg of his pants. "She doesn't get how, for the rest of my life, I'm going to have to live like I'm some kind of shadow."

I sit next to him and slip my hand into his. He glances at me, his big, dark eyes wide and almost frightened.

"Do you regret it?" I ask. "Being here, even with the way things are now. Do you regret coming back?"

"I didn't come back," Noah says. "I was brought back. I didn't really have a say so I don't think I can regret it."

I stay quiet. He has every right to feel however he feels, but *I'm* glad he came back—was brought back.

"I'm going to have to watch her die," Noah says.

185

"What?" I ask.

"My mom," he says. "I'll have to watch her die and not just her either. Everyone. Anyone I love or care about will go before me because I can't die."

I haven't even begun to think that far ahead but now the thoughts come in a rush. "I—I don't know," I stammer. "There's so much I still don't understand. We gotta get to my dad. He'll be able to help us."

Noah nods and grasps my hand tightly. "I don't want this for myself. I don't want this for you. I don't wanna be a burden."

"Don't say that." I push my face into the curve of his neck and pretend I can't feel how cold he is. "You're not a burden. You're just Noah. My Noah."

He slips his hand under my chin and brings my mouth to his. He kisses me like he'd forgotten how good it feels and I swear it feels like a spark of electricity in the places where my skin touches his. His hands move up my back and under my shirt and I wrap my arms around his neck, pulling him closer. His breath in my face is cold and crisp but as I rest my hand on his chest there is no heartbeat. He cups his hand over mine.

"If it could beat, it would only be for you," he says.

My heart ticks up enough for the both of us. Maybe he didn't want this. Maybe he didn't choose it. But he's here now and isn't that the only thing that matters?

There is suddenly a tangle of raised voices from the living room. Noah pulls away from me even though I'd give anything to stay right here in this moment forever.

"It's our moms," he says. "They're still arguing."

It sounds more intense now so I reluctantly get up, adjust my shirt, and follow Noah out into the living room.

"What is happening?" Noah asks. "You're still fighting?"

Miss Cliff thrusts a finger in my direction. "Your mother, Meka, gets to pretend that everything's normal but I don't?" she asks, her voice breaking. "I have my son back and he's going to go back to school, and we're going to have meals together, and we're going to pretend that none of this ever happened!" I glance at Noah and his expression is a mask of sadness.

"Mom," he says. "Just try to calm down."

"I'm calm," Miss Cliff says, smiling like she hadn't just flipped all the way out. "I'm calm. Really."

"I know this is hard," my mom says. "I understand, but Noah needs you to be strong and you've got to follow the rules."

"I—I'm sorry, Kassie," Miss Cliff says, sounding defeated. She shrugs and wrings her hands together in front of her. "I'm sorry. I don't know what to do."

Noah puts his arms around his mom. "I just need to make sure you're safe. Somebody broke into Meka's place and attacked us."

Miss Cliff pulls away from him and looks him over. "Are you okay? Did they hurt you?"

"He tried," Noah says. "Has anybody been by here? Anything weird going on?"

Miss Cliff shakes her head. "No."

"Good," my mom says. "Do you have someplace you can go just for a day or two while we figure this out?"

Miss Cliff looks concerned. "I—I guess I could go to a friend's house, but why?"

"Somebody else knows about us," my mom says. "About

Noah and me and I'm afraid they might come after us again. I'm worried and I can't get ahold of Jonathan. We're on our way to find him now but I think you should go to your friend's house for the time being."

Miss Cliff nods and looks up at Noah. "I'll go to Katrina's but when I come back I need you to be here so we can get you set up for school in the fall. You can go back virtually if you want."

My mom is about to say something but quickly turns away.

"Mom," Noah says softly. "You know that's not going to happen, right? I really need you to understand that things are different now. I know you were hurting. I know it must have been hard, but did you stop to ask yourself if this is what *I* would have wanted?"

Miss Cliff stares at her son. "You're angry with me for letting you come back? This is a gift, Noah! A second chance. It's like a miracle."

Or a curse, I think.

"I'm not mad," Noah says. "Please don't think that. It's not about that. It's just . . ." He trails off and he raises his hand to his face, touching the spot I'd filled in with mortuary wax. "Right now, I just need to know you're safe. Can you get a bag together?"

Miss Cliff nods and goes off to get her things. She gets a Lyft and Noah and I walk her out to the waiting car.

"See you soon," Miss Cliff says as she gets in.

"Love you," Noah says.

"I love you," Miss Cliff says.

The car backs down the driveway and disappears around the corner. Noah and I stand alone under the starry night sky.

"I think something is broken inside her," Noah says. "This isn't supposed to happen, you know? I'm not supposed to be here but I am and I think it messed something up in her mind."

"I get it," I say. Seeing Noah again almost broke my brain too.

Noah turns to me and takes my hands in his.

"I'm sorry for everything," Noah says. "I should have said it before . . . well, just before, you know?"

"What are you talking about?" I ask.

"I love you, Meka," Noah says. "I think you know that, but I need to say it because I waited too long before . . . before—"

"I don't care about what happened before," I say as I try to wrap my head around hearing him say those words to me.

Noah presses his forehead against mine. "You should care. What happened before matters. It was just that I didn't know what to do. I didn't want to say it first in case you weren't ready. I didn't want to pressure you—"

I press my lips to his and stop him from saying anything else. Right now, all I want is him and I lose myself in the closeness of him. This is what I had spent so many days and nights mourning and missing. Noah presses his hands to my back and I wish the rest of the world would just fade away.

"Hate to interrupt," my mom calls out.

Noah breaks away from me but I keep a tight grip on him. I don't care if my mom sees. I don't care if the whole world sees.

"We should get going," she says. "I still can't get ahold of your dad." Her bottom lip begins to tremble and I shake myself out of the haze I'd been in and put my hand on my mom's arm.

"It's gonna be okay," I say. "We're gonna find Dad and figure this out."

"I don't know what there is to figure out anymore," Mom says. "We can't keep going on like this. I can't—" She stops herself, touching her pursed lips with the tips of her trembling fingers. "Never mind. You're right. Let's just go find your dad."

She walks to the car and Noah and I get in with her. Suddenly, her phone buzzes and she almost fumbles it before scrambling to hit the green button. My dad's image flashes on the screen. Mom lets out a high-pitched squeal as she presses the phone to her ear.

"Jonathan! Jonathan! I've been trying to call you! Where are you? We were so worried! We—"

The joy goes out of her voice and her expression stretches into a grimace.

"What is it?" I whisper.

"Yes. I—I'm here," my mom says. She sets the phone on the middle console and hits the speaker button.

"Listen to me very carefully," says a voice that doesn't belong to my dad. "Jonathan is here with us."

My mom grips the edge of the seat. "Are you—are you going to hurt him?"

"Hurt him? We will *kill* him, do you understand me?" the voice says with a tone of malice so sharp I back away from the phone like the person speaking is going to jump out of it.

"We have Jonathan but he is only part of the equation," the person says.

"What do you want?" my mom asks, her voice trembling.

"You already know the answer to that question," the man says.

"No, I don't!" Mom shouts. "I don't know what you want!"

"The book, Mrs. Redwood. All we want is the book."

My mom lifts her gaze to meet mine and in the dark confines of the car the terror etched on her face scares me.

"I—I don't have it," she says.

There's a rustling on the other end of the line and my dad's voice suddenly sounds in the phone but he's not talking to us.

"She doesn't know where it is!" he shouts. "And you'll never have it if you kill me!"

More scuffling and then my dad is yelling. Screaming. I grab the phone and grip it in my fist. "Dad!"

"You can't have it!" my dad screams as his voice moves away from the phone. "I swear on my father's grave you won't ever have it! On my father's grave!"

The other man returns to the phone. "I think you know what you have to do. Do not keep us waiting. Answer the phone next time we call."

The call ends and I stare at the phone in my hand.

My mom grips the steering wheel and presses her forehead into it.

"Who was that guy on the phone?" Noah asks.

My mom sits back and sighs so heavily I think she might deflate completely, like a balloon with a small leak that just can't keep itself afloat any longer. "He was probably one of those people your dad left with. The same people who showed up at the house right before your accident."

I search my memory and find the images of my dad getting up from our dinner table to answer the door. He'd seemed tense but I'd chalked it up to some annoyance at an uninvited guest.

"There was someone outside my school too," I say. "I saw them across the street when I was in film studies. And now that I'm thinking about it, I also saw somebody at the cemetery one time too."

My mom looks horrified. "The blond guy?"

I shake my head. "Somebody else. Whoever it was, they were

way taller than the blond. I couldn't really see their face. But it's gotta be the same people, right?"

Mom angles her head to look at me. "It has to be. They know about us and if what you saw on the blond guy's arm is any indication, they're reanimates too." She shakes her head.

"But they didn't know about you until recently," I say. "Or they would have come for you sooner."

My mom nods. "I think you're right. We covered our tracks after the accident. Nobody would have known anything was amiss."

"So you and Dad thought somebody might be watching you?"

Mom thinks for a moment. "I thought we needed to cover our tracks so the general public wouldn't ask questions. Family and friends, you know? But I guess your dad was always more on edge than I thought was necessary. These people must be the reason."

"And we don't know what they want?" I ask. "Besides this book?"

"And what kind of book is it?" Noah asks. "They're willing to kill somebody over it. It's gotta be something important."

"From what I understand, the book is a sort of tool," Mom says, shaking her head. "It has been with the Redwood family forever. Jonathan's dad passed it down to him."

Images from my nightmare-memory flood my mind. "This book, does it have a leather cover? With strange markings on it?"

My mom sits bolt upright in the driver seat. "I—I've never actually seen it so I don't know but how do you even have any thought about what it looks like?"

"The nightmare," I say.

"You were so little," my mom says in a hushed tone. "I—I

didn't think you'd remember anything except bits and pieces of the crash." She suddenly seems more upset by this than anything else. "You were there when he . . . of course you were . . ." she trails off.

It occurs to me in this moment that the memory of watching my father recite from the book at the head of a prep table had to have been immediately after the crash while my mom was actually dead—*before* the so-called reanimation.

"You were in the room," she says. "Meka, I—"

"I don't want to talk about it," I say. "Not right now." I push away the swell of anger. I'll deal with it later. Noah reaches forward and puts his hand on my shoulder. The weight of it is comforting. "These people, they want the book. So we have to make sure they don't get it. Where is it?"

"I don't know," Mom says.

"You think he hid it?" Noah asks.

"He must have," my mom says.

"Wait," I say as my memory doubles back on itself. "The night me and Dad picked up that old man something else happened." I look down at my hand. I remember the feeling, the way pain had traced across my fingers like a hot knife, the strange tingling sensation in my skin that had lingered for hours. "I think Dad had the book right before Noah died."

"What?" Mom asks. "How would you know that?"

"I think it was in the hearse," I say. "I think I accidentally touched it."

"The night that body sat up?" Noah asks.

My mom looks at my hands, stares at them, then lets her gaze move to my face. "A body—sat up?"

I realize I hadn't had a chance to explain the incident to

her. I assumed my dad would have told her. Noah died right after so I hadn't even thought of it since.

"Yeah," I say. "Scared me to death. Then later that same night I saw Dad go back to the hearse and take something out of it. It had to have been the book. And he had to have used it for Noah but then what? That means it's probably close by, right?"

"Maybe," Mom says quietly.

"Does your dad always swear like that?" Noah asks suddenly.

"Swear?" I ask. "I didn't hear him swear."

"Not like curse words," Noah says. "He swore on his father's grave that he wouldn't let these people have whatever book you all are talking about. I've been around Mr. Redwood a lot. I've never heard him say anything like that."

"He never really talks about his dad at all," I say. "But Grandpa Redwood's been coming up a lot more lately."

"Did you know him?" Noah asks. "Your dad's dad?"

I shake my head and then a thought occurs to me, something I don't even want to say out loud, so I ease myself into it. "Where is Grandpa Redwood buried?"

Mom raises her gaze to meet mine. "He's here in Ithaca."

I touch the back of her hand. "Is he close? Like, somewhere Dad could get to quickly and come back without us noticing?"

Mom inhales sharply.

"What?" Noah asks. "What is it?"

"I think I know where my dad put the book," I say.

My mom turns the car on and slams on the accelerator sending me and Noah back into our seats.

"Sorry!" she says as she wheels the car around and swings out onto the road leading away from Miss Cliff's house. "I think you're right. Let's just hope Grandpa Redwood is still in his coffin."

CHAPTER 16

GRANDPA REDWOOD, 1947-2000

Our car idles in a parking spot just outside the entrance to Ithaca City Cemetery. Me, Noah, and my mom sit in complete silence for probably a solid minute. I don't even look out the window, but Noah does. He stares up the walkway at the place where he's supposed to be buried.

"I'm supposed to be in a coffin in that tomb," he says softly.

"You were never actually in there, right?" I ask.

Noah shakes his head. "I don't think so."

My mom clears her throat. "He wasn't."

"But I—I saw him in his coffin," I say.

"We had to make it seem like we had prepped him," Mom says. "It was all about maintaining the lie." The way she says "lie" is like a curse. It feels heavier than it should.

Noah leans forward from his seat in the back and puts his face very close to mine. "I—I'm so sorry, Meeks."

"I'm not," I say. "I thought it was the last time I was ever gonna see you. I almost didn't go down to the prep room because I was afraid, but I didn't want you to be alone down there. I didn't want to be afraid of you."

Noah's lips part just slightly and he gently touches my shoulder. I put my hand over his. With every passing moment, I care less and less about the strangeness of this situation and try to keep myself focused on the next task.

"Grandpa Redwood is in the mausoleum at the top of the hill," my mom says. "He's in a vault."

"And he's been in there since when?" I ask. He died before I was born. It's strange to think his body's been in a tomb right around the corner from my house this whole time.

"He's been there since he died in 2000," my mom says.

"And we're sure he's dead," Noah says. "Not—not like us?"

My mom hesitates. "Jonathan has never even suggested that Grandpa Redwood was reanimated but I guess stranger things have happened."

"Have they?" I ask. "How much stranger? Because I can't imagine it gets weirder than all of this."

"You saw the blond guy's arm?" my mom says. "You said it was different from the rest of him."

I nod. "It's like it didn't match."

"I'd bet any amount of money the arm didn't belong to him at all," Mom says. "I maintain my body, with all its original parts, but I've thought about what would happen if something catastrophic happened. How could a lost limb be fixed if it was damaged beyond repair, that type of thing. I'm not going to die from it, so how would I fix it? When I talked to your dad about

196

it, he said a transplant might work but the question then became where would the spare part come from?"

"Mrs. Redwood," Noah says, his tone serious. "Are you saying these people are snatching people's body parts off?"

I stare at my mom, waiting for her to deny it, but to my horror, she doesn't.

"I don't know for sure," she says. "But you asked what could be stranger? What could be more awful? I think something like that might do it."

The knife-wielding Mr. Lions had said something about being cut into pieces and I wonder if maybe he had a point. I suddenly feel sick to my stomach.

My mom opens her door. "Come on. Keep your eyes up when we're out here, okay?"

We follow her out into the frigid night air. There is an eerie silence in the dark of the cemetery broken only by the crunching of our shoes across the snow and the calling of ravens circling overhead. In their cacophony, I'm almost certain I can hear something that sounds like a human voice.

We pass under the iron latticework of the cemetery's archway and as we pass the Cliff family tomb, Noah hangs back. I slip my hand into his.

"It's just weird, you know?" Noah says. "I should be in there, right? Like, that's the way this was supposed to work."

It puts an ache in my chest to think about it. "We're way past doing things by the book. You *should* be in that tomb and I *should* be mourning you forever. Is that really how it was supposed to be?" I'd lived in that terrible reality for months. "I don't care what was *supposed* to happen. You're here now."

Noah squeezes my hand and nods.

We continue up the path that leads to the top of the hill. The snow lies like a blanket across the dozens of graves that butt up to the walkway. Some of the grave markers are crumbling, with no discernible names or dates on them. Others look new, with the name of the deceased laser-etched on the stone. Towering birch trees, their branches bare, their pale trunks like shards of bone sticking out of the ground, sway gently in a stiff and frigid breeze. Breath pumps out of me in billowing clouds but nothing is coming from Noah as he huffs along beside me. I glance at my mom. She's trekking through the snow, too, her chest rising and falling, but there's no halo of warm breath in the cold air surrounding her. They also don't seem to be as cold as I am. I'm pulling my hood in around my face like my life depends on it. My fingers are numb. Mom and Noah don't even have their coats zipped.

"Do y'all just not feel the cold?" I ask.

Mom slows her pace but doesn't turn around. "Not really," she says. "My arms and legs feel a little stiffer than they normally do."

Noah inhales sharply. I catch a glimpse of his expression as he turns his face away from me. He opens and closes his hands and tilts his head up toward the dark sky. I can't imagine what learning all of this for the first time is doing to him.

"And the breathing?" I ask. "No heartbeats, but breathing?"

"It's more of a habit," Mom calls back. "Probably a good one to have otherwise we'd be too still, too dead looking."

I decide I'm not going to ask any more questions I don't want honest answers to.

At the top of the hill, a rectangular stone structure emerges from the dark. Its gray stone exterior is festooned with vines that snake up and across the arched entryway. The surrounding grounds are littered with an overgrowth of prickly bracken.

Mom looks around cautiously as she approaches. I do the same. The cemetery is silent, unmoving except for the tree branches shifting in the wind. Shadowy shapes lurk in every darkened corner and I have to shake myself to get out of my own head. Noah takes my hand, gripping it tightly.

"It's okay," he says. "I think."

I smile even though this isn't the time or place. "Is that supposed to make me feel better?"

He shakes his head. "I guess not."

I squeeze his hand. "I'm scared. You're scared. Let's just be scared together."

"Yeah, you're right," Noah says. He kisses my cheek and I pull him toward the gray stone mausoleum.

Mom gently pushes the heavy doors of the crypt inward and disappears inside. A moment later she pops her head out.

"It's all clear," she says, gesturing for us to follow her.

As I step over the threshold, the musty air envelops me. It smells like rotted leaves, moisture, and dirt. There is a faint whiff of decay. I take short, shallow breaths to keep from tasting the air on the back of my tongue.

The interior of the mausoleum is cloaked in somber darkness, with the only light coming from the moon as its glow spills through a few circular windows high up on the wall. Vaults, in a checkerboard pattern, line the walls. My mom takes out her phone and cuts on her flashlight. She sweeps the cone of light across the rear wall. Names and dates materialize—Henry Hullman 1856–1903, Margaret Ellen Gordon 1936–1989, Martin F. Tompkins 1874–1952.

"Mrs. Redwood," Noah says. "I—I don't think I can stay in here too long. This place is . . . I don't know. Something's off."

I can feel it too. It's like a silent vibration permeates the space and I'm having a hard time figuring out if I'm also hearing the hum or just sensing it. Noah presses his shoulder into mine as my mom moves to the wall on the right side of the mausoleum. She shines her light on a vault at the bottom of the wall.

CLARENCE D. REDWOOD

1947–2000

DEATH IS NOT AN END,
BUT A BEGINNING.

"Found him," my mom says.

Noah and I join her at the wall. Grandpa Redwood's grave marker is covered in a slick of green moss and the letters of his name are mostly chipped away. Mom sweeps the light across the tomb and something catches my eye. Usually, in a vault, the granite-facing stone that has the person's name on it is set in place and secured by a small plate in each of the four corners. In older tombs, like this one, the facing stones are held in place with mortar. Grandpa Redwood has a few neighbors in this dark and dank place. The mortar on their graves is nearly black with grime and age. Grandpa Redwood's, however, is a pearly white.

"Somebody's been in here recently," I say. "It had to be Dad."

Mom takes a long, deep breath. "The only question is why? Either the book is in there or maybe . . ." she trails off.

"Maybe he brought his dad back from the grave?" Noah offers.

I shake my head. "No. No way. He wouldn't have done that, right? Could he even do that? Grandpa Redwood's been dead for twenty-five years."

I look to my mom. "Maybe," she says. "I don't really know."

"How's that work?" I ask in stunned disbelief. "Dad could bring somebody back when they've been dead that long?"

"He could but he shouldn't," Mom says. "He wouldn't. Remember what I said about having to work with the body? Your decayed corpse could come back but then you'd have to maintain an already rotted body. You couldn't pass for a living human being at all. Who would want that? You'd have to stay in the shadows. You'd have to be a recluse."

Noah holds up his hand. "I'm gonna throw up."

"No, you're not," Mom says. "You can't. Not really."

Noah takes a step back from the vault.

Mom returns her attention to the seal around the vault. "Stay here," she says. "I'll be right back." She darts out, then returns a few moments later with a small triangular-shaped bag. She tosses it down and fishes around inside, coming up with something that looks like two long wrenches stuck together in the shape of an X.

"What is that?" I ask.

"A lug wrench," Mom says. "It's all I had in the car but I think it should work."

"Are we about to break into the vault?" I ask.

"We don't have a choice," she says. "If the book's not here, we have to go back to square one and time is not on our side." She grips the lug wrench. "These people, Meka, I don't think they're the kind of people we want to mess with." She pulls her bottom lip between her teeth as she tries, and fails, to keep her chin from wobbling. "I can't imagine what somebody who is essentially immortal would do if they had a mind to be awful."

We set to work chipping away the freshly laid seal around the edge of the vault door. We work quickly and in fifteen minutes, we've got the seal completely broken. It takes all three of us to pry off the facing stone and set it on the floor.

Mom shines the light from her phone into the narrow space. A mahogany coffin with brass fittings sits inside. A gust of cold air sweeps through the crypt and a strange tingling sensation sparks in both my hands. It's familiar, painful, like a cut in the skin of both palms. I quickly open and close my fists in front of me, halfway expecting to see an open wound but there's nothing.

"You okay?" Noah asks.

The feeling doesn't dissipate but I lower my hands. "Yeah— I—it's nothing."

Noah doesn't look convinced, and I feel like my expression is betraying everything. I know this feeling. It's what I felt when I touched what I now believe was this strange book as it was concealed under the seat of the hearse.

"We're going to have to pull the casket out," my mom says, her words cutting through my thoughts.

Noah takes a step back. "What do you mean?"

"We have to open it," Mom says. "I don't see anything in the vault itself so if the book's here it's probably inside the casket."

Noah clenches his jaw and while his face shifts, the little area I had repaired with mortuary wax stays unnaturally still. "I don't think I can do that, Mrs. Redwood."

"I'll open it," my mom says. "But I still need you both to help me take out the coffin and put it on the floor."

202

"It's solid mahogany," I say. "Probably three hundred pounds on its own. We can't lift it alone."

"I don't see any pallbearers around here, baby," my mom says. "And we don't have time anyway. We can probably just pull it forward until it drops."

"You want us to drop the coffin?" I ask. It's one of those weird unwritten rules. You don't drop a coffin. You don't even let it touch the ground if you can help it.

"Again," Mom says, exasperated. "We're out of options and we need to look inside." She grabs the brass handle on the foot of the coffin and yanks on it. It barely budges.

I grab one of the ear panels and Noah does the same on the other side.

"Pull on three," my mom says. "One. Two. Three!"

We yank the coffin toward us and it moves about halfway out. It teeters on the lip of the vault like a seesaw. Then it slips under its own weight and slides to the floor. The foot of the coffin slams into the ground with a loud thud as the head end scrapes the inside of the vault before clearing it. It tumbles to the ground, sending a cloud of dust into the air. Noah stumbles back and so do I but my mom rushes in and runs her hand along the panels until she finds the latch pin. She pushes it aside and grips the head panel.

"If PeePaw Redwood is in there, you think he's gonna be pissed we just threw his whole box on the ground?" Noah asks.

My mom hesitates. "He's probably in here and probably very dead. I don't think he cares. Jonathan would never reanimate somebody and then keep them in a box."

Eternity in a box? I can't imagine anything worse.

I'm about to ask my mom to wait but the protest dies in my

throat as she lifts open the lid of the coffin. Noah steps back until he is pressed against the inner wall of the mausoleum. It's a good thing, too, because what's inside the coffin is a horrific sight.

Grandpa Redwood. A man I'd never met, though I had seen a few pictures of him, lies moldering in his casket. In one of the photos I'd seen, he'd been wearing a dark gray suit, a pair of thick, black framed glasses, his facial hair cropped close. He had started to bald in the photo. I step closer as my mom stares down at what's left of the body. I had expected him to look mostly the way he had in the picture, but I'm wrong. Very, very wrong.

"Oh my god, Mom," I say. "He wasn't embalmed?"

Grandpa Redwood is a pile of bones in the remnants of a black suit. The cream-colored satin lining of the coffin is stained dark with bodily fluid. A few bits of emaciated muscle and skin that look almost petrified cling to the yellowing skull, which is wearing a pair of black glasses, and I think Grandpa Redwood had maybe enjoyed candy when he was alive because nearly every exposed tooth has a silver filling. A rancid smell begins to creep up my nose and I quickly pull up my shirt to cover the lower half of my face. My mom's expression falls. She searches around the perimeter of Grandpa Redwood's body.

"It's not here," she says. She's on the verge of tears.

A thought occurs to me. A terrible thought but I figure it can't be much worse than digging up an old man's rotted corpse. "Can we—can we bring him back and ask him where this book might be?"

"What?" my mom asks, her eyes wide. "No. That's backward, Meka. You need the book to bring him back. We don't have that and even if we did nobody here knows how to use it."

"Grandpa Redwood did," I say.

Mom tilts her head and looks at me. "You'd want to do that? Bring him back just because we need something?"

A deep sense of shame washes over me. I guess my idea doesn't really make sense to begin with but what I'm not going to admit to her is that yes, I would bring back Grandpa Redwood's casket of bones if we knew how and if it meant we could help my dad.

"The book's not here," my mom says.

"It's not?" I ask. "Are we—are we sure?" The tingling in my hands and the hum in my ears have intensified so much I almost feel like my bones are vibrating. I move to my mom's side and peer into the casket. "Look," I say.

Grandpa Redwood's hands are crossed over his chest but they're not touching his body. It's as if something invisible is holding them aloft. I lean closer and as I do, the tingling in my hands turns to a burning. A soft green glow begins to illuminate the gore inside the coffin. A rectangular object materializes under Grandpa Redwood's decayed hands.

CHAPTER 17

FATES WORSE THAN DEATH

The book from my nightmare comes into existence right before my eyes in a hazy green light. Mom puts her hand on my arm as she stares in disbelief. Her gaze moves to my face and then back to the book. She leans forward and tries to pull the book out. The bones of Grandpa Redwood's hand shift and several fingers fall off and roll into the interior of the coffin.

"Oh shit," I whisper.

Mom clenches her teeth and grasps the book firmly. "Sorry, Clarence." She yanks the book up and what's left of Grandpa Redwood's arms collapse within the tattered sleeves of his suit. Mom steps away from the casket with the book clutched to her chest. It blinks in and out of existence, still holding its shape but losing the details the farther away from me it gets.

"Can we close the coffin now?" Noah asks. "Please."

I quickly push the lid down and latch it. Noah's posture relaxes a little as he comes over and peers down at the book my mom is holding.

The strange feeling in my hands intensifies as I touch my mom's shoulder. Her arm spasms and her hand clenches into a tight fist. I pull my own hand back.

"What the hell?" my mom asks as she stares at her arm.

Suddenly, there's a loud pop in my ears followed by a low hum, like somebody had snapped on a breaker and sent electricity buzzing through the mausoleum. My head feels like it's vibrating and then, strange symbols on the front of the book begin to take shape.

I touch the front cover and a bolt of energy shoots through my fingertips and up my arm. I snatch my hand back, clutching it to my chest.

"Meka?" Noah asks. He grabs my hand and examines it but there's nothing there.

My mom looks down at the book and then to me. "What do you see, Meka?" she asks.

"You—you can't see it?" I ask.

"I can see the book," mom says. "Barely. It's like it's made of glass. And it's glowing but that's all. Are there pages? A cover?"

I look to my mom and then Noah. "It's leatherbound. There are markings—looks like writing on the front."

Mom shakes her head. "And when you touched it, you felt something." It's not a question really, more like a statement she knows is true.

"What is going on? What is this?" I look at my hands again as the feeling pushes through me. "What are you not telling me?"

My mom holds the book in front of her, squinting like she

can't make out its proportions. Her hands move across the cover. "I didn't know if you were like them."

"Who's *them*?" I ask.

"Your dad and Grandpa Redwood," Mom says. "And your Great-Grandma Redwood, and her mother before her. Back and back and back. They all had the gift but I—I don't know. I was hoping you wouldn't have to bear it. I've seen what it's done to your dad, to his father . . ."

The book glows so bright it hurts my eyes but Mom and Noah don't seem to be as affected by it as I am.

"They were all reanimators," Mom says. "And you are, too."

She puts the book in my hands and before I can push it away, the jolt rockets through me again. I grip the book as the feeling surges through me. My heart races as my entire body vibrates. The book's front cover flies open. On the title page, a name written in smudged burgundy ink reads Johann Konrad Dippel. The pages turn on their own. There are strange symbols and words I don't recognize, diagrams of bodies flayed open, and other horrific images. As the last pages cycle through, names appear in the same burgundy ink—the first ones, Marilyn Leighton, William Burke, Franklin Cabot, are barely legible. Dozens of names follow and the dates scrawled next to them go back as far as two hundred years. On the last page, two names I recognize appear.

Kassie Redwood and Noah Cliff.

Under their names is a small drawing, no bigger than a stamp, that looks like a raven.

A rumbling noise suddenly fills the confined space inside the mausoleum. I try to home in on where it's coming from.

The sound is coming from the vaults.

The coffins inside them are rattling like their occupants are trying to get out.

The hum of electricity crashes through my body. A loud crack echoes through the mausoleum. Grandpa Redwood's mortal remains clatter around in his coffin. There's a terrible pounding in my head.

"Close the book!" Noah shouts. "Close it!

My mom steps toward me with her hands outstretched. The green glow emanating from the book is so bright I want to cover my eyes. I slam the book shut and try to focus but my vision is dancing with green spots as I try to readjust to the dark. Suddenly, my mom disappears from in front of me. The clanging from the vaults ceases but now there are other noises.

Noah grunts, like the air has been knocked out of him. I turn toward him and realize some strange man has him in a headlock.

"Noah!" I shout.

Something impacts the side of my face. Pain rockets through my jaw and down the side of my neck. I stumble to the side, catching myself on the wall. For a moment, I can't see anything. Pain blooms over my eye and the sensation of warm liquid running down my face and into my eye and mouth makes me gasp. I press my hand to my head, and it comes away bloody.

"Get it!" a man shouts.

"I can't see it!" another voice responds.

As my senses slowly come back to me, I see that two men have entered the mausoleum. Noah has managed to get free from the one taller guy with the black hair, but he's now menacing Noah with a long, curved blade. The shorter guy—the same blond guy from the movies and who broke into our house—is struggling with my mom over a handgun. Everything suddenly comes into focus.

I wipe the blood out of my eye and rush the shorter guy, slamming my full body weight against him. He tumbles forward, head over feet, and lands in an awkward heap by Grandpa Redwood's coffin. The gun skitters across the floor and my mom lunges for it. The guy scrambles after her on all fours and I deliver a kick to his ribs. There's a loud *crack* and for a second, I think my foot has gotten tangled in his coat but as I try to shake it free, I realize my sneaker is in this guy's rib cage. I scream and kick at him again, freeing myself. Mom grabs the gun and swings it around.

"Meka, move!" she shouts. I stand behind her as she aims the pistol at the taller guy. "Drop the knife! Now!"

The taller man quickly darts behind Noah and holds the knife to his neck.

"Don't!" I scream.

"Get the book!" the taller man shouts.

I realize I'm not holding the strange book anymore and when I spot it again, it's in the hands of the shorter man, who smiles when he sees me staring at it.

"It's here!" he shouts. "She sees it!"

He rushes out of the mausoleum with the book. I step toward the entrance but the man holding Noah hostage presses his knife closer to Noah's throat.

"Let him go!" I shout.

The man glances toward the entrance. I can hear the rev of an engine outside.

"Put the gun down and I'll let him go," says the man holding Noah hostage. "All we want is the book. We have it now. No need for this to go any further."

"You can't hurt him anyway," my mom says. "Think about what you're doing."

I smile in spite of our terrible circumstances. The guy is holding Noah at knifepoint but Noah can't be killed. He's technically already dead. He doesn't even feel pain. I wait for the man to realize what a stupid situation he's put himself in but his expression doesn't change.

"I can't kill him but I can make existing impossible for him," says the man. "You can patch up flesh wounds but what happens if I cut off his head?"

I'm not smiling anymore. A cold shiver rushes through me. My mom slowly bends and puts the gun on the ground.

"There," she says. "Let him go."

The man takes the blade away from Noah's neck but as Noah steps toward me, reaching for me, the tall man brings the blade up and then back down in one quick motion. There's a quiet thud as Noah's dismembered hand falls to the floor.

CHAPTER 18

TAKE ME BY THE HAND

The sound that claws its way up my throat isn't so much a scream as it is a strangled yelp. I wait for Noah to react but he just stands there staring at the hand, his eyes wide and terrified.

The man with the knife darts out the door and I hear the spinning and screeching of tires as he and his companion make their getaway. I know I should be worried about that. They took the book but all I can think of, all I can see, is Noah. I rush forward and grab his wrist. I squeeze it. That's what I'm supposed to do, right? Put pressure on the wound. I look around for something to wrap around it.

"Mom!" I say, my voice cracking under the stress. "Mom, help me! I need something to put on it. Hurry!"

But she doesn't hurry. She walks up to me and Noah and instead of looking at the wound she looks at me.

"Meka, baby, it's not necessary."

"What?" I ask in a haze of confusion. "No. Help me! Please!

We gotta stop the—" I cut the sentence short. I was thinking I needed to stop the bleeding but there is no blood. "Oh," I say with a little stab of embarrassment. "Right."

Noah's face is still frozen in a mask of disbelief.

"Is he in shock?" I ask. I still have a death grip on his wrist. "Noah? Noah, try to relax."

He's staring down at his hand. Then . . . he screams. The most agonizing, bloodcurdling scream I've ever heard.

"Noah," my mom says firmly. "Baby, please." She gives him a firm shake and his scream fades into a dull whimper. "It doesn't hurt. Your mind only thinks it does because it doesn't make sense. You're okay."

"What—what am I supposed to do?" he asks.

I turn to my mom. She puts her hand on Noah's shoulder. "It's okay. We can reattach it."

"Huh?" Noah asks. "What do you mean? You can't just put it back on, right? That's not how it works . . . is it?"

"Wiggle your fingers," Mom says to Noah.

"I—I can't," Noah says. "How?"

"Just try," my mom says. "Think of your hand, then wiggle the fingers."

Noah does as she asks. I can feel the muscles and tendons in his wrist moving under my grip. On the floor, the fingers on his hand open and close.

"We need to get out of here and figure out a plan B," my mom says quietly. She reaches down and scoops up Noah's hand. She tucks it under her arm and motions toward the entrance. "Let's go."

Outside, we trudge back down the hill and get in the car. Noah slides into the back seat and I get in on the passenger side. As my mom slips into the driver's seat, she sets Noah's hand in my lap. It takes everything in me not to scream. The fingers twitch and then suddenly the whole thing lurches over and gently grips my own hand. I whip my head around to face Noah, who has a little smirk on his lips.

"Sorry," he says. "I just wanted to hold your hand."

"If we all weren't in the most dangerous situation ever, that might be sweet," my mom says. "Aren't people always saying we're like the Addams family? Now we have our very own Thing."

"I actually hate that," Noah says. "No offense, Mrs. Redwood."

I stare at Noah's hand. It shouldn't make sense but it *does*. If I can do the things my dad has done, the things Grandpa Redwood did, it all makes sense when it didn't before. The moving corpses, the quality of my cosmetology work on the dead, it all came back to this . . . power. It stirs a dizzying mix of feelings— I'm scared to death but I'm also relieved. I'm not losing my mind or hallucinating or having nightmares—I am seeing things clearly. I am remembering.

My mom steers us home and parks the car behind the house. I gently lift Noah's hand up and hold it like I'm carrying something made of glass. I take Noah and his hand into the basement as my mom locks up and then joins us a few moments later in the prep room. Noah takes off his coat and lies down on the prep table. I set his hand on his chest.

"Thanks," he says. The fingers on his hand reach toward me.

"Can I hold your other hand?" I ask.

"No," Noah says. "Let's keep it weird."

I laugh and it's the first time I've laughed like this in a really long time. Noah does too. Even my mom can't keep a straight face as she collects the supplies needed to reattach Noah's hand. For one minute, I pretend things are okay. That my dad's at work. That Noah never died. That my mom has no secrets. That my nightmares were just dreams and not memories. It's just a minute, though. Then, the weight of the entire situation falls on me like a brick. There is no getting away from it and there is no going back to normal. Even Miss Cliff wanted so much to go back to how things were before but it's impossible. I look at my hands.

"I need to pack the wound with Vis-O-Guard gel," my mom says softly. "That will control any seepage since Noah is still pretty—well—fresh."

"I'm fresh?" Noah asks. "Like fruit?"

"Sort of," Mom says. "You're newly reanimated. For the first few months some residual liquid that's still in your body might push its way out. It happened to me and let's just say it wasn't pleasant. The Vis-O-Guard gel will keep it from smelling and it'll also help preserve the tissue."

Absolutely nothing is funny anymore.

"I think you'll be able to use the hand," my mom says. "But you're going to have to be very, very careful. You'll have to detach it probably every few weeks and reapply the gel before reattaching it."

"And I do this . . . forever?" Noah asks.

My mom looks at Noah and I can see that she pities him, but it's more than that. She knows what life will be like for him. She knows how hard it will be.

"Yes," my mom says solemnly. "Forever."

The look on Noah's face puts a knot in my throat. He's so dejected. I can't even imagine what he must be feeling.

"If you show me how to do it, I can help," I say. "I'll change it out whenever you need me to."

Noah only looks more upset at my suggestion. "So, you'll just stick by me forever? Patching me up when I fall apart?"

In my mind, the answer is obvious and I'm a little worried that Noah doesn't see it. "Yeah," I say. "That's exactly what I'll do."

"Meeks," Noah says. "That's too much for me to ask."

"No, it's not," I say. "And please stop talking to me like you're some kind of monster who doesn't deserve my help. You didn't ask for this." For the first time in all of this, there's a flare of anger directed right at my dad because he did this to Noah and to my mom. But I shake it off because I know my dad. I know he's strange, but he's good. There has to be something I'm missing.

"I don't want you to have to change your whole life just to help me out," Noah says. "That's not fair."

"It's not fair that you died," I say, fighting back a wave of angry tears. "And now you're back and you don't want me to help?"

"Hold on," my mom says as she pulls up a swivel stool and gently grasps Noah's wrist as she prepares to reattach his severed hand. "Let's all just hit pause."

Noah reaches for me with his intact hand and I take it.

"I need another jar of Vis-O-Guard and I'm all out down here," my mom says.

"There's some in the shed," I say.

"Stay here," my mom says. "I'll get it."

She steps out of the prep room and I step into the hall behind her.

"Want me to go out with her?" Noah asks from his perch on the prep table.

"No," I say. "I think she's good. Just stay there."

Noah nods and as my mom goes upstairs, I go across the hall to the door that leads to the cold storage room and slip inside. Prep room one is where the embalming happens. It feels more sterile in here. I walk to the big metal door at the rear of the room and touch the handle. I peer through the little window into the darkened space beyond.

I need to see something.

I pull the door open and a frigid rush of cold air hits me like a wintery wind. My skin is raised to gooseflesh and I hold my breath for a moment. On the double row of body-size shelves there are two bulky figures lying prone. Two guests have yet to be embalmed and they are patiently waiting their turn. I wave my hand in the air and the motion-activated light in the cold storage room flickers on. I stare at the bodies.

There were other corpses hidden in the walls of the tomb where Grandpa Redwood had been interred and I had heard them clattering around when I held that strange book.

I set my hand on one of the body bags. I try to think of what it felt like as that strange sensation had rushed through me, had made me feel like I'd been struck by lightning. The blowers in the ceiling click on and push the cold air around trying to compensate for me leaving the door open, letting all the cold air out. The bags rustle but only from the airflow, not because the people inside are waking at my touch.

My mom said I had this power and that it had come to me like a gift from my father and his father before him. People pass down curly hair or being tall, not the ability to raise people from the dead. I rack my brain to find a time when my dad might have laid it out for me and all I can conjure up is our conversation in the hearse the night our guest sat up and how Grandpa Redwood had been a topic of conversation more in the past few months than at any other time in my whole life. I think he knew that something was shifting. I think he could feel it and now, I can feel it too.

I leave the cold storage area and firmly shut the door. The light goes out once all is still inside and I sigh. What was I expecting?

"What are you doing?" my mom asks.

I flinch at the sound of her voice. She's standing right inside the prep room door, the new jar of Vis-O-Guard in her hand.

"I didn't see you," I said.

She smiles. "Come on, I need to tell you something."

I follow her into the hall but as I glance back, I notice the motion-activated light in the cold storage room is back on.

"Can I tell you both something?" my mom asks when we rejoin Noah in prep room two.

I don't know if right now is the time for a heart-to-heart but I'm not gonna tell my mom that. She flips the lid off the Vis-O-Guard gel and uses a small spatula-like tool to smear it on the end of Noah's wrist. She coats the entire surface of it and makes sure to get it inside where the cleanly cut shards of bone and tendon are visible.

"When I first came to be . . . this"—Mom gestures to herself before returning to her work—"I patched up cuts and dents myself. Even repaired my own teeth as they fell out of their sockets."

I glance over at her. "I thought you got veneers."

"I did," she says. "But I had to learn how to shape the composite material and do the bonding myself because I couldn't chance going into a dentist's office and getting hooked up to a machine that wouldn't find a pulse or the body temperature of a normal human being."

Another piece falls into place. I realize she's probably never been to a doctor in the years since the accident. No doctor, no dentist, nothing.

"All that to say that I never had anything catastrophic happen outside the wounds I got in the car accident," Mom continues. She picks up Noah's hand and applies more of the preservative gel to the stump. Noah's fingers curl up as she does. "I don't think the reanimated are meant to go on for as long as I have."

I think about having to repair a body over and over again. A body that won't die no matter what.

"What does Dad think about that?" I ask.

"Nothing," my mom sighs. "I don't think he has a full picture of the origins of his power. He knows it's passed down to him, he has the book, but because he was so distant from his father, I think there are things he doesn't know. These people who've come after us clearly can't wield the book themselves or they wouldn't need Jonathan. They can't even see the damn thing much less read from it."

Mom laces a thick cord of waxed mortuary thread through a curved needle and sets it aside before picking up a small drill, something you might see in a nail salon but sturdier. She pulls back the flesh from Noah's wrist, exposing the white bone of the radius which has been cleanly shorn in half and drills a small hole in it. She drills another hole in the other piece of the radius that is jutting from Noah's detached hand. Looping a length of steel wire through the holes, she strings the hand and wrist together, cinching it tight.

"Jonathan reanimated me," Mom continues as she picks up the curved needle and begins to reconnect the bits of flesh around Noah's injury. "It got harder and harder for me to do the maintenance on my own. I can see the toll it takes on him." She presses her lips together. "Imagine watching somebody you love fall apart right in front of you."

A terrible tightness grips my chest as I think about all of this through my father's eyes. "He does it because he loves you," I say. "*We* love you. If he doesn't want to do it or if he gets tired, I'll do it."

My mom shakes her head. "Baby, it's not about that."

"What's it about, then?" I ask. I'm suddenly angry again.

My mom flashes me that check-your-tone look and I try to remember that while some things have changed, others have not. I drop the attitude and just try to be honest with her.

"I don't like the way you and Noah make it seem like you're a burden to me or to Dad," I say. "I'd do anything for either one of you. I'd put you back together a thousand times if that's what it takes."

My mom's expression hardens. "Is that what you'd want if it was you?"

I don't say anything. I don't want to tell her that it's *not* me. It's her and Noah and yes, I'd do it if it meant keeping them close to me.

She finishes reattaching Noah's hand and when she's done patching the outer layer of skin with mortuary wax and painting it to match Noah's skin, it looks almost identical to his other wrist.

Mom sits back and crosses her arms over her chest. "We have to get to your father, and I think the only way to do that is to track down the people who have him."

I head toward the door. "Okay. So let's go."

"We can't," Mom says. "I have no idea where they are."

"Dad was always going to the Cornell campus," I say. "Maybe they took him there. Maybe they're like a secret society or something."

220

"I don't think we can just walk around the campus asking people where their shady secret society hangs out," Noah says. "And they probably have more than one secret club, right? It's a lot of rich old men up there and you know they love a secret club. Skull and Bones, Freemasons, stuff like that."

"Skull and Bones is at Yale, but you have a point," my mom says. "But I also don't know where else to even start looking for him."

We are at an impasse. We have no clue where my dad is but I want to do *something*. Sitting around feeling helpless is pointless.

"Let's go through his stuff," I say. "Maybe there's something in there that can tell us more about who these people are and what they want. Maybe it'll point us in the right direction." It's a long shot but there's nothing else for us to do.

My mom nods and heads upstairs. Noah and I trail along behind her. As she makes her way to the upper floor Noah hesitates and we hang back near the kitchen.

"Hang on," Noah says. He goes into the kitchen and grabs the bracelet I'd left on the counter. He quickly loops it around my wrist and fastens it. "This belongs to you. Promise me you'll keep it this time."

He gently presses his forehead against mine and puts his arms around me. "Promise," I say.

"We gotta find your dad," he says. "We have to make all this right."

"I don't know how," I say.

Noah slips his newly repaired hand under my chin and lifts my face to his.

"We are gonna figure this out together because that's the only way we *can* figure it out," Noah says. "You trust me, I trust you. That's all that matters." He pulls me closer to him.

"I'm the girl whose whole life revolves around death," I say. "You know how lucky you are that it worked out like that? Imagine if it was somebody else."

"Somebody like Caleb?" Noah asks. "Imagine him having to deal with this." Noah holds up his hand and wiggles his fingers. "Or this." He lifts my hand and places it on his cheek where the work I'd done on his wound is still holding up. "He'd be passed out somewhere and I'd be doing all this alone." He sighs. "I would, you know."

"Would what?" I ask, trying to concentrate as I slip my hand around the back of his neck.

"I'd do it alone if you said you couldn't deal," Noah says. "I'd never want to do anything to make you uncomfortable and I get it if you see me differently now."

I stare into his face. Even though it is changed in a way that feels impossible, I still love everything I see. There is nothing he could be that would make me turn away from him.

I stand on tiptoe and press my lips against his. The jolt I normally feel in my hands is in my lips now. I realize that I've been feeling it almost every time we've touched since he came back to me. Everything is changed now that I know what that spark can do but I don't care. He cups my face in his hands and I breathe him in. We will make this new reality our own.

CHAPTER 19

UNDER THE FLOORBOARDS

In my parents' bedroom my mom has every drawer on my dad's side of the dresser open. She's pulling out the contents, sifting through pockets, and undoing pairs of socks to check inside.

"Can you two look in the closet?" she asks. "Go through every coat, every bag. Look inside every shoe."

"I know going through his stuff was my idea but I don't even know what we're looking for," I say. "Do you really think he left a note that has the address of the secret society on it?"

My mom lets her shoulders roll forward. "I don't even know, baby. If you see something weird just let me know, okay? I don't know what else to do." The sadness and desperation in her voice is palpable. "When I tell you this stuff involving reanimation is a secret, I mean it. The only reason I know the little bit that I do is because of what I am now." She looks down at her hands as she clutches my dad's T-shirt. "He had to tell me something. I couldn't stand not knowing anything about what happened to me. I pressed him about it for years until he finally gave me something. Mostly the information about Grandpa Redwood and not much else." She sets his T-shirt down and just stares at it. "It always felt like we were running out of time, like a clock was ticking, but I thought it was because of me. My condition. I thought he was worried about how I'd take care of myself but now I realize it was something else." She looks like she's on the verge of tears and I quickly go to her, putting my arms around her. She hugs me back, then nudges me toward the closet because regardless of how terrible this is, we have work to do.

I open the heavy doors of my parents' bedroom closet. I pull my dad's button-downs and coats off their hangers and search them inside and out. Noah goes through shoeboxes and tote bags. We don't find anything and neither does my mom, who sits on the bed with her head in her hands.

"Let's check the top shelf," I say, even though I'm sure it only contains folded sweaters and extra winter comforters.

Noah steps into the closet and reaches up to pull down a stack of dusty knitted sweaters when a loud crack echoes through the room. Noah stumbles, spilling the sweaters onto the ground. He sits down hard. His foot has gone straight through one of the wooden boards in the bottom of the closet.

"You got termites in here, Mrs. Redwood?" Noah asks as he pulls his foot out of the hole.

I quickly pull up his pant leg and examine his bare skin. He seems okay. No scratches or cuts. I let out a long, slow breath as Noah pulls himself to his feet. My mom comes over and examines the hole in the floor.

"What in the world?" she asks, crouching to peer inside. "Meka. Shine a light in here real quick."

I grab my phone and angle the light downward. It illuminates the space as my mom reaches inside and comes up with a stack of dusty papers.

"What is it?" I ask.

My mom carries the stack of papers to the middle of her room and sits down on the floor. "This stuff belongs to your dad but I—I don't know if you should look at it. I don't know if *I* should look at it."

"Why?" I ask as I sit down on the edge of her bed.

"He hid it," my mom says. "He doesn't want us to see this."

"I don't care," I say. "We have to find him."

My mom thumbs through the stack and begins to lay the different things out on the floor. She picks out a photograph and hands it to me. It's of my dad. He's wearing a cap and gown, smiling his familiar little half smile. There is already sadness in his eyes.

"High school graduation," my mom says.

"Do you think he already knew what he could do when he was that young?" I ask.

My mom nods. "He's always known."

I can't help but look at my hands again. Hadn't a part of me always known something was off about me too? I picture Grandpa Redwood telling my dad what he could do when he was little. It must have been a heavy burden for a kid and I'm sure this is what he was trying to shield me from by not telling me.

Noah sits down on the floor near my mom. She hands me another photo. This one is of me and her together. She's got me slung on her hip and I'm giving the camera a wide grin with no more than three teeth in my mouth. Mom's smiling wide. I stare at the photo—her smooth brown skin, her hair down;

she's got on a tank top and shorts like we've been outside in the sun. The picture is so completely normal, but I can't look away. Something about her is different.

The realization that I'm a baby in the photo and it had to have been taken *before* settles on me like a dark cloud. She was alive in this photo.

I glance over at her and she's got four more photos from before spread out in front of her. Her hands are trembling as she arranges and rearranges the pictures.

"I don't remember anything about the reanimation process," my mom says, keeping her voice low and steady. "I remember being in the car with you and your dad and we were . . . running."

A chill runs up my back. "Running?"

My mom shuffles through more papers—one of which is a sketch of a body with markings eerily similar to the ones on my mom's chest and back.

"When I think back, it's hard for me to piece together," my mom says. "I thought it was just the road, the driving conditions, but no." She closes her eyes like she's trying to resurrect a memory. "We just got in the car and left. I—I remember now." She blinks repeatedly. "We were running from them. These people. But they found us, didn't they?"

My heart ticks up as images of the dream—the memory—blaze to life in my head. I'm in the back seat, Mom and Dad in the front, the song on the radio, and . . .

"There was someone in the road," I say.

"What?" My mom's head whips around. "I—I didn't see anyone. At least I don't remember—I don't even remember the crash. I only remember looking into your face and feeling that we needed to go." Mom sets down the papers and stares at me. "Who was it? What did they look like?"

The image burns bright in my mind's eye. There was someone in the road that night—someone standing in front of our car. I saw him through the front windshield. He loomed over the hood as my dad jerked the wheel and our car tumbled off the road. His face is a blur in my mind, like it's made up of different parts my memory and imagination have cobbled together. He has the face of the man I thought I saw in my window when I was five but that, too, is a blur, like someone had smudged his features.

"I can't remember clearly," I say. "It was a man, I think. He was standing in the road. I saw him through the window."

Mom sits quietly for a moment. "They've been here all along," she whispers more to herself than anyone else.

Noah reaches out and picks up another piece of paper.

"It's embalming but for . . . pets?" Noah asks, a clear look of confusion on his face as he reads the paper. "Can Mr. Redwood bring back animals too?"

"I've never seen him do that," my mom says softly, taking the paper from Noah and handing it to me. "He's never mentioned anything like that to me."

The paper shows a sketch of a dog with various incisions and markings on it. I had a dog named Vick when I was three. He died unexpectedly when I was six and I remember how devastated I was. I stayed in my room, didn't eat, and I cried myself to sleep for weeks. If I had known I had this power, that it could work on pets, I might have done something unspeakable.

I quickly flip the paper over and push it away from me.

As Mom and Noah look through the papers, a newspaper

article catches my eye. A woman with red hair is pictured as she holds up a plaque with her name on it.

"Look!" I say, scrambling off the bed and joining Mom and Noah on the floor. I snag the paper and point to the woman. "This lady was here the night we got takeout before Noah died."

Mom takes the paper and reads the caption. "Camille Phelps wins prestigious Holcomb prize for her work in furtherance of Thiel embalming."

"What's that?" Noah asks.

"The Thiel technique is used to embalm a body that's going to be used for medical research," Mom says. "It makes the body and organs appear more lifelike. Medical students use corpses treated with the Thiel technique to practice on."

Noah holds up his hand. "You sure I can't throw up?"

My mom nods; then her expression changes. "It says this woman, Camille, died of an aortic aneurysm." She glances at the paper. "This paper is from 1998."

"So I'm guessing she's reanimated now too," I say. "Otherwise, how was she standing on our porch?"

Mom stacks up the papers and I spot another article. This one had been paperclipped to several others just like it.

"Man from homeless encampment in Ithaca goes missing," I read aloud. I flip to the next article. "Two women missing from Ithaca encampment." I glance at Noah. "That guy you bum-rushed while we were in the shop, his name was Mr. Lions and he was saying someone was gonna get him and cut him into pieces." I hand Noah the stack of articles. "Maybe he wasn't out of his mind."

My mom puts her hands over her mouth. "I can't even wrap my brain around what he was implying."

Noah stands and continues his search of the closet as I thumb through the rest of the papers. At the very bottom of the stack is an opened envelope with my dad's full name and an address I don't recognize scrawled on the front. I take out the piece of paper inside and it falls apart in my hands, like it had been torn up and stuffed back in the envelope. One scrap reads, *It's not like it is in films, Jonathan. This is not a fiction. The stories are so close to the truth of our family but they leave out the most important part . . . why? Why would we do these things? Why must we do these things? If only they knew.*

Nothing else in the letter is legible but there is a slightly yellowed photograph mixed up in the fragments. It's Grandpa Redwood lying still and stiff in his mahogany coffin. His black glasses are perched on his face, and if I didn't know better, I'd say there was a slight smile on his lips. I shove the picture and the papers to the side. I'm more confused and frustrated than ever.

The closet is nearly empty now but Noah snags a big leather tote from the deepest corner.

"Wanna check inside this?" Noah asks, handing it to me. "It's the only thing left."

I take it from him and toss it on the bed, pulling open the top flap. The smell that wafts out is familiar and strange all at once. Mom comes over to peer inside the bag. There's some kind of blanket or robe bunched up inside. I pull it out and the smell hits me again—sweet and smoky, like incense or something. I realize this is the same smell and, from the looks of it, the same cloth that had been in my dad's suitcase. I shake it out and hold it up.

"What is that?" Noah asks.

The garment has a deep black hood and is long enough to brush the floor even though I'm holding it over my head. "It's a cloak. I think my dad said it was Grandpa Redwood's."

Mom and I exchange puzzled glances.

"So, your grandpa was, like, a cosplayer or something?" Noah asks. "He liked to dress up as what? Emperor Palpatine in his off time?"

"I've never seen this," my mom says as she touches the fabric. "And the smell. It's like church. My grandma was Catholic, and I used to go to Mass with her when I was little, Christmas services, Easter." She smiles a little. I only know my grandmother from pictures. A little pang of sadness ripples through me. "They burned it in a censer," Mom continues. "The place would be filled with the smoke and the smell of it." She lifts the cloak and sniffs it. "Almost the exact same smell."

"Grandpa Redwood was at church?" I ask. "Wearing this?"

My mom shakes her head. "No, I don't think so. That man was many things and religious was not one of them."

"So Dad brought back you and Noah," I say, thinking through everything. "Who brought back the redhead, and the blond guy? Was it Grandpa Redwood?"

"Maybe," my mom says. "I don't know why he'd do it. He knew what we'd become. Maybe he didn't care."

"Why did Jonathan do it, though?" Noah suddenly asks. "His dad must have told him how it was gonna work. He knew it was gonna be hard for us, right?"

I glance at Noah and he has his bottom lip tucked between his teeth. His jaw is tense.

"Jonathan told me right after I was reanimated that he panicked," Mom says. "That he didn't know what he would do without me. He said he looked at Meka and couldn't stand to let her be without me. I never questioned it. We've had so much more time together because of what he did but—"

"But?" I ask. Something in me expects that there has always been a "but." Did she regret it? The way she has to live now, is it too much? Too difficult?

"But," my mom continues, "Jonathan made the choice for me." Mom lets her gaze move to the floor. "He loves me more than he loves anything besides Meka. He did what he thought was best at the time but that doesn't change the fact that I didn't have a say."

"Like my mom," Noah says. "She made that choice for me too."

My mom nods. She and Noah share something I can barely understand. I wish I could take away their hurt and confusion.

"Would you have made a different choice?" I ask. "If you knew and you had a say, would you have let him?"

My mom grasps my hand and holds it over her heart. A heart that no longer beats. "I wouldn't change anything about what happened. All I'm saying is that I can make my own choices now."

I put my arms around her and hug her tight. So tight I worry I might be hurting her and when I'm reminded that she can't feel a thing, I squeeze tighter.

From down the hall there is a small thud. I freeze. Noah steps toward the door and listens.

"What was that?" I whisper.

Noah peers down the hall. The heat is kicking on and the pipes begin their annoying percussion of knocks and bangs, but between the familiar sounds of the ancient heating system is something else.

Tap. Tap. Tap.

I look around the room for something to use as a weapon.

I reach for the floor lamp in the corner, but Noah puts his hand on my arm and shakes his head no.

Tap. Tap. Tap.

"I'll go out there first," Noah says.

"What?" I ask. "Whoever it is might attack you!"

"Whoever it is can't hurt me," Noah says. He holds up his newly attached hand and wiggles his fingers.

"They can't *kill* you," Mom says. "And you can't feel pain but that doesn't mean they can't do serious damage. Enough to make your existence unbearable."

Tap. Tap. Tap.

"You think it's those weirdos again?" I ask, my voice barely audible.

"I don't know," my mom says. "They have the book. They have Jonathan. Why come back here?"

Noah steps out into the hall and my mom and I follow close behind him. The tapping noise is louder and more frantic now. My heart is beating so hard I worry everyone can hear it.

Tap. Tap. Tap. Tap. Tap. Tap.

We ease onto the stairs and they groan under our collective weight. The tapping continues.

"On three," Noah says.

"On three what?" I ask.

"One. Two. Three!" Noah says with no other instructions. He launches himself off the step and lands with a crash at the bottom. He rolls on the floor, then pops up with his fists raised in front of him. He looks down the entry hall toward the back door.

I scramble down after him, afraid of what I might see or who else might be down there but I'm not about to let him face

232

whatever it is alone. My mom rushes down and stands beside me. The hallway is empty.

"You good?" I ask, trying to get a good look at Noah.

"Yeah," he says, avoiding my gaze. The hot heat of embarrassment wafts off him.

I touch his arm. "That was . . . special."

Noah presses his mouth into a tight line.

Tap. Tap. Tap. Tap. Tap. Tap.

The sound is coming from the little window to the right of the back door. On the platform my dad had built for his feathered friends sits the biggest raven I've ever seen. It's tapping its beak so hard against the glass I think it might break.

"It's a bird," Noah says, exhaling. "I almost had a heart attack. If I even could have a heart attack."

He glances at my mom, who solemnly shakes her head no.

The bird continues rapping at the window and even though I now know it's a bird and not some weird undead corpse coming to kill us all, it doesn't make me feel any better.

"Why is it doing that?" I ask.

"Maybe it's one of your dad's regulars," my mom says.

The tapping continues. Maybe it's one of the birds my dad feeds. Maybe it came to eat or maybe it came to leave him a trinket. Still . . .

I walk toward the little window. The raven is situated on the lip of the perch. It's so dark outside, the bird looks like a shadow, aside from the eyes . . . the milky-white eyes. I had jokingly called the ravens "beady-eyed" one time and I thought my dad was gonna cuss me out. I apologized immediately and he told me it was okay, that the ravens did in fact have beady eyes—black as night and shiny like onyx. But not this one, apparently. Its eyes are the only part of it I can see clearly and they are a cloudy white with a slightly bluish hue to them. They are not the shining eyes of a living thing—they are the eyes of something that has been dead for a good long while.

CHAPTER 20

CASTLES IN NEW YORK

"Mom," I say, parsing out my breaths in quick puffs to keep myself from hyperventilating. "I think it's reanimated."

Mom takes a tentative step toward the little window, where the raven is still tapping on the glass. "I—I don't think so," she stammers. "No. That can't be."

"There was something about reanimating animals in those notes we found," Noah says.

Images of the strange book flood my mind. I had seen Noah's name there alongside my mom's and there had been something else. The small figure of a bird . . . a raven.

I go to the window and flip the latch, sliding the pane up. The bird hops onto the inner ledge and stands there, its head tilted to one side. Tufts of black feathers are missing from its chest and the ribs beneath are visible through tears in the gray-colored flesh. Something small and white and wriggling falls off and lands on the floor.

"What the hell?" my mom whispers.

Another white object no bigger than a grain of rice falls to the floor and begins to inch its way toward the kitchen. It's a maggot, and the crow's broken chest is filled with them. The wriggling creatures have already made meals of the rotting organs and they continue to fall, plump and squirming, onto the floor in front of us.

"Did Dad do this?" I ask. It's the only thing that makes sense.

"Why would he?" Noah asks. "What's the—" He stops short as he approaches the bird. "There's something on its leg."

I step closer, crushing a few of the maggots under my shoe. Affixed to the bird's leg is a small cylindrical tube about the size of a crayon. I reach for it and the bird pecks the back of my hand.

"Shit," I say. "He's vicious."

Noah steps in and removes the little cylinder from the bird's leg. It pecks him too. Takes a chunk right off the back of his hand but he only gives me a little smile and hands me the makeshift container.

It's made from the barrel of a stick pen that's been broken in half and sealed on the open end with tape.

"What is it?" my mom asks.

I give it a shake. "There's something inside."

Peeling back the tape, I tip the contents into my hand. It's a rolled-up piece of paper. As I unroll it, my heart begins to race. It's a note.

I read it aloud. *"Beware; for I am fearless, and therefore powerful."*

"What's that mean?" Noah asks.

The raven squawks, then lowers its head. The white of its cervical vertebrae show through a patch of open skin and missing feathers. A grumbling noise erupts from its chest and then . . . it speaks. The same not-quite-human voice that had come from the raven by the falls echoes through the hall.

"Roscoe." It pecks at the few remnants of seeds that lie on the ledge but doesn't eat them. "Roscoe," it repeats.

Noah steps back, his mouth hanging open. "Everybody heard that, right?"

I nod. So does my mom.

"They can do that," I say, recalling what my dad told me.

"Who the hell is Roscoe?" Noah asks.

"No idea," I say.

My mom takes the paper from me. "Meka, this is your dad's handwriting."

My dad had sent the bird. There's no other explanation and I suddenly feel like I'm running out of time, like maybe it's already too late to save him.

"Google it," Noah says.

I go into the office and sit down at the desk. I quickly type the quote into the search bar and the results come up immediately. I'd worried it would be some obscure thing that we'd have to go searching for but it's not.

"It's from *Frankenstein*," I say as I look over the results. "Except for the Roscoe part. The rest is from the book."

Mom stares down at the screen, the pale light illuminating her worried face. Her eyes are searching and glassy, like she's on the verge of tears.

"Have you ever read *Frankenstein*?" my mom asks.

Noah and I both nod. "We read it for English last year," I say. "We watched a movie too. The one from the thirties."

Mom sighs. "I don't know how that helps us."

Noah leans over me and types "Frankenstein Roscoe" into the search bar. The only thing that comes up is some novel written by an author with the last name Roscoe but nothing about the quote.

I huff and shove the keyboard away from me. "What do we do?"

Mom paces in front of the desk as Noah gently rests his hands on my shoulders.

"What do we know?" Noah asks. "Let's think about this."

"Those people, those other reanimates, have my dad," I say. "We know that. And now they have the book, too."

"But they can't use it without him," Mom says. "They can't even really see it. They need him. At least, they need someone *like* him."

I look down at my own hands. I'm like him. I'm like him and everyone before him.

"We don't let them get anywhere near Meka," Noah says. "We do whatever we need to do to keep that from happening."

My mom gives a firm nod. "Meka, baby, google 'Roscoe' again but put 'New York' after it."

"It's a place?" I ask.

She nods. "I'm pretty sure it is. Sounds familiar but I can't think straight."

I do as she says and a few minutes later I'm knee-deep in fishing and camping accommodations for Roscoe, New York. "It's all outdoor activities and stuff. Nothing useful—" I stop short. As I'm scrolling through the page, there's a small picture of what looks like a castle. I click on the photo. "Dundas Castle," I say. "A castle? In New York?"

"There's a few actual castles upstate," my mom says as she comes back around the desk to stare at the screen. "Rich folks love to build outlandish things, don't they? People also use them as wedding venues, retreat locations, stuff like that." She sighs. "It's pretty but I don't see how it helps us."

Noah points to a small caption on the screen. "It says exterior shots of the castle in the 1931 movie *Frankenstein* were filmed there."

My heart ticks up. "That's gotta be the connection, right? That has to be what Dad was talking about, right?" The word "castle" is highlighted and appears to link to an external source. I click it to see if there is any more information and am taken to a page about the actual Frankenstein's castle in Germany. "Wait," I say, confused. "This says *actual* castle. Frankenstein was real?"

"No," my mom says. "It's made up. Like Dracula or the Wolf Man. But it looks like this castle in Germany was the inspiration for it."

I scroll down the page and read about the history of the real Frankenstein's castle. "It says Mary Shelley may have known about the legends of the castle which included rumors of a mad scientist who lived there at some point. It even says she might have visited it in person." I continue reading, when about halfway down the page I stop. There is a name I recognize but it takes me a second to remember where I'd seen it before. When I finally put it together, I stand up, pushing my chair back.

"What?" Mom asks. "What is it?"

"Look," I say. "That name, Johann Konrad Dippel, his name was in the book."

My mom cranes her neck to read the information on the screen. "He's one of the reanimated?"

"His name was at the beginning of the book, not the end like all the others," I say. "Like, maybe he wrote it?" I lean over the computer, reading the rest of the information. "He was an alchemist, and he was born in the real Frankenstein's castle in Germany. It says he may have been the inspiration for Doctor Frankenstein in Mary Shelley's novel."

"Wait," Noah says. "The monster was a doctor?"

"Did you even pay attention in class?" I ask.

"I was too busy paying attention to you," Noah says.

Heat rushes to my face. This is not the time or place but damn.

"Frankenstein is the doctor, not the monster," I say.

"Oh, okay," Noah says. "That makes way more sense. But I'm still confused. What does that have to do with you or where your dad is?"

"One thing's clear," I say. "My dad is trying to tell us where he is. The quote is from *Frankenstein* and this place, this Dundas Castle, is a dead ringer for the actual location. This has to be where my dad is."

"Why not just send us the address?" Noah asks. "Why all the codes?"

"Maybe he was worried he'd get caught," my mom offers. "Maybe he doesn't know the actual address."

"It doesn't matter," I say. "We know and now we can go get him."

"Hold on," Noah says. "We're just gonna gloss over the fact that *Frankenstein* is like a fictional version of your actual family. The guy who inspired that story has his name in a book you own—that's not weird to you?"

"Everybody needs a mascot," my mom says. "Even a group of reanimated dead people, apparently."

I take out my phone and type "Roscoe NY" into the maps app. "We're only about two hours away. We gotta go. We have to get him."

Mom and Noah exchange glances, then my mom grabs her purse off the little table in the hallway and slings it over her shoulder.

"Wait," Noah says. "Should we bring a weapon?"

"Like what?" Mom asks.

"Maybe like a chain saw or something?" Noah suggests.

"You think I have a chain saw just lying around?" Mom asks.

"I don't know," Noah says. "Maybe? I thought maybe Mr. Redwood—"

Mom huffs out a laugh. "Baby, that man couldn't wield a chain saw if his life depended on it."

She heads out the back door and Noah hangs back as I shrug into a thick sweater and try to pretend like I'm not scared out of my mind.

"Ready?" I ask.

I grab Noah's hand and step toward the back door but Noah stops me.

"What's wrong?" I ask.

"Nothing," Noah says. "Well, maybe everything, right?"

I squeeze his hand. "This whole situation is like something out of a really bad movie."

He nods. "I know we're in a rush, but I just need a second to catch my breath." He frowns. "Not literally but you get what I mean."

I run my hand up Noah's arm and my fingers brush against the threads holding his right hand to his wrist. The thread is already showing through the mortuary wax. The skin is stretched apart and the inner pieces of severed muscle are visible. The fingertips of his hand are slightly lower, like the internal sutures are loosening. A twinge of guilt ripples through me.

"We gotta find a better way to keep this attached," I say. "It'll fall off if we don't fix it."

Noah looks at his wrist, then quickly readjusts the sleeve of his jacket, hiding the wound. He shakes his head. "I don't want to talk about it," he says. There is something in his tone, a profound sadness that echoes through.

I lean in and press my lips to his. His skin is cold to the touch. He smells like Smithfield's. I hate that I notice all these little details but I remind myself that I don't care about any of it. I kiss him deeply, madly, like I'm gonna lose him if I stop, like I already have. When he pulls away from me, I'm crying. He wipes my face with his hands and pulls me to him.

"I love you," I say to him.

I don't know why I had put off saying it. I think about all the opportunities I'd had to tell him how much I care about him and didn't because I just *knew* we had tomorrow or the day after or the day after that. It felt like we would always have time but as it turned out, we didn't have any time at all.

"I love you too," he says. "I should have said it sooner."

"Me too," I say.

Noah sighs and holds me close. "Promise me something."

"Anything," I say.

"Promise me that no matter what happens, you'll keep going."

I stare into his big brown eyes that suddenly seem sad. "What do you mean?" I ask.

Noah presses his mouth in a hard line. "Just keep going," he says. "If something happens to me, you have to save yourself, you have to help your dad."

"Noah, I—"

Noah shakes his head and I quiet myself.

"Just promise me," he says.

"I promise."

The sky is still dark as we start the drive south to Roscoe. The roads that wind out of Ithaca are slick with snow and it slows our pace when my mom steers us up the rolling hills and through the endlessly dark woodland. People think of New York and they think of the city, the bright lights, the impossible number of people jammed into every available space, but outside the city there are forests as old as the Amazon, thousands of miles of wilderness sheltering ground that existed before dinosaurs walked the earth. Monsters lurk here and I wonder if, in some strange way, my mom and Noah are now counted among them.

As my mom follows the GPS to Roscoe, the shadowy forms of tree-covered hillsides go by in a blur. The interior of the car is warm and my mom's got the radio on. Noah is stretched out across the back seat.

"You want me to drive?" I ask.

Mom laughs lightly. "No, baby. I'm trying to get to where we're going as intact as possible."

"My driving really that bad?" I know it is. I just don't like hearing it.

Mom doesn't say anything. She just keeps her eyes forward and smiles. That's all the confirmation I need really. I yawn and my eyelids feel like they might close on their own.

She sighs and reaches over to pat my leg. "Try to get some rest. I'll wake you up when we're closer."

I don't want to go to sleep. The familiar fear of sleeping creeps back in. I'd almost been able to put it completely out of my mind with everything else going on but now, as sleep descends, I almost don't care if the nightmare memory will replay itself. I'm so tired.

Sleep consumes me and I fall into its gaping maw, my heart racing, my chest tight. I'm in the car. My mother is looking at me in the rearview mirror. The music plays on the radio. I see the strange man in front of the car, his face a terrible blur like too many watercolors mixed together. Suddenly, everything changes. I am in the unfamiliar prep room and my dad is conducting his ritual. The book in his hands, the same one I'd found in Grandpa Redwood's coffin, glows green. My mother's body lies prone in front of him. Her eyes are open but she's not alive. Tears stream down my dad's face as he dips the tip of some kind of pen or quill into the trail of blood that has dripped out of my mom's mouth and collected on the table beneath her head. I stare in abject horror as my dad uses the blood to write something in the book. Smoke billows all around us as he takes a deep, wavering breath and recites an incantation, reading it directly from the book. My head pounds as that strange sensation of buzzing rattles my brain. My hands feel like they are on fire. I cry out as my dad continues to speak.

"Alive. Alive. Alive!" His voice is like a siren, and it splits the air around us.

The muscles in my hands seize involuntarily as I curl my fingers around my mom's bare ankles. The electric shocks reverse stream and instead of traveling up my arms, they shoot out of me and into her. Her body jolts violently—once, twice, three times. It's as if she's being electrocuted. Her hands ball into fists and her mouth opens so wide I think her jaw might come unhinged. Her body jerks upright and now she's sitting on the prep table. She grabs me by the shoulders, digging her bloody fingertips into my skin.

"Let me go," she says in a voice so mournful, so filled with sorrow and agony that tears well in my eyes and then spill down my cheeks. "Meka," she gasps. "Let me go."

CHAPTER 21

THE MORE DEAD, THE MERRIER

I awaken with a start. Noah's hands are on my shoulders and my mom is staring at me from the driver's seat.

"You were dreaming," she says quietly.

I was remembering, wasn't I? Isn't that what I'd come to realize? But if that's true, had I been more than just a witness to my mom's reanimation?

I glance back at Noah, who lowers his gaze. My face is wet with tears. Mom reaches over and puts her hand on my leg but says nothing. I wipe my face, a little embarrassed.

"We're here," my mom says.

I check the time on the dashboard. It's just after 5 AM. The sun hasn't come up yet but the sky is starting to warm.

"What's the plan?" Noah asks. "Is this castle in town?"

"It's about twenty minutes outside Roscoe," my mom says. "We should go straight there but we'll have to keep out of sight.

I'm worried that if anyone sees us coming, they'll hurt Jonathan."
She grips the steering wheel. "I can't let that happen."

"We won't," I say. "But we can't just drive up to the castle.
We'll have to park somewhere and walk to it."

"Is that sweater going to keep you warm enough?" my mom
asks.

I nod. "I'll be fine."

Mom looks doubtful but doesn't protest as she steers us through
the little town of Roscoe. It reminds me of a miniaturized version
of Ithaca. It's surrounded by rolling hills on all sides and the town
itself is nestled in among the trees. We pass what has to be the
town's only main street. It's lined with little shops but within a
few seconds, that's all behind us and the road winds into the thickly
forested outskirts.

The trees crowd the road, their leafless branches swaying in a
stiff breeze. Twenty minutes later Mom pulls into a rest stop where
only a single other car is parked.

"I think we can make it from here," Mom says. "It'll take us
maybe thirty minutes to get to the castle on foot."

"What do we do when we get there?" Noah asks.

"We should probably watch for a little bit, right?" I ask.
"See if anybody is going in and out. Even if we find the castle,
that doesn't mean we know what's going on inside or where
Dad is."

"If he's for sure in there," Noah adds.

Mom and I both look at him.

"Sorry," Noah says. "I'm not trying to upset you, but we really
don't know what we're getting into here. We have the note but
maybe it was a trick? Maybe these people want us to come here

so they can finish what they started." He holds up his hand and I can see the stitches holding his wrist to his arm.

"He's right," my mom says. "You two should stay here. I can go up there by myself and look around."

A sudden stab of panic ripples through me. "No. We're not splitting up. I'm not letting you go up there alone." I zip up my sweater and make sure it's snug around my neck. "We do this together or we don't do it at all."

"Meka," my mom says. "Baby. You have to let me go."

The words from the dream replay in my mind. *Let me go.*

"No, I don't," I say. I open the door and get out before she can say anything else.

Noah gets out and puts his arm around me.

"I have a really bad feeling about this," he says.

So do I but I don't want to say it out loud. My mom joins us and I slip my hand into hers.

"Okay," she says. "Keys for the car are in the visor in case any of us need to make a break for it. We try to stick together but if I tell either of you to leave, just do it."

I nod but I know I'm not leaving her or Noah behind for any reason. I think she knows it, too, because she shakes her head and mumbles something under her breath about me being hardheaded.

A blanket of crisp white snow covers the trail leading away from the rest stop. My shoes are laced tight but cold is creeping in, numbing my feet. Shoving my hands in my pockets as the wind whips my face, I keep my head down and follow my mom into the increasingly crowded forest. The trees offer some cover once we're far enough in so that the branches are blotting out the early skylight. Noah trudges up beside me and loops his arm through mine.

"You okay?" he asks.

"No," I say honestly. "You?"

Noah grins and to my horror the mortuary wax plugging the defect in his cheek lifts at the edge, exposing the bone underneath. I reach out and press it flat.

"It's the cold," I say to him. "The wax isn't meant for these kinds of temperatures. It's gonna keep lifting until we're somewhere a little warmer."

"Maybe I should just let it fall off," Noah says. "It'd be easier."

Easier for him, maybe, but would he be able to blend in with a huge hole in the side of his face? Does he even want to blend in? Everybody who knew him thinks he's dead so it's not like he can go for a walk around town or be seen anywhere in public. The more I think about it, the more I wonder what our life will be like. *Our life.* I guess I've made the decision to walk with him down whatever path he wants to go.

"Maybe another twenty minutes walking," my mom says.

Might as well be an hour. I can't feel my face anymore.

When we arrive at the end of the trail, the castle still isn't visible but I feel like I can sense it just beyond the crest of the driveway. This place was designed to keep prying eyes off it.

There's a gate closing off the long stretch of driveway and there are several signs affixed to it. One reads No Trespassing, Violators Subject to Prosecution. Another reads Private Property, Keep Out. Smaller laminated papers describe construction permitting and dates for town hall meetings that have come and gone years ago. A metal pole with a busted-up control panel sits to the right of the gate.

"Is there anybody even in here?" I ask.

There is suddenly a sound like something heavy approaching

from behind us. I grab my mom by the arm and rush her off to the side of the gate where a low brick wall stands. Noah joins us and we duck behind the wall. The noise is louder now. I peer around the wall just as a snowcat with a bright orange cabin emerges from another trailhead. It shudders up to the gate and rolls to a stop. The door opens and someone gets out. They're covered head to toe in cold weather gear—a hooded puffer jacket, boots, and snow goggles. Noah grips my arm.

The person strides up to the gate and flips open the control panel, punching in some kind of code. The gate rolls open, groaning in protest as the stranger gets back in and steers the snowcat through the open gate. As it closes behind them, I collapse against the brick wall.

"So, there are definitely people inside," I say. "We can't just walk in without being seen."

"And what do we even do when we're inside?" Noah asks in a hush. "We don't know the layout or if your dad is even here."

He's right but I can't think that far ahead. Our best option is to check for him here. If he's been moved or worse—a shudder runs through me—then we'll think about plan B or C or D.

I stand and brush the snow off me but my body is shivering violently. I have to grit my teeth to keep them from clacking together. Noah puts his arms around me but it's like being embraced by a cold wind. He takes off his coat and puts it around me.

"I don't even know why I'm wearing a coat," he says. "I should have put this on you sooner. Sorry."

The extra layer helps but only a little. I huff into the palms of my hands, trying to breathe life back into my numb flesh. I wonder if this is how Noah and my mom feel all the time—stiff and cold. I push that thought away immediately.

"Let's see if we can get through the fence," my mom says. "We can't go through the front gate without a code anyway."

Following her around to the right of the drive, we walk along the perimeter of a neglected fence until we find a break in it, a place where the metal has been warped by time or disuse and we squeeze through. The inner courtyard is overrun with fir trees that stretch up to the sky. It's like a nightmare version of a Christmas tree farm. The trees are huge and their branches are so intertwined in some spots we have to take detours around them. For a minute we lose our bearing, and I can't tell if we're headed toward the driveway or back toward the fence.

"Here," Noah whispers suddenly. "Come look at this."

There is a small gap in the trees. Through it, the castle finally comes into view. It's less like a castle and more like a mansion made to resemble a castle. There are turrets and a covered portico but some of the windows are boarded up or completely broken out. It looks like it was a fancy place once—a long, long time ago. It's vaguely familiar. Maybe I had some image of it from the *Frankenstein* movie but I'm still unsure. Dilapidated as it is, the snowcat and two other vehicles are parked out front in the circular drive. Shadows move behind the few intact windows on the lower floor.

"We should wait till it's dark to go in," Mom says.

"She's not gonna last that long," Noah says, glancing at me.

He's right. The numbness is spreading through my body like ice in my veins. I'll be a popsicle before nightfall. Mom glances back in the direction of the trail.

"No," I say. "I—I'm not go—going back to the car."

"I'm not asking you," my mom says. "I'm telling you that—"

"Look," Noah says suddenly.

From the lower level of the castle, a door opens and a tall older woman steps out. She has a shock of red hair flecked with gray spilling over her shoulders. The rest of her is draped in something similar to the robe I found in my father's belongings.

"It's the redhead," I whisper. "That was her picture we found in Dad's closet."

My mom nods. "Camille Phelps."

Camille stands still in the frigid air, her head moving slowly from side to side, like she's looking for something. Suddenly, a man in a heavy coat emerges from behind her. He shoves her roughly as he goes past.

"Excuse you!" Camille shouts at him.

The man doesn't even turn around. He stomps through the snow toward the snowcat.

"Where the hell are you going?" Camille asks.

"The package is ready for transport," he responds. "Everything's almost ready so I'll go get it and bring it back."

"Well, hurry up," Camille says. "I want to get started."

The man moves around to the side of the castle.

"I'm going with you," Camille says. "Make sure you don't screw this up for me."

"No," the man responds. His tone is harsh, like he's annoyed with her. "I don't want your company and besides—" He stops short, looking around. "Where are the gas cans I left over here?"

A smile spreads across Camille's face. She saunters up to him, limping a little, leaving the door behind her open a crack. "Wouldn't you like to know?"

"I don't have time for games," the man says. "Tell me where they are right now or—"

"Or what?" Camille asks. "What will you do?"

The man looks at her in a way that makes me scared for her but she doesn't budge.

"Tell me I can go with you and I'll show you where the gas is," she says.

The man grumbles something I can't quite make out and then Camille leads him around the side of the building and out of sight.

My mom stands up and grabs me by the arm. "Come on," she whispers.

"Where are we going?" I ask.

"Did you see Camille?" Mom asks. "She didn't even have a coat on. That means it's probably warm inside."

"It means she doesn't need it," Noah says. "The paper said she died, remember? She's reanimated."

We sit in silence for a few seconds.

"Regardless," Mom says. "We need to get Meka inside."

"They'll see us," Noah counters.

"Just come on," my mom says.

She pulls me through the trees and out into the open area in front of the castle. The wind whips up once we're out of the shelter of the trees. Tears sting my eyes as we move toward the door Camille had come out of. We duck inside and press ourselves against the wall as Camille's voice returns outside. My heart leaps into my throat. She's arguing with the man again and then the engine of the snowcat turns over and their voices are drowned out. A moment later the rumble of the engine dissipates, and I breathe deep.

"Look at this place," Noah whispers as he looks around.

We are in a narrow hallway with windows on one side and doors on the other. It's cold in here but better than being outside. Lights in decorative sconces line the hall. The place is wired for electricity and apparently, it's on and working. There is a strong musty smell in the air, like damp earth and smoke mingled together.

A murmur of voices sounds from somewhere behind us. The sound moves closer and panic grips me like a vise. I rush toward the closest door only to find it locked. Noah stumbles toward the next one and it opens for him. We duck inside and find it filled with dusty furniture and moldering boxes. We shut the door and lean against it as the voices move down the hall and past the door. After a moment, they're gone, and I collapse onto the floor.

"How many people do you think that was?" Noah asks.

"Two? Maybe three?" I say. "That's what it sounded like. I'm not really sure." I rub my legs trying to push some feeling back into them.

"What do we do now?" Noah asks. "Where do we even start?"

Mom squeezes her eyes shut and rubs her temple. "Let me think." She paces back and forth in front of the door as Noah crouches next to me. "We can't stay here," she says. "We should keep moving. Maybe we should follow the people who just went by."

"I don't like this," Noah says.

I take out my phone and google Dundas Castle, New York. Pictures of the exterior come up. I erase my search and start over. I tap in Dundas Castle blueprint. A schematic of the interior of the castle pops up. I show it to my mom and Noah.

"I think we came in here," I say, pointing to a doorway marked Carriage Entryway. "The castle is built in an L shape with a square inner courtyard. If we're here, the people who passed by us are headed toward"—I glance at the blueprint again—"the remains of the spa and bath."

"The bath?" Noah whispers, confused.

"It's probably underground," I say as I study the picture. "It says 'sublevel.'" A little circle appears on my screen, then all my bars disappear, replaced by the SOS symbol. "The signal's gone." It feels like we are out of choices and maybe out of time. I get to my feet and go to the door. "We follow those voices to see if Dad is with them," I say. "We get him and then we make a break for it. We get back to the car and get away from here."

My mom gives me a quick nod and Noah does the same but this won't work. The plan is simple enough—get Dad and get out. Nothing we've tried to do so far has gone to plan and something tells me this won't be any different.

I press my ear to the door and listen. There's only a low murmur but I can't tell exactly where it's coming from. After a moment, I pull the door open and peer out into the hallway. It's empty so I slip out and turn left, following the path of the people who came by just a few minutes before and heading in the direction of the sublevel. Mom and Noah stay right behind me.

Pushing down the hall there's a sharp right turn. The hallway terminates in a narrow wooden door. There are no other passages or entryways in this length of hallway so the other people must have gone through this door. I don't hesitate. I put my hand on the handle and push it open. A spiral staircase twists down into the earth like a corkscrew. Noah peers over the rail.

"What the hell," he says under his breath. "We gotta go down there?"

I take his hand and hold it tight. "Just keep moving," I say.

I take the stairs and as we descend the cold dissipates, replaced with a warmth that at first feels like heaven compared to the bitter cold outside. But as the staircase loops over on itself again and again, the heat becomes stifling. I shrug out of Noah's coat and hand it back to him, all the while moving deeper into the dark below. By the time we reach the bottom, my back is sweaty and I pull the neck of my sweater open to try and circulate some of the hot air.

"Is this hell?" I ask as Noah joins me at the bottom. "It's hot as shit down here."

We've entered another hallway, at the end of which is a small arched doorway. It's damp and it smells even worse down here than it had above. The stones that make up the floor are so worn, there's a slope in the center of the hall where water has collected.

A noise wafts through the tunnel—the murmur of voices.

"Listen," I whisper.

Moving toward the archway, my heart beats wildly as panic invades every part of me. I focus on my breathing, try to calm myself. When I reach the opening, I peer inside.

A room is situated another full floor below us. It's surrounded on all four sides by towering marble columns. There is a raised platform in the middle. The floor around it is tiled in a black-and-white checked pattern. The air is thick with a familiar smoky smell, the scent from my dad's strange robe. I don't see anyone but I can hear voices from somewhere below.

Whatever plan I'd had about bursting into a room, grabbing my dad, and fleeing into the snowy woods leaves my mind as I look into the space below. Everything I see here makes me believe more than ever that none of us have any idea what we're walking into.

And that there may be no walking away from this at all.

Suddenly, from somewhere behind us, there is the sound of footsteps. I lurch forward and trip down the stairs that lead to the room below. Noah steps on the back of my heel as we emerge in the strange space. The columns holding up the ceiling are massive and between each of them is a curved arch. Torches light the dank space but the shadows are deep.

The footsteps are closer now and my mom's eyes grow wide in the dark. I grab her hand and we rush forward, skirting the platform in the center of the room and ducking behind what can only be described as an altar—a large rectangular stone draped in cloths and topped with small bowls and lit candles. We press ourselves behind it, and Noah barely manages to join us as the other people enter the space.

"Everyone's here?" asks a voice, the same man's voice who had been looking for the gas cans earlier. He grunts and then sighs heavily. There's a thud, like he's just set something heavy on the floor.

"No," Camille says. "Roger and Morris aren't back yet. They have the book, though."

I slide down the back side of the altar, getting as close to the ground as I can manage, before shimmying my way to the edge so that I can peer around the side. Camille and the man we'd seen outside are standing near the platform in the center of the room and it takes everything in me not to scream when I see what they've brought with them. On the platform, which had been completely empty when we rushed past it, now lies the body of a young woman.

CHAPTER 22

SPARE PARTS

The dead woman is draped in a sheet and from the looks of it has been deceased for maybe a day or so. When they adjust her position on the platform, there's no give. They've placed her on her back and the redhead delicately arranges the woman's long hair around her shoulders. My stomach turns over.

"Plucked her right out of that camp in Ithaca," Camille says.

"We've gotten a few from there," the man says. "We'll arouse suspicion if we get them from the same place over and over."

"Who even cares?" Camille asks. "No one's going to come looking for her. Nobody cares about her. It's perfect." There's a tone of excitement in her voice that makes me nervous. She traces her fingers over the outline of the woman's leg under the sheet. "I'm lucky we found one so young. The parts will last longer."

The man gives a huff and the two of them exit the room through a door to the left of the altar. I quickly stand and rush to the platform. The woman is probably in her twenties. Her eyes are closed and her hands lie at her sides. Her long hair is flecked with bits of leaves and her skin is tanned like she's spent most of her days out in the sun.

My mom steps to the platform. "What is going on here?" she asks. "What are they doing with her?"

I don't know for sure but I can guess. "Camille said the parts will last longer." Images of the blond man flash in my mind. He was wearing another person's arm as his own. "They're going to use her for parts."

"Parts?" Noah asks.

My mom looks like she'd be sick if she could.

Noah approaches us but doesn't come too close to the girl. "It's—it's not right. They can't do this . . . can they?"

"They already have," Mom whispers. "Who knows how many times."

Suddenly there is the sound of a door opening. My mom and Noah scramble back behind the altar but I get tangled up in my own steps and have to duck behind one of the massive stone pillars. Noah reaches for me but my mom pulls him down to the ground. I press my back to the pillar as footsteps enter the room. I hold my breath and peer around.

Four people come into the chamber, all of them in hooded black robes except one . . . my dad. As they shove him forward the torchlight illuminates his broken, bloodied face. His lip is split open and he has a black eye. The people position themselves around the woman on the raised platform. My dad stands at her head and looks down at her.

"What is this?" he asks. His voice is taut with fear.

"Oh, come now, Jonathan," Camille says from beneath her cloak. "Don't be dense."

My dad looks at her and she lifts her gaze to meet his. Her face is drawn tight, her lips pursed.

"Camille," my dad says.

Camille smiles but there's a strange glassy look in her eyes. "We go way back, Jonathan. Took you a moment to place me, though, didn't it?"

"You died when I was a kid," my dad says. "You shouldn't be here."

"But I am," Camille says. "Thanks to your dear old dad."

My dad blinks repeatedly. "My father."

"Bingo!" Camille's voice rings out like a maniacal bell. "But he's dead and buried, so now it's you in his place." She looks him over from head to foot. "Pathetic."

"Whatever it is you want, I'm not going to participate," my dad says. "I am not my father."

I'm a little taken aback. He never talks like that to anyone.

Camille's face twists up and she's about to say something else when another one of their order touches her shoulder.

"Not now," the man says to her.

Camille jerks away from him. "Get off me, Roger. Morris got his arm fixed! It's my turn!" She pulls her cloak away from her body, revealing her badly mangled right leg. The muscles and even some of her bone are visible through the torn flesh. "No more patch jobs!" she yells. "Take off her leg"—she pokes the dead woman on the table—"and put it on me."

My dad gasps and so do I. I clap my hand over my mouth and press myself against the pillar.

Please don't see me.

"You don't need me to do that," my dad says. "Patch yourself up on your own."

Camille grips the edge of the platform so hard I think it might break. "The patch jobs never last because we're using dead flesh." She sticks out her neck and tilts her head like she doesn't understand how my dad doesn't get what she's trying to say. "The woman has to be reanimated first. Regular body parts don't last long enough."

My dad looks horrified. "You want me to reanimate her just so you can have her leg?"

Camille rolls her eyes. "What do you want? Money? We can arrange something."

"Is that what my father did?" Dad looks absolutely disgusted. "He took your bribes?"

Camille grins. "He was paid handsomely for his work. He never did this sort of thing, though. Frankly, we hadn't thought that far ahead. We were content to use the parts from people off the street. There were always fresh supplies and really, who would miss them?" Camille looks down at the woman's body. "We'll destroy what's left of her when we're done."

"Reanimated flesh is dead too," my dad says. "That's the whole reason you have to take care of your bodies."

"Reanimated flesh is more durable," Roger says. "Our experiences have shown this to be a fact."

"And I don't have the privilege of living with Ithaca's most deft mortician, like your pretty little wife, do I?" Camille asks, a ring of sarcasm echoing through her angry words. "Must be wonderful to have every little injury fixed right on the spot."

"But we're correcting that problem, aren't we, Jonathan?" Roger asks. "You've forgotten where you belong. A reanimator's place is here with us. But you've always known that, haven't you? You always knew this day would come."

"I'm not staying here," my dad says. "I can't."

"It's not a request," answers another hooded man.

"Langan, please," Dad says to him. "We don't have to continue this way."

Langan, the man from the snowcat, shakes his head. "It's too late for all of that. I was reanimated before you were even born. Your father brought me back and he was agreeable to everything we asked of him. He lived a productive life, you can too."

"My father was absent, uncaring, and cold," my dad snaps. "He chose this work over his family. I won't do that."

"We've recovered the book, Jonathan," Roger says. "Morris is preparing it right now. You'll stay with us, and you will dedicate your considerable skill to us and us alone."

Langan leans toward my dad. "You will do this or we will kill you and then we'll go get Meka. She can take your place."

My heart lurches in my chest.

"Leave her out of this!" my dad shouts.

"No," Camille says bluntly. "And now that we know what you've been up to maybe we should kill you regardless. I think Meka would make a wonderful servant."

My dad is trembling, his jaw clenched. My head spins. Dad is being forced to do this work but I can't understand it. These people are what—four or five strong? Why do they think they should control him? I'm missing something. I can feel it in my gut.

I silently move across the pillar, looking for my mom and Noah but they are still hidden behind the altar. The sound of a door opening again cuts through the room. Footsteps approach but these are different from the ones that had come before. They are heavy and each step sends a little tremor through the tiled floor. The reanimates fall silent as the footsteps echo in the room. The hair on the backs of my arms stands straight up. A pit forms in my stomach. It's like a sudden and terrible dread washes over me and I'm more afraid than I've been at any point until now. Trembling, I peer around the pillar in the direction of the altar. A figure comes into view.

Whoever it is is dressed like the others, draped in a thick black cloak, but I cannot see their face. They approach the altar and my heart trips into a furious rhythm. This person is well over six feet tall. Their shoulders are massive even under the flowing black robes. They stand still as a final hooded figure comes into the room holding the strange book we uncovered in Grandpa Redwood's coffin. I can see it clearly, but the person holding it can't. I can tell by the way their hand slides across the cover, finds the edge, then grips it tightly. The reanimates all bow their heads in the direction of the tall figure. My dad does not.

"We're ready to proceed," Camille says.

"No, we're not," my dad says.

Panic grips me. They've already threatened to kill him and I know that it's not an empty promise.

"Yes, we are!" Camille shouts. She grabs for the book, misses, then finds it after grasping at the air for a moment. She shoves it into my dad's hands. "Get to work."

My dad shakes his head as the book begins to glow softly. A jolt of electricity shoots through my palms and I have to bite my tongue to keep from crying out. I press myself into the pillar, struggling to keep sight of my dad.

"I won't do this," Dad says. "Reanimate her so you can take

her apart? Are you insane? All for what?" He sighs heavily. "Maybe if the upkeep of your body is too much of a burden, you shouldn't exist in the first place."

Camille glares at my dad. "You're a goddamned hypocrite!" she spews, with so much venom in her voice the words strike my dad like a fist. He steps back.

The tall figure at the altar doesn't move.

"I am a man who did something because I couldn't live with the grief," my dad says. "I did something to keep myself from the pain but the pain came anyway. It grows in me every day." His voice catches. "And it's your fault," he says, looking toward the robed figure. "If you had just let us go . . ."

He knows this person?

"I want to be what I was and I don't care what I have to do to get it!" Camille shouts. "You will do this for me! You will restore my body and you will do it as many times as I order it!"

My dad shakes his head. "I won't." He sets the book on the platform near the woman's head and he gently touches her forehead. "You will never be the way you were before. You don't even deserve to be. My father made a mistake reanimating all of you. You are abominations."

A pair of hands clamp down on my shoulders and suddenly I'm being pulled violently from my hiding spot. I'd been so focused on my dad I hadn't realized the last man to enter the room, the one who brought the book in, had moved around and spotted me. He wrenches my arm behind my back as he shoves me forward. The tall figure at the altar turns around but doesn't raise their head. I still can't see their face.

"Meka?" my dad asks, confused. "Morris, let her go right now!"

I shove Morris and he lets go of me. As I turn, I get a good look at him and realize he's the blond guy who'd been in the movie theater with me and Noah and who'd attacked us at home. I run to my dad and he puts his arms around me.

"What are you doing here?" he asks as he takes my face in his hands. "You shouldn't be here."

"Of course she should!" says Camille. She reaches out and grabs me by the wrist. Her icy cold fingers dig into my skin. "It's a family reunion, in more ways than one, isn't that right, Jonathan?"

I don't know what that's supposed to mean but I don't care. Camille reaches into the folds of her robe and produces a knife. She presses it to my throat and I almost stop breathing.

"Don't!" my dad yells. He steps forward but the other reanimates hold him back.

"I'll kill her," Camille growls. "And I will see to it that your other—what did you call us, abominations?—are unmade."

Unmade.

The look on my dad's face as Camille says these words scares me.

"Dad?" I ask, my throat tight.

"They cannot be unmade," my dad says.

"You think we don't know what is in that book?" Camille asks angrily. "You think your forebears didn't leave an out?"

"Nothing like that exists in the book," Dad says. "You can't even read it! You don't know what it contains! That power lies with me and me alone."

Camille grabs my hair and yanks my head back. "Not you alone," she shouts. "Isn't that right, Meka? You've got something special in you too, don't you?"

My dad steps toward me.

"We know all about that night in the hearse," Camille whispers against my ear. "We know what you did. We know why your funeral home has the reputation it does. *And* she's a mortuary assistant? It's perfect."

"I didn't do anything," I say, but as the words leave my mouth I know they are a lie.

Camille laughs. "And she didn't even know. But now, well, now things are different, aren't they, Meka?"

Dad takes another step closer.

"Get to work!" Camille shouts. "Or I'll cut her up so bad there won't be anything left to reanimate."

My dad seems to implode on himself. His shoulders roll forward and the light goes out of his eyes. I glance toward the altar and catch a glimpse of Noah's sneaker sticking out from behind it. Camille presses the knife into my skin and a warm rivulet of blood dribbles down the front of my sweater. For a second, I think it's all over and I wonder if my dad will bring me back. But the blood stops flowing after a few moments and the fear seated in my gut won't let me feel any pain.

"Last chance, Jonathan," Camille says.

"All right!" my dad screams. "I'll do it! Please. Please don't hurt her."

I try to push Camille's hand away from my neck but she's stronger than I would have imagined. A surge of adrenaline pumps through me. Time slows to a crawl.

The man called Langan approaches and drapes a black cloak

over my father's shoulders. My dad opens the book on the platform next to the dead woman. Morris produces a small brass orb, the top of which opens on a hinge. He lights whatever is inside and smoke begins to billow out in thick waves. The smell is the same one that clung to Grandpa Redwood's robe and it sparks something in my memory. I know what is about to happen and it has all happened before. Everything has come back around.

Langan hands my dad a quill that looks like it's been crafted from the feather of a raven. My dad's gaze flits to me and in his eyes there is a solemn sort of regret, and fear.

He pages through the book, mumbling an incantation under his breath. The smoke billows and begins to fill the room. The firelight cuts odd shapes in the haze. The tall person at the altar is still unmoving and silent, a statue.

The book glows green and my hands feel like they're burning. Camille grips me tight. She's saying the same words as my father. She knows the incantations, but she can't do this work herself. It's not just about the book, it's about my dad, it's about *us*.

My dad speaks the incantation faster and his voice gets louder. He's almost yelling now, and the green glow of the book illuminates his face and the body of the young woman at the same time. The haze of smoke makes everything blurry. The tall figure at the altar shifts their weight from one foot to the other, remaining silent. My dad presses the quill to the woman's shoulder and when he pulls it away, the tip is soaked in thick, red-black blood. He touches the pen to a blank page of the book.

A jolt of electricity cuts through the air and my vision goes white for a second. My head is buzzing and the shock of it makes me stumble back. I reach for the edge of the platform but accidentally touch the dead woman instead. She sits straight up. Her eyes pop open and the milky-white orbs dart around wildly. Her mouth opens and the smell of rot wafts out. Vomit makes its way up the back of my throat. The tall figure at the altar shifts. I think I hear whoever it is gasp.

There's a sudden yelp and when I blink, my vision clears. Noah is out from behind the altar and is grappling with Morris.

My dad slams the book shut and picks it up as my mom rushes to him. I remove my hand from the dead woman and she flops back onto the platform. Camille lowers her knife just long enough for me to sidestep her. I spin around and punch her directly in the face. Her nose explodes in a hail of greasy pieces of waxy skin but no blood. Pain blooms in my knuckles as she stumbles back and I dart away from her. I reach my dad as Roger lands a glancing blow on his cheek. My dad stumbles. Mom picks up the brass orb and cracks Roger over the head with it. His skull collapses in on one side. I cup my hands over my mouth to stifle a scream. Roger lurches sideways, then catches himself. I can't understand how he is still upright. He turns around and when I catch a glimpse of his face through the billowing smoke I do scream. I can't hold back. His left eye is dangling from its socket by a bundle of twisted nerves . . . no. Strings? Wires?

My heart backflips into my throat as Roger scoops up the eye and shoves it back into his now deformed head. He is reanimated. Just like my mom. Just like Noah. He is one of them.

There is a sudden, thunderous boom, like the clap of thunder. Everyone turns toward it at once. The tall figure who'd been standing at the altar has clapped their massive hands together sending Camille, Langan, Morris, and Roger into a strange, almost reverential silence. They bow their heads. The one called Langan even takes a knee.

My dad pushes me and my mom behind him. Noah stands just a few feet away from me. I stare up at the hooded figure.

"What have we come to?" the figure asks.

The voice is the most awful thing I've ever heard. It's less of a voice and more of a noise—grating and harsh and unnatural.

My mom cowers at my dad's side. My dad doesn't move but when I put my hand on his back I can feel him trembling uncontrollably. I glance at Noah, who looks like a statue—frozen where he stands.

We should be running. We should be making our way back to the car and driving away. I never wanted to be here in the first place. An anger uncoils itself inside me and I don't try to hold it in. I step in front of my parents.

"Who are you?" I ask. "What do you want?"

The figure lifts his head slightly and while the shadow and smoke are thick, I can see the eyes—one brown, one blue, the sclera yellow and shot through with blackened veins. My blood turns to ice.

He leans toward me and the overwhelming and unmistakable stench of rotted flesh wafts into my face. "You don't know what you are," he says. "The truth of it all has been kept from you."

"Don't," my father says quietly. "She's just a child."

"As am I," the man says, his voice grating and inhuman. "The child of a selfish and hollow man." He steps toward me and I get a real sense of how disproportionate he is compared to every other person in the room. He is taller than all of us, broader too. His footfalls make the floor rumble under my feet. He stands in front of me and I don't look up into his face right away. I can't.

I can feel him looming over me. Maybe this is where it all ends. All these things have come to light only for me to die before

I can fully understand them. I swallow my fear and turn my face up to his. He is still cloaked in shadow, the cowl and hood of his robes swallowing the important details of his face. I can't see him clearly but I still want to scream. The feeling is like being in the presence of a wild animal—dangerous, unpredictable.

"If you, Meka, are the last in a long line of reanimators descended from the man who started all of this then you and I are as close as any creator and their creation could possibly be," he says. I want to run but I can't make myself move. "I have crossed oceans and endured the relentless passage of time to keep you near. Frankenstein was the doctor. The original reanimator. But I—I am the monster. His greatest creation."

CHAPTER 23

A MONSTER AMONG MONSTERS

The man pulls back the hood from his head and I cannot fathom what I am seeing. He is a grotesque approximation of a human being. His crumbling flesh is so badly decayed around his watery right eye that the yellowed bone of the socket is plainly visible. The scattering of hair on his head is black and greasy. His teeth are visible even though his mouth is at rest. It is as if the skin has been pulled back too tightly. That skin—it's not a smooth canvas but a patchwork of pieces held over the bone by ragged stitches.

"Is it all clear to you now?" he asks.

In his horrible face I see something from a nightmare and then, with a sudden and dizzying terror, I realize he is familiar to me. I feel as if I know him, as if I've seen him. I grasp at the threads of the memory, hauling them up from somewhere deep in my mind.

"The window," I manage to stammer. "And in the road the night of the accident . . . you were there."

The man—or whatever he is—smiles. "The school, the cemetery, a hundred other places you've been. Always with you. As I was with your father, and his father before him."

I'd seen the man at my window when I was little. The same man who had stood in front of our car on that rainy night of the accident. The man I'd convinced myself was partially a figment of my imagination is real, and now he is standing in front of me.

"I have kept a watchful eye on you for so very long," he says.

"Why?" I ask. It is the only thing I can think of to say.

I look to my dad, whose gaze is locked on the monster.

"Tell her," the monster says.

My dad lets his gaze wander to the floor. "I don't know where to begin."

"Dad," I say, my heart pounding in my chest. "What is this?"

My dad lifts his gaze to meet mine and there is nothing but fear and sorrow in his eyes. He clutches the book to his chest. "There was a man, a very long time ago. A doctor. We are descended from him. He is the man who inspired the tales of Victor Frankenstein." The defeat in his voice is clear. He never wanted me to know about any of this. He was trying to save me from it.

"Dippel," I say. "The name in the book."

My dad nods and the monster . . . smiles. It is a grotesque and terrible sight. Saliva fills my mouth as I try desperately to stifle the urge to vomit.

"He made you," I say to the monster, my mind racing.

The monster straightens up and clasps his hands together in front of him; the fingers look like they've each come from a different person. His palms are in such a state of decay I can see the bones and emaciated tendons moving beneath as he opens and closes his hands. "There was no harnessing of the lightning." He

272

sighs almost mournfully and his breath is the scent of rot. "No. Dippel had a power, given to him by right of his birth. The spark came from him. *You* have that same power. You are what is left of my maker and I am the keeper of his gift to you."

The monster grabs hold of my wrist and wrenches it up. I cry out as my shoulder pulls, like it's going to be ripped away from my body. Noah sprints toward me but the monster backhands him so hard his feet leave the ground and he flies into the altar, knocking over all the bowls and candles. He lies motionless. I kick and scream and try beating against the monster with my free hand but it is useless.

He shoves the dead body of the young woman onto the floor and sets me roughly on the raised platform. Camille rushes to the woman's side and examines her now exposed leg.

"I have spent these many years making sure Dippel's descendants know their place," says the monster as he paces in front of me. His steps are uneven, heavy. "Your grandfather was blissfully compliant. Your father, on the other hand, has strayed from his sacred mission."

"Get away from her!" my mom shouts.

Roger, his skull still dented in, grabs her and as my dad goes to push him away Langan knocks my dad to the ground. His head strikes the corner of the step that leads up to the altar with a sickening thud. He sits up, dazed and bleeding. I try to slip off the platform but the monster shoves me hard in the chest, knocking me back. Hot, angry tears sting my eyes.

"And you," the monster says, turning his attention to my mom. "You were not meant to exist at all."

My mom narrows her angry gaze at him as she struggles against Roger.

"Come," the monster says. "Let us see what you are capable of."

The monster moves toward my father and roughly takes the book from him. He returns to the platform and grabs my arm, squeezing it so hard I think it might break. He pulls me to my feet as Camille wrestles the dead woman's body back onto the platform.

"I want *you* to reanimate her," the monster growls.

"I—I can't!" I stammer. "I don't know how!"

The monster leans down and presses his mouth to my ear.

"You have always known. Do it," he says. "Or I will kill your father and destroy your mother and this other." He gestures to Noah's crumpled frame. "I will tear down everyone you have ever loved, everyone who has ever known you. You can run but I will follow you to the ends of the world, just as I did my maker. I will sit at your side at the moment of your death."

"Don't!" my dad shouts. His voice sounds far away, like he's still dazed.

Morris kicks him in the back and he winces.

"Stop!" I shout. "Please stop!"

"We will not," the monster says. "Never." He leans closer to me, pressing his body against mine. "Your father would have you believe he is a virtuous man but what has it gained him? Think of your grandfather. He was a paragon of gracious servitude. You could be as Hebe was to Zeus . . . cupbearer to a god." He sets the book on the raised platform and opens it.

"I can't read it," I say. "I don't know how."

The monster says nothing. He only smiles hideously. "I think you know what you need to do."

I don't want to. I shouldn't. But I can . . . I know it.

The monster suddenly grabs my wrist and wrenches it toward

274

the dead woman's feet which are now facing me. I grip her ankle, feeling the waxy, cold flesh beneath my palm. I can do this—appease the monster and his creations and maybe save my dad and mom and Noah all at once.

I squeeze her ankle. Her body jolts.

"But the book," Camille says. "The incantation."

"Silence," orders the monster.

Camille lowers her eyes and shuts her mouth.

I grip the dead woman's other ankle with my free hand. My body feels like it's on fire. The pain building in my sweaty palms is almost unbearable. The woman's frame jerks violently under my grip. The monster steps back, his eyes locked only on me, his gaze burning through me.

I look at the open book but I can't understand the language written there. The dead woman sits up, her chest heaving, her mouth a blackened, open maw. The milky-white orbs beneath her lids roll lazily under her purple-tinged lids.

My hands ache, my head throbs, and I feel . . . alive. Strangely, horrifyingly invigorated.

"You feel it as all who have come before you have," the monster says. "The power you possess can only be guided by me. I can help you wield it." He moves behind me and puts his hands on my shoulders. "I will decide who lives, who dies . . . who will become a god, and you will become worthy of your gift."

I stare into the woman's terrified face. Is this what my grandfather saw when he reanimated the dead? He wielded this terrible power, too, and he left my father to struggle on his own for the sake of it.

"Kill—kill me," the woman says, her voice a husk of what it should be. "Kill me."

I let go of her ankles. She gasps and falls back, tipping off the side of the platform and falling in a heap onto the floor.

"I don't want to," I say. "I won't do it."

Some nightmarish understanding flickers in the monster's eyes. "Destroy the mother," he says. "Kill them all."

"No!" I try to scramble backward off the platform but the monster grabs my thigh and squeezes it so tight I think it might break.

He holds me in place as Roger and Langan take my mom by her arms. Morris emerges from behind the altar with Noah in his grip.

"Reanimates exist because I will it to be so!" the monster bellows. "*That* is my power. *That* is my charge. To guide the reanimator to a higher purpose." The monster stares at me. "Their purpose—your purpose—is to serve unquestioningly and without hesitation. Dippel cursed me to this life and now I ensure the bearers of his power wield it appropriately." He tilts his head back and the gaps in the skin of his throat open like many hungry mouths. "This is my purpose. The reanimator and the reanimated together, in a dance. One and the other. Always."

"You're salvaging body parts from dead people," I say angrily. "You can't even maintain yourselves. You're trying to force me to reanimate that woman to do what? Experiment with reanimated flesh? That's our higher purpose?"

The monster stares at me, through me. "You should be thankful I allow any of you to exist."

Allow?

I think of all that has happened, about my dad and Grandpa Redwood, my mom, Noah, the other reanimates . . .

"You can't do any of it without us," I say as a terrible anger sparks inside me. "You don't have any real power. You're some sick, twisted creation, and if the stories are true, your maker thought you were a mistake—an abomination. *You* are the one who doesn't deserve to exist."

The monster's terrifying gaze flits to me and for a moment I see something distinctly human in his eyes—it is bitter sadness and if I'm not wrong . . . pain. But it is almost immediately overtaken by a kind of anger I've never seen before. I can almost feel it rolling off him in waves. He is seething.

"Reanimators are simply the tool," the monster says. "But I am the god called forth by their magic. I have spent my existence in the shadows, but no longer. I am Prometheus, but I refuse to be chained. I am the light in the void."

The other reanimates bow their heads as I look to them for some sense of reason, some sign that any of them are willing to help me.

"The light?" I ask, my voice trembling. "You're not a light! You said it yourself. The spark that made you came from Dippel." I face the monster's lackeys. "You're not his creations. He's the same as you! If you are the dark, he is in there with you!"

Something flits across Roger's face—something that almost looks like regret or sorrow. I can't tell. The monster grips my leg harder and I scream. Noah pulls himself up and staggers forward. The monster shoves me back and I go skidding across the raised platform and onto the tile floor, slamming into one of the pillars. My vision goes blurry for a moment and when I regain my focus, Noah is crouched beside me and the monster is stalking toward my mom. I try to get up but my legs won't cooperate; I can't get my feet under me.

The monster grabs hold of my mom and pulls her right arm

with a loud grunt. There is a pop as the arm comes away from her torso. The monster flings it to the floor.

"No!" I scream.

My mom's face is a mask of shock as the monster grasps her by the waist. My dad springs up and strikes the monster in the face over and over but I don't think he feels it at all. In one quick motion, the monster violently twists my mom's torso so that her upper body is facing backward. He lets her go and she collapses in a heap.

I scramble to my feet, willing my body to work. Someone catches Noah by the arm but I slip away and manage to grab the only thing within reach, a heavy brass candlestick. I charge the monster and plunge the end of it into his back. It sinks into his flesh right below his bottom rib. He spins around and catches me by the neck. He squeezes and everything goes black, though I can still hear the terrified screams of my dad and of Noah. I can't breathe. I kick against the monster but it's no use. The sounds from all around me begin to fade until there is only blackness.

CHAPTER 24

AN ACCUMULATION OF ANGUISH

When I open my eyes again, I'm lying on the floor on my back. I turn my head and find the broken body of Morris lying next to me. His eyes are blinking rapidly but his head is no longer attached to his neck.

I sit up even though it hurts; each breath brings with it a wave of pain and nausea. A sickening noise, like the ripping of wet paper, sounds to my right. As my vision comes into focus I catch a glimpse of Camille hunched over the dead body of the woman, removing her right leg with a long serrated knife. I gasp and Camille looks up. She has a faraway look in her eyes.

Langan's body is crumpled next to the platform in the center of the room. His arms have been removed from his torso and he stares angrily at Camille, shouting at her.

"You did this to me!" he screams. "Traitor!"

I think Camille has gone out of her mind. She carefully cuts away the woman's leg and because the woman wasn't a reanimate, there is blood. So much blood but it is black and sticky, like tar. She holds the leg against herself, measuring, assessing. She pays no mind to Langan as she presses the knife against her own leg, tearing at the flesh, and begins to cut.

The door the monster had come out of sits ajar. The monster, Noah, and my dad are all missing. My mom's crumpled body lies on the floor but I cannot look. It's like my mind cannot accept what I'm seeing regardless of everything I've witnessed up to this point. I stand and start to move toward the door. Morris's head begins to spit and sputter. I give it a swift kick and it bounces into the shadows.

"Get her!" Langan shouts. He can't get up and I look to Camille. She doesn't even glance at me. She has situated herself on the floor and is slowly sawing through the decayed flesh of her own upper thigh.

Roger stumbles back into the room and approaches Camille. His wobbly gait and broken skull make him look like something out of a horror movie—a shambling corpse brought back from the dead, stalking us through the bowels of this cursed castle. I back away, fearing he'll come after me but he is focused only on Camille.

"Camille, stop," he says softly.

She doesn't stop her cutting but he kneels next to her and gently puts his hand on her shoulder. The sight of him and her together, their bodies all but destroyed—this is the impossible price of immortality.

Camille, her chest heaving, her jaw clenched. "I can be who I was before. I can put my body back together if no one else will."

Roger glances up, but he doesn't move. The fight has gone out of him. He simply watches Camille sever her own leg. She gets through the last of the bone and tosses the knife down on the floor.

Langan starts yelling again but soon quiets himself. They're all irrevocably broken.

A small, muffled cry comes from where my mother had collapsed. The noise pulls me out of this terrible unreality and I rush to her side. She lies face down near the altar. Her body is twisted unnaturally and I'm afraid to touch her. She turns her head to the side and smiles at me.

"I—I thought you were—gone," I say.

"It doesn't hurt," she says. "Help me turn over."

I take her by her one good arm and roll her over onto her back. I don't want to look at the place where her other arm used to be. She says it doesn't hurt and I know she's telling the truth but I still can't stand to see her like this. Can we even fix this? Do I have the skills to put her back together? Tears sting my eyes as she takes my hand in hers.

"The monster took your dad and Noah ran after them," she says. "We can't let this continue, Meka." Her gaze splits to Camille, who is sitting silently, next to Roger. Morris's head lolls to the side. The arms and legs of his detached body twitch. Langan has lowered himself to the floor and lies on his back, staring up at the ceiling.

"We used to be something," Langan rambles. "He was our god."

"He's a monster," I say quietly.

Langan turns to me. "The monster of all monsters."

My mom touches my arm. "Go. Now."

I grab Camille's discarded knife and cut across the room, entering the open door on the opposite side. Behind it are spiral stairs that wind up to the floors above. I take the steps two at a time as I grip the knife until my palm aches. The room I emerge into on the uppermost floor is empty and spans a wide swath of the castle. The wooden planks that make up the floor are rotted away in some places, leaving gaping holes. Clear on the other side I see the hulking silhouette of the monster. I race toward him not knowing what I'm supposed to do when I reach him. I only know I need to get to him.

As I approach, the monster has my dad by the front of his shirt and is lifting him off the ground. The boards groan under his feet. Noah is there, pounding wildly on the monster's back, screaming at him. The monster either doesn't feel it or doesn't care, I can't tell which. The monster steps toward the open window, whose glass has been broken out. I scream as he dangles my father over the edge.

"Get away from him!' I shout, wielding the knife in front of me. My hand is trembling and my heart feels like it's in my throat.

The monster turns his head to look at me and again he smiles the most unsettling and unnatural grin. "He doesn't need to live," says the monster. "I have you now, my dearest Meka. And you are special. You are so much more than anything your father or his forebears could ever have been and I think, maybe, you don't even know it yet. You have only just begun to see, when others have kept their eyes closed for so very long."

"I know what I am!" I scream, allowing all my anger to bubble up and spill out.

"Do you?" the monster asks.

Noah strikes him hard across the back with some broken piece of wood he'd scrounged from somewhere. The monster turns and knocks him aside with one colossal blow. Noah hits the ground and skids across the floor coming to a stop at the base of the wall by the window. He lies still and I try to remind myself that he can't be killed that way.

"What do you want?" I shout as tears run hot down my cheeks. "Why are you doing this?"

The monster blinks once, then twice and turns his face up to the ceiling. "Because I must. Because it is only fair and right and just that I, who have been denied so much, should be able to determine who will receive this gift."

"You haven't been denied anything!" I yell. "You shouldn't even be here in the first place!" I don't know what Dippel's motivations were for creating this creature but even if the power to reanimate someone was Dippel's to command, he should never have done it.

Dad grips the monster's robe and yanks hard on it, trying to free himself. The billowing black cloth slips down revealing a jagged line of stitches at the monster's shoulder. The skin of the arm is a different color and texture than his torso. The monster watches me watching him and he narrows his gaze at me. In the daylight streaming through the window a row of poorly mended stitches running directly across the top of his forehead stretches open. The white bone underneath shines like a crescent moon.

"Have you ever beheld anything so destroyed?" the monster asks. "There is almost nothing left of them," he continues. "Of the men whose bodies were taken from the ground and fitted together to shelter what is left of my soul." He breathes deep. "Daniel Allen, Simeon Cady, William Lewis—I suppose I owe my existence to them. Their flesh made me what I am."

"You owe your existence to Dippel," I say angrily. "He made you."

"And look what I have become," the monster says. "I have existed for over two hundred years. A living shadow." There is sadness, real human sadness in his words but I am unmoved.

"So why don't you just let yourself die," I say through gritted teeth. "Let yourself rot away. Turn to dust."

"And miss the opportunity to see what you will become?" the monster asks. "I would never."

"What she'll become?" my dad rasps.

The monster turns, looks him in the face.

He drops my dad, who grasps hopelessly at the monster's cloak tearing it away as he falls.

"No!" I scream.

Noah stirs on the floor but can't seem to get his feet under him. The monster is now nude and while his limbs are proportional, they don't go together the way they should. His right arm is shorter than his left and the skin on each side is a different color. The bone in his upper thigh is exposed, the flesh around it decayed to almost nothing. He has an array of stitches and patches as if he's been mended and re-mended over and over again since he first came into being, two hundred years of stinking putrid flesh, melded together. It is the most terrible thing I've ever seen.

He steps toward me, unashamed of his exposed state and unwilling to let it hinder him. I hold the knife in front of me. The monster lowers his head and charges forward. I try to duck out of the way but he stiffens his shoulder and puts it directly into my chest. A bolt of pain rips through me as I tumble to the floor. I'm rolling up onto my side, gasping for the breath that's been knocked out of me, when something impacts my leg. I scream out in agony. The monster has stepped on my ankle, crushing it. My vision blurs. Vomit rises in the back of my throat.

From the window there's a scuffling sound, and when the haze of pain briefly clears I catch a glimpse of Noah hoisting my dad in from the window as he clings to the remnants of the monster's cloak. He hadn't fallen after all. The monster turns toward them and I pull myself up and limp after him.

"Your time has come," the monster says to my dad as he advances, backing my dad up to the window again. "You're not worthy of the power you possess."

Noah is still going at the monster as my dad cowers in front of him. I look down at the knife, at my broken ankle, at this impossible situation. Is this how it will be? I'll lose my dad and Noah and my mom and then be at the beck and call of the monster?

No.

No, I can't accept that.

I still myself. Adrenaline saves me from the pain as I put my injured foot down. I lurch forward with all the strength I can muster and slam into the monster's back with the full weight of my body, sinking the knife in at the base of his skull. We tumble forward through the open window and land on the snow-covered ground below.

CHAPTER 25

ALL THINGS MUST END

The pain hasn't reached my brain yet but I know it's coming. It's like a train approaching from a distance. When it hits me I can't even scream. I just lie on the ground wondering if this is what death feels like and how—if I somehow manage to survive—I'll never lie to anyone again by telling them that death is peaceful.

I try to roll over but find that I'm still maybe a foot off the ground. Turning my head just a little farther hurts like hell, but it's then that I realize I've landed on top of the monster. I scramble off him as he lies face down in the snow.

"Meka!" my dad's voice cries out. He's looking down on me from the window three floors above.

My body begins to register my injuries. My ankle is shattered but now there's a blooming pain over my ribs on the right side. A coppery taste fills my mouth. I groan and try to stand but it's impossible now. A wave of nausea overtakes me and the world tilts.

Suddenly a figure stirs in the snow and I realize with a sudden stab of panic that Noah has tumbled out of the window, too, and without the benefit of having anything to land on. I scramble over to him, pulling myself through the snow, ignoring the pain.

Noah's left leg is broken at the thigh and it juts out at a ninety degree angle from the rest of his body. His hand, which was barely holding on anyway, has come loose and is lying in the snow several feet away from him.

"Noah!" I scream. "Noah, get up!"

"I can't," he says.

"No, I know," I say, resting my head against his chest. "Your leg is broken."

Noah looks down the length of his body and shakes his head at the exposed bit of bone sticking out of his leg. "Oh, man. We're gonna have to fix that."

A rustling sound draws my attention. Like the slasher at the end of some shitty horror movie, the monster is attempting to get up one final time. I scramble back, knocking my ankle into Noah and sending a new jolt of pain through my body. The monster's torso shifts as he lifts his arms to push himself up but as he does, his head tumbles back down into the snow. I scream. I couldn't have stopped it if I tried.

The head rolls forward, then stops with its eyes fixed on me. I'd put the knife in at the back of his neck and the force of the fall must have pushed the blade all the way through. The silver point of it is sticking up out of the snow near the monster's lower body, which is now feeling around on the ground in front of it. By sheer will I draw myself up, trying desperately to not put any weight on my ankle.

The monster captures his own head and sets it atop his severed neck where a portion of the spinal column is exposed. He spears his own head, using the spine as a pike. The head sits at the wrong angle, but its gaze finds me again. He lunges forward and I have to throw myself into the snow to get away from him.

I scramble across the frozen ground on hands and knees. When I look back, he's readjusting the angle of his own severed head to find me again. He lurches through the snow as I pull myself up and stagger back.

"Get away from me!" I scream.

The monster bounds forward and catches me in a bear hug, lifting me off the ground. He smiles as he presses me close to him. I can't smell him because I can't inhale, he's squeezing me too tight, but I can feel the rot on him.

Shapes dance around the edges of my vision when suddenly there's a flurry of footsteps and a loud *thwack!* The monster's head flies away from his body and my dad stands panting, gripping a plank of wood like a baseball bat. The monster's hold loosens, and I wriggle out of his arms. My dad slams the board against the backs of the monster's knees. They buckle and the body collapses into a kneeling position.

"Finish it, Meka," Noah shouts. "Hurry!"

I hop through the freezing snow and grab the knife. The monster's arms strike out, missing me by just a few inches. I hold the knife in my trembling hand, dragging my crushed ankle behind me as I find the monster's head. I look into his eyes, eyes that were maybe human once but not anymore. I reach down and shove the head toward Noah who shrieks but corrals it near him as my dad and I shove the monster's body flat against the ground.

I remove the monster's arms and legs from his torso. Cutting through the rotted flesh, it's clear to me that this abomination had no one of any skill to care for him. His body is in all stages of decay all at once. The newer flesh stinks and in his lower limbs maggots have made themselves at home. I vomit into the surrounding snow twice before we're done.

The head continues to blink and the mouth moves as if the monster is trying to speak but can't. When the terrible work is finished, the monster lies in six separate pieces, all of them squirming and wriggling together.

"What do we do now?" I ask.

"We take it back inside," my dad says. "And then we burn this whole goddammed place to the ground."

I help move Noah to the hallway just inside the door, and then my dad and I carry the dismembered pieces of Dippel's monster— Frankenstein's monster—back into the bowels of the castle. I am in so much pain my vision blurs but we have to do this. Camille is still there with Roger and what is left of Morris and Langan. They are still as corpses and none of them speak or move as we work.

We pile the pieces of the monster on the raised platform in the center. The head tries to bite me as I arrange it alongside the other body parts so I quickly remove the lower jaw, breaking it off at the joints, and toss it away. I consider taking out the eyes with the knife but I worry my dad and Noah will think I've lost my mind. Maybe I have. All of this feels like a terrible dream.

Mom watches, her gaze far away as my dad kneels down next to her. She turns her face toward him. "You have to destroy the book so that this can never happen again."

"No," my dad says, shaking his head. "I won't do that."

"No, Dad," I say. "That's a good idea. We should get rid of it. I don't want this—this—whatever this is to go on. If we destroy the book, nobody can ever bring back some monster from the dead."

"You don't understand," my dad says. "I—"

There's a shuffling noise from the top of the stairs. Noah has managed to drag himself down to the lower level. I limp up to him and help bring him the rest of the way down. He sits next to my mom.

My dad glances at me, then my mom, then Noah. "I lied," he says. "About the unmaking ritual. It exists but not in the way they thought."

"I don't understand," I say. "We can unmake them?" The wriggling pile of limbs is visible out of the corner of my eye. "Let's do that, then."

My dad shakes his head. "The unmaking is simply the destruction of the book. It holds the names of all the reanimates. We destroy the book, we destroy them. *All* of them."

I look to my mom, to Noah. I'm about to say something when my mom grabs my hand and holds it tight.

"Meka, baby, I need you to listen to me," she says.

"No," I say. I don't want to hear it. I can't. This isn't going to happen. We will find another way."

"Listen," my mom says sternly. "What your dad did, it was done out of grief. I don't fault him for it. I probably would have done the same thing."

I try to pull away from her but she holds me. My dad puts his hand on my back.

"I wanted us to have more time," my dad says quietly. "I didn't think about what it meant for your mom. I wanted her with me, with us, and I—I was wrong."

"No," I say. I can't form any other words. "No."

"Yes," Mom says. "I don't regret it. I don't regret being here with you all these years. I wouldn't trade it for anything, but look at me, Meka. Really look at me. I am literally falling apart. I am tired. Exhausted, if we're being honest. Every day is like a race to keep my body from decaying and I am losing. I have been for a while."

"I—I couldn't tell," I say as the tears stream down my face. "You're always perfect to me."

My mom pulls me closer and I lie on her chest.

"You have to let me go," she says.

"No," I say. "I can keep you alive. I can make you stay."

"That's not what I want," my mom says firmly. "This is the way it should have been all along. We have been living on stolen time. It's okay to let me go, baby."

I don't want to even though I know that makes me selfish. Maybe I'll be selfish. It's better than this pain that's threatening to choke the life from me. I stare at my mom. She's suffering and I want her to continue to suffer because I love her? I want her to stay even though that's not what she wants? No. No, that can't be right. I lift my head and stare into Noah's face. He doesn't have to say anything for me to know he agrees with my mom.

"I wish I could stay with you forever, Meeks," Noah says. "That's really all I ever wanted anyway." He holds out his good hand and I take it. "Burn the book. Tell my mom I'm sorry. I know she didn't know what would happen, but I need her to know I'm not mad."

I can only nod.

"I love you, Meeks," he says. "I wish I had told you sooner. I'm sorry about that."

"It's okay," I say through a torrent of tears. "I know now. That's all that matters."

My dad sobs openly as he embraces my mom. I pull Noah

closer to me and kiss him, breathe him in, touch his face and his hair. This must have been what my dad felt when he knelt by my mom's body on the road that night. This is the grief, the longing that drove him to do what he did. I don't think I fully understood until this moment.

"I wish we had more time," Noah says. "We were supposed to have more time."

When I let him go, I turn back to my mom.

"I love you," I say.

"I love you," she says. "More than anything in this world."

My dad takes the book and sets it on the floor. Roger cradles Camille and it's then that I realize Langan's body had been torn into multiple other pieces. From the blank expression on Roger's mangled face, I think he might have been the one who did it.

Noah sits next to my mom. They put their arms around each other and then, I can't watch anymore. I close my eyes.

I hear my dad remove one of the torches from its place on the wall, his hollow footsteps, a soft *whoosh*, and then a wave of heat breaks across my body. When I open my eyes, the book is nearly disintegrated and Mom, Noah, Camille, Roger, Morris, and the jumbled mass of dismembered reanimate parts that used to be the monster lie still. They're all gone.

I collapse into a heap and my dad comes to me and wraps me up. We stay this way for what feels like forever until my dad takes my face in his hands.

"We need to go home," he says. "And we need to take Mom and Noah with us. They don't deserve to be here with these—these monsters." He casts an angry glance at the pile of body parts.

We move Mom and Noah to the snowcat one at a time. A somber procession performed in complete silence. Then I help my dad tear up a pile of wooden planks from the upper floor and haul them down to the sublevel. We make a bonfire of the boards and of the monster parts. My dad empties three cans of gasoline that had been stored for the snowcat and tosses a torch into the center. We rush outside and wait for everything inside to be engulfed before we finally get into the snowcat and leave the castle, the monster, and the horrors of our strange family tree behind us.

We don't have a funeral for my mom. People around me think she died after a brief illness, and we let them come to the house to offer condolences. There is no wake. No burial.

Later in the week, after my ankle has been set and put in a cast, I take the small box that contains her ashes and scatter them into the waterfall by my house. I think that's what she would have wanted. Not only to always be in a place that was so beautiful but to know, without any doubt, that if somehow the book were to be recreated, if me or my dad found that we could read from it again, that there was no way of bringing her remains back. That's how it should be. Death is meant to be final. The period at the end of a sentence. Her death had been more like a comma, with more yet to say. I think she's at peace now and I can't be anything but grateful that we had the time we did. I miss her every second of the day, but she's never far from me. Not really.

Noah's second funeral is small. Just me, my dad, and Miss Cliff. Nobody knows why we all decided to gather at the Cliff family tomb on a random Wednesday morning, but I think they'll probably say it is grief and that visiting the place is how we cope. The second visit which occurred only four days later would probably have been harder to explain so I just hoped no one would ask. In the process of prepping for Noah's second funeral, we realized that in our haste to get the bodies of my mom and Noah away from the castle we had left Noah's dismembered hand in the snow. My dad and I had to travel back to Roscoe to reclaim it, which was a task in and of itself because the entire property had been cordoned off after the blaze. After some searching and damn near getting frostbite on my own hands, we found Noah's missing piece and brought it to the cemetery to be reinterred with him. I couldn't stand the thought of removing his casket and opening it again so we simply removed the facing stone and placed the hand just inside before sealing it back up. We didn't invite Miss Cliff along for this small ceremony. It seemed like a little too much for her to handle.

One night, in the weeks after, as my dad and I settle into our new normal, I wake from a dream in the dead of night. The nightmare memories are gone but are now replaced with a vision of Noah standing at the end of a dark hall, his hand outstretched.

"I wish we had more time," he says. "Just a little more. You could do that for me, Meeks. You could bring me back."

CHAPTER 26

ALIVE! ALIVE! ALIVE!

I'm sitting with my dad on the couch, watching *The Addams Family*, eating takeout, and discussing the sloppy delivery of our latest guest.

"Guests need to be delivered in a timely manner," my dad says, a slight tone of annoyance in his voice. "It's important for the preservation, for the families."

Our latest guest had come in a poor state of decomposition and my dad had, surprisingly, gone off on the delivery driver, the hospital, and anyone else he thought shouldered some of the blame. I'm proud of him for sticking up for himself and for our guests. I think it's a new way of being for him but something he'll have to do more of now that my mom's not here.

An ache invades my chest and I try to breathe through it. This is how it's been for three months. Just trying to breathe, trying to move forward. It's been hard. Harder than when Noah died—the first time—and with every passing day, I hold my dad less accountable for what he did when he brought my mom back. This pain feels like too much sometimes.

A pecking sound draws my attention. My dad's beloved ravens are here for their nightly meal.

"My babies," my dad says as he pulls himself off the couch. He opens the hatch next to the back door and scatters a handful of seeds as two ravens peck at it. I wouldn't say my dad is less haunted now, but maybe he's haunted in a way that is more bearable. He doesn't seem like he's going to break under the weight of our mourning.

A commercial interrupts our movie and the local duo of reporters tells us that on the six o'clock report they'll be discussing a tribute to Vincent Hollowell, who only a few months prior had seemed fine, but who had dropped dead seemingly out of nowhere.

My dad eyes me knowingly. Hollowell had clearly been a reanimate of Grandpa Redwood's making.

"What if they knew he wasn't alive to begin with?" my dad asks. "That would be breaking news."

"Alive," one of the ravens repeats in a voice that sounds almost identical to the tone and pitch of my dad. "Alive!"

I don't think I'll ever get used to how human they sound.

"Anyway," Dad says. "Despite the ineptitude of the hospital and the delivery, I prepped our guest. She's ready for you whenever you're up to it."

I've taken over the mortuary cosmetology for all our guests until we can hire on some help, but right now I'm happy it's just me and my dad.

"Dad," I say. "I need to ask you something."

My dad closes the bird hatch and rejoins me on the couch. "Go for it."

The impossible nature of everything that happened will stick with me forever. I know that. But there was something that stuck in my head, not because it was horrific or traumatizing, but because it was odd.

"When we were there at the castle," I say. "The monster kept saying things to me that didn't make sense." I pull my legs up and tuck them in close to me. "He said I was special. He said he couldn't wait to see what I would become. The way he was looking at me when I reanimated that poor woman . . . what was all that about?"

My dad is lost in his own thoughts for several moments before he answers. "We all have this gift that when coupled with the book gave us the power to bring back the dead. I don't know if 'special' is the word I'd use to describe it but you are indeed special."

"Dad, I love you," I say. "I really do and I love that you think that way about me but I guarantee that is not what the monster meant."

My dad shrugs but I can tell he's holding back.

"It's something else," I say. "Like they knew something you didn't."

"I don't see how," my dad says. "My family has passed this knowledge down through the generations."

"You mean the things Dippel knew?" I ask.

"Yes. It all started with him."

"And we know that Dippel authored the book because he had the power to reanimate people, right?" I ask.

My dad nods.

"He was the first," I say, more to myself than to my dad as an avalanche of thoughts tumble through my head. "How much of the Frankenstein story is true and how much is made up?"

"I don't know what you mean," Dad says.

I think for a moment. "In the story, Doctor Frankenstein had a theory that he could create life and he used electricity to spark that in a monster he created from a bunch of dead bodies. But the monster himself said that that wasn't true. He said Frankenstein—Dippel—*was* the spark. It almost sounds like the power reanimators have existed before the book. Almost like Dippel was trying to work out something he already knew existed."

"But the names were all in the index," my dad says, his voice low and serious. "Every reanimate was listed there. They have to be. That's part of the ritual, recording the name in blood."

"When Dippel made the monster, he wrote down the process and started keeping track of the reanimates," I say. "He wrote down the process, the words, the rituals." I huff and sink back into the couch. "There is something missing."

"Like what?" my dad asks.

"Did you get a chance to write that woman's name down? The one on the platform?"

He thinks for a moment. "I didn't. I was in the process when she sat up. The book was open, I was saying the words, performing the ritual."

"Can I ask you a question?" I say softly as the thought takes shape in my mind.

My dad says nothing but I take this to mean yes, I can ask, but tread lightly.

I ask him the only question that makes sense to me in this moment. "Have you ever tried to reanimate someone without using the book?"

He hesitates, swallowing hard and then leveling his gaze with mine. "I have."

I sit straight up. "What?"

"My father tried to force me to do it when I was very young," he says. "It's one of the many reasons we were estranged."

"He thought you could do it without the book," I say.

"I could make bodies move, make them shift around on the prep table in the mortuary he worked in," my dad says. "That had never happened to him. He thought it meant something, but it never went any further than that. So you see, there *must* have been some power in the book and if I'm being honest, I'm glad it's gone." He stares off for a moment, then shakes his head. "Meka, I don't think there is anything else to discover. "I don't think we have to worry about any of that anymore. We can let it all go now."

He pats my knee, then stands up and walks to the hall.

"Meka," he says over his shoulder.

"Yeah, Dad?"

"The book is destroyed," he says. "It's not possible to reanimate someone anymore, not as far as I know anyway, but if it were . . . they couldn't be destroyed. The book being gone makes that impossible. You understand that, don't you?"

"Dad, I—"

"Just tell me you understand," my dad says firmly, using a tone my mom would have used to let me know she was serious.

"I understand," I say. "You're right. I'm gonna go get started on our new guest. Love you."

"Love you too," my dad says.

My dad goes upstairs and I slip off to the basement and wheel our new guest, one Miss Shelby Ryan, who'd fallen from a mountain bike and landed on her neck the wrong way, from the freezer to prep room number one. Her skin is badly discolored and she is definitely going to have to go into a turtleneck or a high-collar shirt because the bone in her neck is sticking out at an odd angle.

I use the lift to transfer her to the table and slip on my apron, still thinking about what the monster had said to me and what it means. My theory about Dippel using the book as a means of recording still stands but if I'm right, it means there was no book at that very first reanimation. It was just Dippel and the dead body made of other dead bodies. Was there some magic connected to the book? My dad was right. There had to be, otherwise destroying it wouldn't have ended all the reanimates, but that still doesn't feel right. The book was a means of controlling the reanimates, and the reanimator. Even Grandpa Redwood thought it was possible a reanimation could be done without the book.

I take up a seat on a stool at the head of the table and begin setting down a base for Miss Ryan's makeup. I think of how my mom would have proceeded and it makes me feel like she's still here, keeping watch. I can almost hear her voice in my ear telling me that we have a reputation to uphold and we gotta live up to it.

I touch Miss Ryan's cheek. Pain, like a knife slicing my fingertips, rockets through my hand. But this feeling is familiar now and I don't jerk my hand back. I don't stand and stumble away from our guest. I sit very, very still. I know this feeling but it's not possible. My hand aches and there's a buzzing in the back of my head. Scrambling to the door, I almost scream for my dad but something stops me.

All those years ago I'd stood at the foot of a prep table as my dad performed those archaic rituals—rituals he'd been taught were the only real way to perform a reanimation. Dippel wrote down what he knew but Dippel didn't need the book before he created it. Those who had come after him did . . . but what about me? My dad hadn't had time to put that dead woman's name in the book before she sat up, before I touched her.

Hadn't this been building up? With my dad even admitting that our funeral home saw more than its fair share of moving corpses, many of them in my presence? I'd seen it happen in the back seat of the hearse. The book had been near but not open and I wasn't reading from it. Everything suddenly falls into place. I *had* done something in the hearse that night. I'd reanimated a man without using the book and I'd done the same thing that terrible day in the castle in Roscoe.

I am a reanimator.

And much like my forefather, I don't need the book because I am the spark. This is what the monster meant. That I would become like his very own maker, raising the dead without a book or a ritual of any kind.

I approach the foot end of the prep table, where Miss Ryan's bare feet are sticking out from under the white sheet. Her pink toenail polish is still intact. I breathe deep and put my ungloved hands around her naked ankles. A spark, painful and electric, shoots through my hands and into Miss Ryan. Her body jerks and her eyelids flutter. I stare at her for what feels like a long time as the current flows out of me. Something deep in my gut tells me if I hold on much longer, she will open her mouth and speak to me, she'll look around and wonder how she got here. She will ask to be freed from the curse of reanimation and I won't be able to help because the book is gone and there can be no unmaking. I let go of her ankles and she falls back onto the table.

My heart is knocking in my chest, but as I stare at my aching hands, I cannot help but feel something unspeakable, something that has been needling at my insides for as long as I can remember but it didn't have a name. Now, I know what it is . . . power. And it's not just some vague thing that me and my dad have spoken about in whispers. It is real and it is in me.

I am the spark.

I let Miss Ryan rest in peace. For whatever reason, she's here on this table and she's not asking for more time. I don't know if that's what she would have wanted . . . but I know someone who did want more time. Someone who asks me for more time every time I close my eyes.

In the dead of a summer evening, I stand in the confines of the Cliff family tomb alone. Noah's name, dates of birth and death, are etched into the facing stone. I stare at it for a long time.

"You are probably asking what I'm doing here," I say aloud. "I don't know. This is the first place I wanted to be when—when I put it all together." I take a deep breath and lean my forehead against the facing stone. "This is what my dad felt like when he thought he lost my mom. I know it." I press my hand over my heart. "It hurts." I sigh. "We let her go and we let you go. It was the right choice."

Wasn't it?

It has to be, because the alternative is a selfish act, an unthinkable undertaking. And still . . .

"I wish you were still here," I whisper into the dark. "I wish you were still alive."

I press my hand to Noah's name. A little ripple of energy tickles the inside of my palm.

Outside, ravens circle overhead. I can hear their song and their voices cawing, *Alive! Alive! Alive!*

ACKNOWLEDGMENTS

Make Me a Monster is the most macabre story I've ever written. When I began drafting this tale, I told myself that I would lean into all the things that felt uncomfortable and difficult. I wanted to write a character-driven horror novel inspired by my favorite gothic horror stories. I didn't anticipate having to delve so deeply into explorations of grief, consent, moral ambiguity, and death—but here we are, and I think all those things are what make this story what it is. Meka and Noah's story is tragic, but sometimes we love a tragic tale. Like Orpheus and Eurydice, like Dani and Jamie from *The Haunting of Bly Manor*, like Charity and Bezi from *You're Not Supposed to Die Tonight*—sometimes tragedy is at the heart of the story and even when it hurts, we tell it again. This is a tale of the monsters we make—of ourselves and of others, and so it was bound to get a little dark. I hope it makes you think and most of all, I hope it made you feel something.

I'd like to thank my daughter Amya for reading an early draft of this and giving me the feedback I needed to keep pushing. I'm sorry it traumatized you, my love! I love you! Big thanks to my family—Mike, Nye, Elijah, Lyla, and Spencer. I love you all so very much.

A massive thank-you to the entire team at Bloomsbury both here and on the UK side—Mary Kate, Erica, Lily, Kei, Katie, Sarah, Emily, and Beth. Teamwork makes the dream work! I love this work and could not do it without your support.

I'd like to thank my readers for rocking with me all this time! Look at us. Look at all the stories we get to share! It still feels magical after ten novels and as long as I can still feel like this, I'll keep writing. Thank you for showing up for me and my work. It means more to me than I can properly express.

Happy reading!

At Camp Mirror Lake,
terror was meant to be a game ...

What if everything you thought you knew
about the fairytale was quite simply ... a lie?

AVAILABLE NOW

Cinderella is dead, but
Snow White fights on ...

New York Times bestselling author of CINDERELLA IS DEAD

SLEEP
LIKE DEATH

KALYNN BAYRON

BLOOMSBURY

AVAILABLE NOW

To break an ancient curse
Briseis must let her power bloom ...

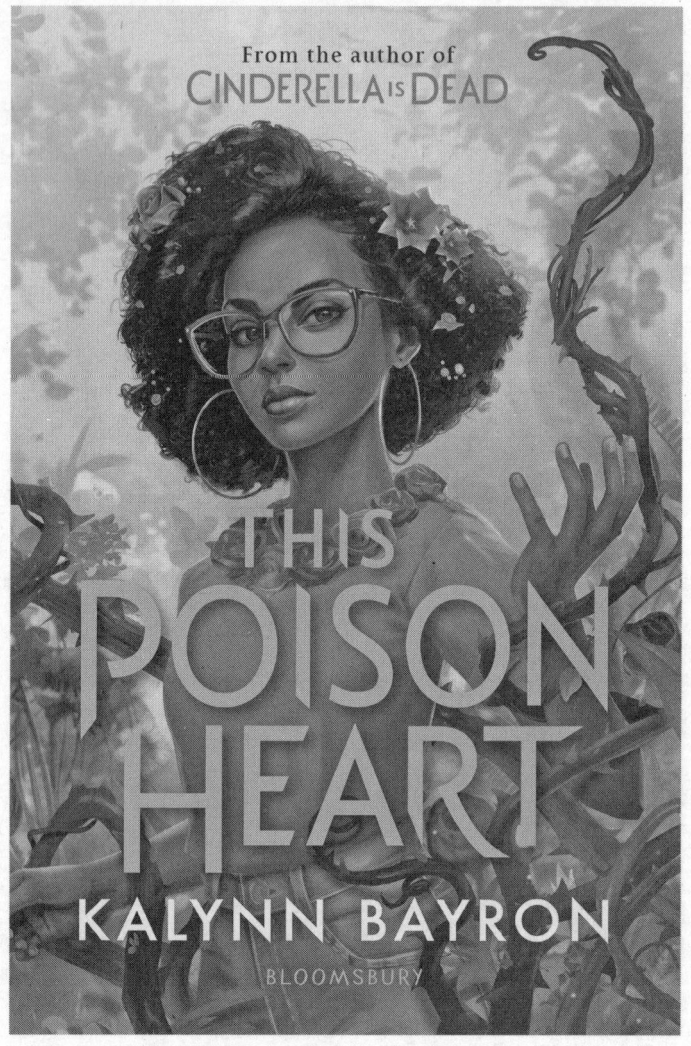

From the author of
CINDERELLA IS DEAD

THIS
POISON
HEART

KALYNN BAYRON

BLOOMSBURY

AVAILABLE NOW

To save the people she loves
Briseis must make her power blossom ...

AVAILABLE NOW

ABOUT THE AUTHOR

Kalynn Bayron is the bestselling author of the young-adult novels *Cinderella is Dead*, *This Poison Heart*, *This Wicked Fate*, *You're Not Supposed to Die Tonight* and *Sleep Like Death* as well as the middle-grade series *The Vanquishers*. She is the winner of the Books Are My Bag Readers Award for YA Fiction 2020 and Wordery's Children's Book of the Year 2020, and has been shortlisted for the Goodreads Choice Award for YA Fantasy 2020 and nominated for the CILIP Carnegie Medal 2021. When she's not writing, you can find her listening to Ella Fitzgerald on loop, attending the theatre, watching scary movies and spending time with her kids. She lives in Ithaca, New York, with her family.

kalynnbayron.com